HOLIDAYS
with
Jane

CHRISTMAS CHEER

JENNIFER BECTON
MELISSA BUELL
REBECCA M. FLEMING
CECILIA GRAY
JESSICA GREY
KIMBERLY TRUESDALE

THE WORK OF AN
Instant

JENNIFER BECTON

Instantly crossing the room to the writing table, [Frederick] drew out a letter from under the scattered paper, placed it before Anne with eyes of glowing entreaty fixed on her for a time, and hastily collecting his gloves, was again out of the room, almost before Mrs. Musgrove was aware of his being in it: the work of an instant!

—Jane Austen, *Persuasion*

"I THINK THE guy in the Santa suit might be having an identity crisis," Anne Elliot mused over the rim of her coffee cup. "He can't decide if he's a Navy version of Saint Nick or a wish-granting genie."

As if to prove her point, the mixed-up Santa raised his arms, offering Anne a good look at his costume: a pair of camouflage BDU pants paired with a fuzzy red

Santa coat, hat, and fluffy white beard. Then, he burst forth with a robust, "Ho, ho, ho! May your fondest Christmas wish come true!"

Camo Santa's proclamation drew the notice of everyone in the Mansfield Perk coffee shop, including Dr. Anne Elliot, her boss Dr. Russell, and nurses Henrietta and Louisa. The four civilians worked together at the Naval Health Clinic at Joint Base Charleston, a US Air Force and Naval Weapons Station, and had stopped for a post-work cup of joe.

"He's full of the Christmas spirit," Henrietta said, watching him in her quiet way.

"He's full of something, all right," Dr. Russell intoned, her face implacable as she raised her mug of herbal tea to her lips. "Someone should remind him that he's out of uniform."

Anne's own lips drew into a smile as the costumed gentleman made a great pretense of assisting a party of women to a vacant table.

"He's probably had a near-fatal dose of espresso," she conjectured as he bounced to the next table to clear away some dirty plates.

"Well, I like him," Louisa said, plunking her enormous whipped coffee concoction onto their table. "He's making this dull old place interesting for once."

Having completed his task, Camo Santa turned, scanned the room, and caught Anne's eye. He smiled hugely at her.

"Uh-oh," Anne said as he gave her a wink. "I think he's coming this way."

"Good," Louisa said, shifting so that she could

wave him over. "We need some holiday cheer over here."

Dr. Russell pushed aside the garland centerpiece with disgust. "We need more of this? I think I'm going to have an allergy attack from all the fir in here."

Dr. Russell was right. The usually sedate shop was in full holiday mode. A live tree stood in the corner, and each table boasted a live centerpiece. The ceiling was bedecked in twinkle lights, and Christmas music piped through the sound system. In addition to the rich scent of roasted espresso beans and fir trees, the scents of peppermint and chocolate pervaded the room.

Many sailors were home on leave, and the shop overflowed with both military and civilian patrons who came to sip some of their miracle elixir and enjoy the varied society an off-base establishment offered.

The place was packed, and Camo Santa seemed to know everyone. As he headed inexorably closer to their table, he called out Yuletide greetings to people by name.

When he finally reached their table, he leaned down to offer Anne a cheery smile.

And of course, every eye in the crowded coffee shop now focused on her. Anne fought to control her embarrassment at suddenly becoming the center of attention.

"Hi, Santa," Louisa chirped from beside her.

"Ho, ho, ho!" Camo Santa returned. "Merry Christmas!"

"I've been a bad girl this year," Louisa said, batting

her eyelashes at him. "Will I get coal in my stocking?"

"No, indeed, not this year," he replied without hesitation or an ounce of flirtation in his tone. "This year, everyone's fondest wish comes true."

"In that case," Louisa said, beaming at him. "I want a hot man with the heart of a hero and the soul of a poet."

"I'll see what I can do," he said seriously.

Anne hoped he would permanently transfer his attention to the clearly willing nurse beside her, but it was not to be. He returned his merry blue gaze to her.

"What about you, young lady? What is your Christmas wish?" Camo Santa asked Anne as he plucked a sprig of mistletoe from his lapel and held it over her head. "Perhaps a kiss from Santa?"

Anne pushed the mistletoe aside but gave Santa a genuine smile. "Sorry, buddy. I'm a little too old to believe in Christmas wishes."

"No one is too old to believe in a little holiday magic," Camo Santa said, looking completely unfazed by her rejection. He leaned closer, giving Anne a whiff of his pepperminty breath. "I understand you. You don't want to kiss just any man. Your heart harbors an entirely different Christmas wish. A powerful one."

"Yeah, right," Anne said, looking away from his intense gaze as a face from her past formed itself in her mind.

She shook her head, dashing the man's image away.

Camo Santa gave Anne a quick wink, as if he knew

precisely whom she'd been thinking of, and she swore his blue eyes actually twinkled at her. And they twinkled *merrily*.

Beside her, Louisa giggled. "Don't be offended, Santa. Dr. Elliot is not free with her kisses, especially during flu season. But you look like a healthy specimen to me. I'll kiss you!"

With that, the young nurse leaped up, put her arms around him, and planted a smacking kiss on his rosy cheek.

Totally nonplussed by Louisa's antics, Camo Santa turned to Henrietta. "And you, my dear? Do you have a kiss for Santa?"

Henrietta shook her head and displayed her engagement ring. The diamond reflected the festive twinkle lights that decorated the walls. "I'm spoken for. I only wish I could finally make myself set a date for the wedding."

Camo Santa nodded and turned to Dr. Russell. Before he could make the same overture to Dr. Russell, she crossed her arms and glared at him. "Don't even think about it. I've got a can of mace with your name on it."

Camo Santa grinned and returned the mistletoe to his lapel.

"Such a shame," he said with mock sorrow. "A table full of beautiful women, and only one kiss to be had."

Camo Santa shifted his focus to Anne. "But, Dr. Elliot, I shall grant your Christmas wish. Everyone's wishes in fact, including yours, Dr. Russell."

And with that, Camo Santa turned and disappeared into the crowd.

"How did that man know our names?" Dr. Russell asked Anne, casting a hard stare in the direction Camo Santa had gone. "None of us are wearing our nametags from the clinic."

Anne shrugged, hoping Dr. Russell didn't dig the mace from her purse and go after the poor man.

"He didn't look familiar to me, but we treat a lot of sailors on base. He was wearing Navy-issued BDU pants, so maybe he knew us from the clinic."

"That explains it," Henrietta said, peering after him. He was now behind the counter taking orders. "I wonder who he is. With that beard, it's hard to see his face."

"Who cares?" Dr. Russell demanded, scowling. "That man is delusional. Probably dangerous. Plus, I don't have a Christmas wish."

"I wonder what *your* Christmas wish is, Dr. Elliot," Louisa said, ignoring her boss's warning. "You have to tell us. Otherwise, we won't know if it comes true."

Anne shook her head and took up her coffee again. "I don't have a Christmas wish."

As the words fell from her lips, Anne realized that they were not precisely true. She did have one wish.

One secret wish that she kept tucked in the deepest reaches of her heart.

Again, the man's image reappeared in her mind, but this time, Anne could not dislodge it before the memories of her past returned.

She had met Frederick Wentworth the summer between college and medical school. Anne had loved him, and he had loved her. But their lives had taken them in completely different directions, and there was no reconciling them. Anne planned to finish medical school and residency, and he had aspirations of one day captaining his own ship, a career path that would take him away for months at a time.

Still, Frederick had proposed, and for a time, they had been giddily engaged. Then, though it broke her heart, Anne decided she could not bear to marry a man only to have him absent from her daily life.

She called off the engagement.

He claimed to understand her reasons, but Anne had wounded him.

He had not spoken to her again. After seven years, Anne believed she'd gotten over him. She even managed to be happy. She had a prosperous career, good friends, and even a few entertaining dates, but often, in the depths of the night, she wondered if she had made the right decision.

Anne shook herself. There was little point in wondering what would happen if the past could be changed.

It couldn't.

She must be content to keep him as a fond memory and nothing more.

"Well, it looks like *my* Christmas wish just came true," Louisa said. She sipped at her frothy drink and then sighed. "I just described the man of my dreams, and there he is now."

Anne followed Louisa's gaze out the window of Mansfield Perk, expecting to find some handsome specimen outside, but what she saw had her sucking in a shocked breath.

Frederick Wentworth.

The very man her mind had just conjured now stood in the flesh just on the other side of the window.

Blood drained from Anne's cheeks, and she barely managed to put her coffee down without sloshing it across the table.

All at once, the Mansfield Perk suddenly ceased to be. The aroma of coffee evaporated, and the sounds of the patrons—including Camo Santa, who was now running the espresso machine—went silent.

Frederick was all there was.

Feeling something between delight and misery, Anne's hands began to shake, and she hid them in her lap.

"Mmm-mmm!" Louisa said, breaking into her hazy thoughts. "If that man comes in here, I guarantee he'll leave with me on his arm. He is hot!"

Anne said nothing, but she could not tear her focus from Frederick. Seven years had only improved his already good looks. His handsome face had matured into sharp chiseled lines, and his shoulders seemed even broader and more solid than before. Despite the dull winter sun, Frederick's skin remained tan, and short blond hair peeked from beneath his cover. He was summer sun in the midst of the damp chill of the Charleston winter.

"I don't recognize him from the base," Louisa complained. "Who is he?"

"He's an officer," Henrietta said, squinting at his uniform. "Lieutenant Commander."

"Surface Warfare Officer," Anne added without thinking. She had followed Frederick's career and knew he was last deployed on the USS *Kellynch*, a guided missile destroyer. But she didn't dare divulge that information.

No one knew of her former relationship with him, and now that he was in Charleston, apparently on leave, she didn't want her friends to find out. If he intended to continue his purposeful disregard of her existence, it was better to bear her sorrow alone than to share it with silly young girls who would not understand.

"That means he might command his own ship one day," Louisa said, clearly awestruck.

Anne would never admit it aloud, but even all these years later, the mere sight of Frederick Wentworth left her feeling a little awestruck too. He was a force all unto himself. She wanted to press her nose against the Mansfield Perk window to get a better look at him or, better yet, to go outside and throw herself at him.

But neither of those two things was going to happen.

Just as in the past, Frederick Wentworth stood right

before Anne Elliot, and yet he remained completely out of her reach.

"Oh!" Louisa gasped and straightened. "He's coming in. Do I have lipstick on my teeth?"

Anne managed to tear her eyes from Frederick in time to check Louisa's makeup and assure her it had not escaped her lip line. When she turned back to the window, she found him almost to the main door.

Panic surged through her. She could not face him. She could not bear seeing the disappointment and resentment on his face when he saw her.

Anne stood abruptly, drawing the notice of everyone at her table.

"Excuse me," she said, yanking her phone from her purse. "I'm…uh…getting a phone call."

Everyone looked at the inert phone she gripped.

"I mean," Anne hedged, hiding the phone in her palm. "My message light is blinking. I'll be right back."

Feeling the absurdity of her actions, Anne hurried to the side door of the shop, intent on making a cowardly escape. Her hand on the door handle, she paused.

Anne was preparing to flee from the man she had once loved. Certainly, she could be in the same room with him, carry on a conversation with him, drink blended coffee drinks with him.

Couldn't she?

She was a mature, intelligent doctor. But this mature, intelligent doctor was also a woman who had once loved a man. That man. Frederick Wentworth.

She may have outlived the age of blushing, but she certainly had not outlived the age of emotion.

Her heart hammered. Her hands shook, and her stomach fluttered.

She closed her eyes as she tried to rally herself. If only she knew what might happen if she stayed and faced him, her decision would be easier. Would Frederick reject her? Would he pretend not to know her? Would he think her ravaged by time?

Anne opened her eyes and considered her reflection in the glass door. Her mulberry colored sweater and tailored trousers flattered her trim figure, and her boots struck just the right balance of practicality and sex appeal. But what would Frederick think of her now?

Her hand flew to her hair as if a stray strand might make a difference, and she felt incredibly foolish.

She must do something, and yet rooted by indecision, Anne stood still.

Finally, she heard herself whisper, "I wish I knew what would happen if I decided to stay and face Frederick Wentworth."

THE SLEIGH BELLS that hung on Mansfield Perk's main door jingled loudly, and without looking, Anne knew that Frederick Wentworth stood in the very same room as she did. Though she and Frederick were separated by tables and people and seven years, she could sense him. The very air of the coffee shop shimmered with his energy. Anne inhaled sharply and swore she could even smell his sun-kissed skin.

Her decision was made. She would stay and meet her former lover. With one last look at herself in the glass door, Anne turned and faced her future.

Frederick stood in line with two other sailors. Easy confidence radiated from him as he talked with his buddies. He had always exhibited a fearlessness of mind that could not be shaken, and she could see clearly that he had not changed in that regard.

But then Frederick saw her, and his expression registered sudden shock from which he couldn't immediately recover.

Anne smiled at him, her eyes never leaving his. She could not decide how she felt about the fact that the mere sight of her caused rock-solid Frederick to show surprise.

"Anne."

He said her name. From her place across the crowded room, Anne could not actually hear his voice, but she felt it in her bones. As if drawn by an irresistible force, she walked toward him. As she progressed across the room, Frederick's surprised expression drifted into regret, as if he wanted to take back his utterance, and then his features went blank.

Before she was cognizant of having covered the distance, Anne stood before him.

She extended her hand and heard herself say what was proper. "Hello, Frederick."

His large hand enveloped hers, and Anne restrained herself from shivering at the contact. He felt exactly the same. Strong, warm, magnetic. A little ray of hope glowed in her heart, but that little fledgling ray of hope was extinguished when he spoke. He greeted her with severe politeness. He spoke her name, but his tone held none of the affection she remembered in it. Instead, she heard coolness and pride. He released her hand with something near disdain in the gesture.

This was not *her* Frederick, she reminded herself. This man wanted nothing to do with her.

"Welcome to Charleston," she managed to say, her tone stiff and formal.

"I did not know you were here," he said as if he would have avoided the city altogether if he had known she lived there.

Anne laughed lightly, and some of her tension dissipated with it. "It gets worse. I work at the health clinic on base."

Before Frederick could say another word, Louisa appeared beside Anne.

"Hello!" she said, wedging herself between Anne and Frederick. "Anne, won't you introduce me to your friend?"

Anne recovered from the interruption and found herself rather grateful for it. She introduced Louisa to Frederick, and in turn, he introduced his shipmates: Lieutenant Harville and Lieutenant Benwick.

Before Anne even knew what was happening, Louisa had become the center of the three men's attention.

"How perfect that your ship should arrive for the holidays!" she enthused. "You are just in time for all the best parties. I hope you will not think me too forward, but I must invite you all to the Nurses' Christmas Ball. The event is held every year, and this year, I am the chairwoman. It's going to be the highlight of the season."

Frederick offered Louisa his confident smile, and the young nurse nearly swooned beneath it.

"Did someone say something about a ball?" Lieutenant Harville asked. "My wife would love a reason to get glammed up."

Louisa gave Lieutenant Harville an open smile. "Then you are all invited," she said, including the quieter Lieutenant Benwick in the invitation.

With that, she reached into the bag she carried on her shoulder, pulled out a small stack of invitations, and began handing them out. Louisa held the last card out to Frederick, but she refused to allow him to take it from her.

"I have no escort for the evening, Lieutenant Commander," she said slyly. "And since Dr. Elliot can vouch for you, I am confident that you are no scoundrel. Would you care to be my date?"

Anne gaped at Louisa, and for the first time since the nurse joined them, Frederick looked at Anne. A self-satisfied smile played about his lips, and she knew that any reply he made was for her benefit alone.

"I'm surprised that a young lady as beautiful as you would be without a date," Frederick said, returning his focus to Louisa.

"I've been so busy planning the event that I just never had time to pick a lucky gentleman to escort me."

"In that case," Frederick said, casting another surreptitious glance at Anne. "Nothing would make me happier than to be your date."

Louisa grinned and let the card slip from her fingers to his.

"What about you, Doc?" Lieutenant Harville asked Anne, putting on a gentlemanly air. "Do you need an escort?"

"What's your wife going to think about that?" Anne asked.

Lieutenant Harville grinned. "Oh, my wife would keelhaul me, but I was asking for Benwick here."

Anne turned to Lieutenant Benwick and offered him a genuine smile. "Though I appreciate the thought, I already have a date."

Though Frederick appeared unaffected by this news, he looked at Anne with fresh eyes, as if assessing her as a woman for the first time since the conversation had begun.

AND THEN IT was over. The worst was over, and Anne was at home alone again.

She had seen Frederick, spoken to him, and now she knew what she must face every time she was in his company. She could prepare to see him with Louisa at the Nurses' Christmas Ball, and she would pretend that nothing he did could hurt her.

If she had to hide her unresolved feelings for Frederick, at least she would do so looking fabulous.

Anne rarely took the time to sit on the small tufted stool at her built-in vanity, but tonight, as she prepared for the ball, she indulged herself.

Wrapped in a thick, white robe with her supplies scattered around the counter, her makeup and hair were done. All that was left was to put on her gown and shoes.

She reached over and stroked the dress that hung on the door frame beside her. The 1950s-inspired design had a nipped-in waist and full skirt. Rather than the expected basic black, the dress was made of rich midnight blue satin.

Far too practical to spend a small fortune on a gown, Anne had purchased a redesigned thrift dress from an online shop called Cate's Creations. She'd ordered it on a whim, and she could not make herself regret it.

When she wore it, she felt like Old Hollywood royalty.

She smiled as she slipped on the gown and stepped into her heels. She turned, studying herself from every angle.

If Frederick wanted nothing to do with her, then this gown would definitely make him regret that decision.

Anne took a sort of devilish delight in the idea of

making him jealous, but the practical side of her wondered if his cold indifference could be breached.

Then, she recalled that fleeting look he'd given her when she'd revealed that she had a date to the ball. She had not wanted to indulge in foolish hope at the time. But perhaps, he had been a little jealous.

She almost laughed at the idea of Frederick Wentworth being jealous of Dr. William Cousins. Her escort was a talented cardiologist, but Anne had no interest in him romantically. In truth, she only agreed to the date in order to please Dr. Russell, who had been courting him for a vacant place on the clinic staff.

But Frederick didn't need to know that.

Anne took one last look at herself in the mirror and was pleased with what she saw. She was Dr. Anne Elliot, respected physician, and she looked pretty darn good. Then, on impulse, she twirled, making the skirt swirl around her, and laughed with delight.

Let Frederick be jealous. It was only fair.

THE NURSES' CHRISTMAS Ball never failed to be one of the most drama-packed events of the year. At least that was how Anne had always perceived it. Colleagues who behaved reasonably at every other time of the year seemed to lose their good sense around the holidays. She suspected the spiked eggnog played a large role in the lowering of inhibitions, and she always steered well clear of it.

Anne arrived on base at the Uppercross Ballroom a bit late, and she found her escort for the evening, Dr. Cousins, already at their table and engaged in conversation with Dr. Russell, who had insisted on chauffeuring him personally to the event.

Dr. Cousins had probably been lean and handsome at some point, but time had gotten the better of him. He sported a slightly receding hairline, which he endeavored to cover with his remaining blond curls, and his face had a swollen look, as did the rest of his body.

A little socially awkward, Dr. Cousins possessed a breadth of health knowledge, which he enjoyed sharing at the least provocation, and he often told charming stories, even if they were clearly rehearsed. Still, he was tolerably pleasant company.

Anne approached the table to hear her date finishing the story of how he thought he'd once met former Surgeon General C. Everett Koop at a fast food restaurant, only to find out it wasn't him. Everyone at the table laughed politely even though the anecdote didn't have a good punchline.

Anne surveyed the group at the table. Henrietta sat beside her fiancé, Charles, a sailor on the USS *Winthrop*. Lieutenant Harville sat beside his wife with Lieutenant Benwick on her other side. Louisa and Frederick came next, leaving an empty chair for Anne between her former fiancé and her current "date."

Anne sucked in a fortifying breath and smiled hugely at her friends.

"Merry Christmas!" she said, standing behind the vacant chair.

The greeting was returned, and Dr. Cousins rose, making a great pretense of assisting Anne to her seat.

"You look beautiful," Dr. Cousins said, leaning in close to take a sniff of her hair. "Smell good too."

"Thank you." Anne tried not to recoil from his sudden closeness, and she definitely did not cast a look at Frederick to see his reaction. "You look handsome too."

Dr. Cousins was the only gentleman at their table who wore a traditional tuxedo. All the other men wore their dress whites, and the effect was striking. Dr. Cousins looked like an ink stain on an otherwise pristine piece of cloth. He came off as soft and ridiculous when compared to Frederick, whom she definitely was not admiring out of the corner of her eye.

Not at all.

"Good evening," Frederick said after she'd taken her seat.

Anne returned a stiff nod.

Then the conversation began to swirl around them. Dinner was served, and libations were consumed.

Soon, an easy camaraderie fell upon the table, and if anyone noticed the awkwardness between Anne and Frederick, they did not say a word about it. Anne fancied that she'd caught Frederick studying her once or twice, but she could not be certain.

Despite the hidden tension, the meal managed to be pleasant.

Louisa, being the most outgoing in the group, led the conversation. She flirted with every gentleman, including those who were engaged or married, and even drew out the quiet Lieutenant Benwick, who had apparently just been dumped by his long-term girlfriend.

Frederick did not appear to mind that his date had eyes for every man at the table, but he did appear to mind Dr. Cousins's increasingly intrusive attentions to Anne.

"Here, Anne. Try a bite of this fruit," Dr. Cousins said, offering Anne a berry from his fork.

Anne blocked his invasive fork with her chocolate-covered one. "No, thank you."

"I have only just finished reading a paper about the effects of processed sugars on the body's functions," he said, seemingly oblivious to the implications of his comments. "The natural sugars in fruit are so much healthier than that chocolate concoction."

"It's Christmas. I feel like being decadent."

"Women of your age are prone to perimenopausal weight gain. It would be advisable to cut back wherever you can."

Stunned silence followed as everyone awaited Anne's response.

"How old do you think I am?" she choked.

"Oh," Dr. Cousins said, realizing his *faux pas*. "I did not mean to imply...errr.... I do apologize if I gave the impression that...."

Beside her, Anne heard Frederick grunt and then lean slightly closer, saying under his breath, "Ass."

Surprised, Anne gave him a quick look.

Her intention had been to make him jealous, but perhaps he was showing his support for her in the face of Dr. Cousins's thoughtless comments. Or was she reading too much into the word?

She looked at Frederick's plate—he'd also chosen the chocolate—and smirked at him.

Perhaps he was not so indifferent toward her after all.

AFTER DINNER, THE dancing began. Anne accepted Dr. Cousins's invitation to a waltz. Frederick and Louisa took to the floor behind them. Though Dr. Cousins was her partner, Anne felt her eyes pulled continually to Frederick, and she fancied she could feel him watching her too.

And what must he see? Could he see how uncomfortable she was with Dr. Cousins? He held her far too closely for her liking, and she spent the dance trying to lever herself away from him while not offending him and thus ruining Dr. Russell's plan to hire him.

Anne hoped no one saw how relieved she was to turn Dr. Cousins over to Dr. Russell at the end of the dance.

She was supposed to be making Frederick jealous, but all she seemed to be doing was getting herself into one awkward situation after another.

The whole plan seemed silly and petty. She was tired of playing games.

She needed a moment to think, regroup.

She returned to the table, which she had expected to find empty. But Henrietta sat alone. Anne slid into the seat beside her.

"Having fun?" Anne asked, taking a sip from the water glass she'd snagged from her place setting.

"Not really," Henrietta confessed, her voice quavering. "Charles and I had a fight."

"I'm sorry to hear that. What happened?"

"Charles seemed to get the idea in his head that tonight I would finally set a date for our wedding."

"And you hadn't planned on doing that?"

"No," Henrietta muttered. "It's not that I don't want to get married. It's just...I'm scared."

"Have you told him that?" Anne asked. "Sometimes ending a disagreement is as easy as just saying what's in your heart."

Both women considered the advice silently for a moment, but Anne was the one more struck by her words. Could anything be changed between her and Frederick if they just spoke honestly with each other and stopped playing foolish games?

Henrietta looked increasingly despondent. "I'm not even sure what's in my heart anymore."

"You know," Anne said, patting her hand. "Sometimes I don't either."

"Maybe I'll go try to find him," she said, looking around the ballroom. "Besides, I think someone is waiting to talk to you."

Anne looked behind her to find Frederick waiting at a respectable distance, and she wondered how much he had overheard.

Henrietta went off in search of Charles, leaving Frederick free to approach her.

"One dance?" Frederick asked softly, surprising Anne. "For old times' sake?"

Anne glanced at the dance floor to find Dr. Cousins now clinging to Dr. Russell. She turned back to Frederick and stood.

"Well, it certainly appears that my escort will not mind," Anne said, grinning at Frederick.

He offered his arm. Anne took it, sliding her manicured fingers across the stiff, white cloth of Frederick's dress uniform. It was easy for her to imagine that something had altered between them since their first meeting at Mansfield Perk. She could almost believe that some of his angry pride had fallen away, revealing the Frederick she'd fallen in love with.

But she must face the truth. Even if his heart was returning to her, nothing in their circumstances had changed. He would soon leave Charleston, and he may never return to this port again.

This could be their last moment together for all she knew.

Determined to enjoy this dance with Frederick, Anne tightened her grasp on his arm.

She wanted to remember every detail: The way he smelled of sun and sea air. The way the light from the disco ball reflected off the gold buttons on his uniform. The way his green eyes looked as they met hers.

No matter what came next, Anne would cherish these memories for the rest of her life.

They took a place in the middle of the dance floor, and Anne came easily into his arms. Frederick held her at a proper, polite distance, the way one might dance with a friend.

Frederick performed the basic steps of the waltz without much thought. Anne followed easily, enjoying his confident lead.

Just as Anne was beginning to wonder if their dance would be carried out in complete silence, Frederick grinned, leaned slightly forward, and sniffed. "Your date is right. You do smell good."

Anne laughed at his unexpected joke.

"Yes, but I should not eat so much sugar, especially not at my age!"

Frederick laughed and then sobered. "What made you accept that buffoon in the first place?"

Anne decided to follow her advice to Henrietta and tell the truth. "Dr. Russell has been courting him for the clinic, and I was apparently one of her lures."

Frederick scowled and then smiled slyly. "I never would have pegged Dr. Russell for a pimp. She just doesn't seem the type to wear gaudy fur coats and feathered hats."

Anne laughed at the image of prim Dr. Russell dressed as a pimp. "She does drive an obscenely enormous Cadillac."

Frederick smiled. "You had no other date for the evening?"

Anne probably should have been affronted by the question, but she could not muster the sentiment. She was past playing games.

"I could have asked any number of men. That's one of the great things about working on base. The odds are always in favor of the women." Anne shrugged, causing Frederick to readjust his hold on her, and he seemed to draw her in closer. "But the truth is that most of my dates have had entertainment value, but little else. I just never got serious with anyone."

Anne did not add "since you," but she felt sure he understood her. She felt his arm tighten on her waist, and she was drawn even closer. Her breasts nearly brushed the ribbons that were pinned neatly on Frederick's uniform.

"Aboard ship, the odds are definitely not in my favor," he said, returning her honesty with some of his own. "And my date with Louisa does not seem to be going so well."

Frederick looked pointedly to his left, and Anne followed his eye line to where Louisa danced very closely with Lieutenant Benwick.

Surprised, Anne let out a little laugh. Who would give up Frederick for Lieutenant Benwick?

"I should be offended, but I just can't bring myself to it," he confessed. "I haven't had much luck with women."

Again, there was the implied "since you."

"Do you mean that you don't date much?" she asked, trying to maintain a light tone. "I cannot believe that! There must be a reason why 'a girl in every port' is a Navy cliché."

"For some, it's true," he agreed. "But you know me, Anne."

His tone implored her to believe him, and she found her eyes drawn to his solemn ones.

"Do I?" she asked softly. "So much time has passed. You may have changed a great deal."

He pressed his lips together. "Perhaps, I have changed a little, but I do not believe that even time can alter a person of strong character. You haven't changed."

"Haven't I?" she whispered.

"No," he murmured, causing Anne to realize that she was pressed against the length of Frederick's body. Her hand was tucked protectively against his chest. If she just inclined her head slightly toward him, she could rest it on his shoulder.

Anne could feel his voice vibrating through his chest. Her body seemed to liquefy with the intimacy of it.

"I have not changed either. Not in the fundamentals. I still like Southern rock and despise game-playing." He waited a beat. "And I have always been a one-woman man."

Anne's heart stopped for a millisecond. She was sure of it.

What did he mean? Was Anne the one woman to whom he referred? Or was she reading too much into his statement?

The way he held her, their bodies so close that she

could feel the steady rhythm of his heart, told her that he had not been able to shed himself of his feelings for her. His dislike of Dr. Cousins told her that he could not bear to see her with another man.

But still, their lives were so disparate. How could they ever be together?

She dared not raise her eyes to his and risk breaking the magic spell that had been cast between them. If she looked up and saw the hopelessness in his expression, she would not be able to bear it. She knew as well as he did that this moment together was all they were to have.

Anne laid her head on his shoulder, inhaled the masculine scent of him, and just enjoyed her fleeting moment of perfection.

THE DANCE ENDED too soon, and it was with great reluctance that Frederick and Anne walked arm in arm back toward their table. The crowd in the dining area had thinned considerably, leaving a maze of empty chairs for them to navigate.

Anne knew that her magical moment with Frederick was over, but she refused to regret it. She had once more been in his arms, and that was the best she could hope for.

"I suppose I must return to my date," Anne said, scanning the room for Dr. Cousins and found him still dancing with a very pleased-looking Dr. Russell. Perhaps her boss's secret Christmas wish was coming true.

"I get the feeling that Dr. Nutrition is happier where he is," Frederick said. "But I don't appear to be so lucky. Here comes Louisa now."

"It's okay. I—"Anne began.

"Anne," Frederick interrupted, leaning toward her with sudden urgency. He looked over his shoulder to see Louisa bearing down on them.

He grasped Anne's hand. "There is something...." He faltered and began again. "If circumstances were different, would you ever consider—"

Louisa burst between them, pulling Anne's hand from Frederick's grasp and yanking her in the direction of the main ballroom door. "Dr. Elliot, you must come with me now."

Anne jerked her arm away, her eyes still locked with Frederick's.

"Not now!" Anne hissed to Louisa, her feet planted firmly where she stood.

What had Frederick been about to say? Anne must know.

"But it's an emergency," Louisa insisted, her tone serious.

Anne tore her eyes from Frederick's serious face and darted a look at Louisa. "Emergency?"

Her mind immediately conjured images of drunken brawls or other alcohol-induced medical emergencies. If someone needed medical help, it was her duty to provide it.

"Yes. In the parking lot." Louisa took her arm again.

This time, Anne followed, but she sent a longing glance at Frederick. He kept his eyes downcast, and Anne wondered if she would ever discover what he would have said if Louisa had not interrupted.

"I should be angry with you, Dr. Elliot," Louisa said airily as she pulled Anne toward the double doors that led out of the ballroom. "My date only has eyes for you."

"Please tell me *that* is not your emergency," Anne said, annoyed.

"Of course not," Louisa said, oblivious to Anne's quickly degrading mood. "I found solace in the arms of one of his shipmates. You remember Lieutenant Benwick from Mansfield Perk, right? Now, *he* has the soul of a poet. Did you know he plays the violin?"

Anne stopped in the middle of the lobby and sucked in a deep breath. She barely noticed the scent of the fir trees that lined the room. "Louisa! What is the emergency? Do I need my medical bag?"

"It's Henrietta. She had another fight with Charles. He issued her an ultimatum about setting a wedding date."

Anne pressed her lips together in frustration. She had been ripped from Frederick because of Henrietta's indecisiveness. Of course, neither Louisa nor Henrietta had the least idea of what they had interrupted. They viewed her as some sort of asexual problem-solving machine.

And perhaps that was all she was destined to be.

Well, if that were the case, then she would be the best asexual problem-solving machine possible.

"I understand that you are worried about Henrietta, but I don't see how this qualifies as an emergency."

"She had a panic attack—hyperventilation, heart palpitations, the whole shebang—and had to leave the ballroom. I examined her myself, and I think it's just anxiety, but I wanted to be sure. All my equipment is already there."

Anne found Henrietta sitting in the passenger seat of her small sedan. Even from a distance, the bright lights of the parking lot revealed how agitated the young woman was. Her hands shook, and her breathing appeared jerky and irregular.

"Hi, Hen," Anne said softly as she knelt before the open car door. "Tell me what I can do to make you feel better."

Henrietta gave a despondent shrug, and Anne began to check her vitals.

"Water," she said finally.

"Louisa," Anne said to the nurse who hovered behind her. "Go get her some water."

Louisa disappeared while Anne finished her examination. She found that she concurred with Louisa's diagnosis. Henrietta showed all the signs of panic.

"You should be feeling better soon," Anne assured Henrietta. "You may shake for a while yet, but that's normal."

"Is it?" Henrietta asked. "I don't feel normal. I feel completely lost."

"Why is that, dear?" Anne asked softly, though Louisa had already told her the gist of the story.

"I don't know what to do!" Tears began to streak down Henrietta's freckled cheeks. "Charles says our engagement is off if I don't set a date for the wedding."

Forgetting to be careful of her gown, Anne sat on the running board of the car and put her arm around Henrietta.

"What makes you hesitate? There has to be some reason why you continue to put off the wedding."

Henrietta dropped her face into her hands and made a snuffling sound. "I don't know!"

"I think I do," Anne said. "When Charles is gone on ship duty, you wonder if your relationship is worth it. He has his life on the *Winthrop*, and you have yours here."

Henrietta nodded vigorously, but slowly began to gather control of herself. "He's supposed to be my other half, my soul mate. When he's gone, I feel like half a person. I don't want to be half a person!"

"Half a person?" Anne tilted her head to the side and studied her friend. "But, Henrietta, you're not half a person. Even when you're part of a couple, and you both live in the same house, you are a whole person all by yourself."

Henrietta rolled her eyes. "You don't have a romantic bone in your body, do you?"

Anne tried not to be offended by Henrietta's accusation. After all, she had told no one about her romance with Frederick and had shown little interest in serious dating. It was logical for the younger woman to believe her devoid of fanciful feelings.

"You just can't understand the way I hurt," the nurse said. "Nobody can imagine what it's like to miss someone the way I miss Charles when he's away."

"It may seem hard to believe, but I do understand," Anne said, giving Henrietta another squeeze. "And what's more, I know what it's like to face just such a choice. When you love someone, you want to be with him as much as possible. Anything else seems like too great a compromise to consider. Every time the one you love leaves, your heart breaks a little more. One day, you fear it will be beyond repair."

Henrietta turned her face toward Anne. Her freckled cheeks were streaked with the trails of her tears, but her eyes were wide with shock. "You loved someone? A sailor?"

Anne huffed. "You sound as if you thought me incapable of any emotion at all!"

Henrietta flushed. "I just never thought men interested you."

She gave her a gentle smile. "You were wrong. I was once in the very same situation you are now."

"You loved a sailor and were engaged to him?" Her eyes searched Anne's face eagerly. "What did you do?"

"I called it off," Anne said simply. She lowered her eyes to disguise the depth of her emotion, but she could not completely hide her sorrow. "The thought of saying goodbye to him so often and for so long...I imagined a life of constant heartbreak and loneliness when he was away. I thought it would be easier if I just made one clean break."

"But you regret it now," Henrietta surmised. She waited expectantly for Anne to explain.

"I do not want to make this moment about myself," Anne said, fearing she had revealed too much. "Besides, I cannot change the past."

Henrietta's forehead creased. "But you know things. You described just how I feel about Charles. I don't want to regret my choice."

Anne sighed as she considered Henrietta's words.

"I do not care for the term 'regret.' Recalling past mistakes and longing to go back in time to correct them is pointless. What is done cannot be undone. I made a decision, and I created a life that I enjoy." She paused and met Henrietta's gaze. "But I often wonder if the life I created is just a little emptier than it could have been."

Henrietta frowned. "You confuse me. Just tell me what I should do about Charles!"

"I cannot tell you what to do. No one can. You must make your choice on your own, but consider this: nothing lasts forever. Neither the good nor the bad is eternal."

Henrietta thought for a moment. "I don't understand."

"Charles will not always be aboard ship," Anne said. "One day, he will return to shore."

"It is the meantime I do not like," Henrietta said. "If I am to marry him, I want to be with him. I want to wake up beside him every morning and go to sleep beside him every night. I want to raise our children together. I want it all, but that's not what I'd be getting. I'd be getting a long-distance relationship, and you know how well those usually work out."

Anne nodded, her eyes suddenly misty. "I thought much the same way myself."

The two women remained silent for long moments. Anne could think only of Frederick and what could have been. She wanted to advise Henrietta both to hold on to her true love and not to compromise her ideals. Yet both could not be accomplished at the same time.

A truth Anne knew far too well.

"Oh!" Henrietta moaned. "It's all so impossible."

"So it seems," Anne agreed. "There seems to be no right answer to this dilemma, does there?"

Henrietta shook her head. "One moment, I think I must marry Charles, or my heart will break, and the very next moment, I think if I *do* marry him, my heart will break. No matter which choice I make, my heart will end up broken."

Anne could say nothing to dispute her.

Finally, after a long silence, Henrietta asked, "If you had to make the same choice again right now, would you do the same thing? Would you marry your sailor?"

Though she already knew her answer, Anne considered her words carefully.

"If I truly loved the sailor," she began slowly, already knowing that she still loved Frederick

Wentworth just as much as she ever did, "and he loved me, then I would attempt the impossible for love."

Henrietta's tears flowed once again, and Anne's misty eyes threatened to spill over as well. She took a deep breath and closed her eyes against the pain that arose from her admission.

WHEN LOUISA RETURNED with a bottle of water for Henrietta, Lieutenant Benwick was with her. Though he said very little, he seemed quite drawn by Louisa's vivacious personality. And Anne could not fault his politeness. He offered to drive both nurses home and help them recover their vehicles in the morning.

No sooner had Henrietta, Louisa, and Lieutenant Benwick departed from the parking lot than Anne felt her phone vibrate.

She groaned aloud. Her head ached, and her chest felt raw with emotion. She considered ignoring the blasted phone, but what if it were a patient with a medical emergency? Even though she was not on call over the holidays, she could not bring herself to leave someone without help.

Instead of finding communication from a patient, Anne discovered an email from Frederick.

So flustered by the message, Anne did not even think to consider how he'd discovered her email address in the first place.

Her fingers shook as she began to read. His first words nearly caused her to drop her phone: "I would ask you to forgive me for eavesdropping on your conversation with Henrietta just now, but I do not regret it."

Frederick was here? Listening to her conversation with Henrietta? Anne's head shot up, and she quickly looked around the parking lot for any sign of her eavesdropper, but she could not find him. In fact, she saw no one in the lot at all, only empty vehicles.

Frederick must be gone now too.

Heart hammering, Anne returned to the message.

I cannot listen any longer without reaching out to you, and this phone is my only means of doing so. 'Would you marry your sailor?' she asks you, and torn between agony and hope, I find myself leaning forward to catch your response. 'If I truly loved the sailor, and he loved me, I would attempt the impossible for love,' you say. I feel my heart stop. Are you thinking of me, Anne, when you murmur those promises? Because I have never stopped thinking of you. I wish I could say that I returned to Charleston for you alone, but I cannot. Instead, I can tell you something far better. I came to Charleston to accept a post on shore. And here you are. Appearing before me just as all the obstacles of the past have been removed.

Henrietta is leaving, and my date is leaving with Benwick, so I will go too. But know this, Anne. I did not plan to find you here when I arrived, but I am glad I did. The truth is that I have never stopped loving you. I don't know how it's possible, but I love you even more than I did all those years ago.

If you love me too, then let's attempt the impossible together. I will be waiting. Find me when you are ready. A word, a look, will be enough to decide whether I approach you with my heart or never speak of this again.

Frederick.

Frederick's words blurred, and the tears Anne had been holding back began to fall. She indulged herself in a good, loud sobbing cry right there in the middle of the empty parking lot.

Though tears blurred her vision, she could see the future suddenly opening up before her.

And she would seize it immediately! She must speak to Frederick right away.

But where had he gone? Home? Anne did not even know if he had lodging on base. She briefly considered emailing him, but then decided against it. She had to see him in person. She needed to see the expression on his face, hear his voice, feel his heartbeat against her chest.

Leaving the email open on the screen, she tossed the phone into her purse and dashed to her own car. She shoved her purse onto the passenger seat and then tucked herself and her dress behind the wheel. On impulse, she reached down, yanked off her ridiculous heels, and threw them in the backseat.

That's when she noticed the empty Mansfield Perk cup in the cup holder.

Mansfield Perk.

That was where she had first seen Frederick.

Maybe she would find him there now.

For some reason, that idea sounded right, and Anne started her engine and squealed out of the parking lot, intent on getting to the coffee shop as quickly as she could.

ANNE PARKED HER car in the exact spot she had used the night she'd first seen Frederick at Mansfield Perk. Forgetting her heels in the backseat but remembering to grab her purse, she leapt from the vehicle and ran barefoot across the cold, damp asphalt.

She flung open the side door of the coffee shop, eyes frantically scanning the room for Frederick Wentworth in his dress whites. But some idiot in a Santa coat and hat blocked her view of the room.

Camo Santa. What was he doing here again? Had he been hired for the whole season? Anne had pegged him as an overzealous sailor home on leave. Now she wasn't so sure.

"Excuse me, Santa," Anne said as she tried to duck around him. "I've got to find someone."

"In a hurry to find your true love, are you, Dr. Elliot?" Camo Santa asked, a smile on his rosy lips.

Anne goggled up at him. "How could you possibly know that?" Then her eyes narrowed with suspicion. Maybe Dr. Russell was right, and he was truly a dangerous individual. "Are you some kind of crazy cosplay stalker? Because I'll call the cops."

She reached into her bag, producing her cell phone as evidence of her intent to involve the authorities.

Santa laughed heartily. "You know who I am, Anne. I have come to grant your Christmas wish. To give you your heart's desire." He nodded at the phone. "And you know who I'm talking about."

Anne clutched the phone to her chest.

"Frederick will be here soon," Santa said. "But not quite the way you expect. He'll look just as he did when you first saw him here."

Anne's brow furrowed. "I don't understand. I just saw him at the Nurses' Christmas Ball. We danced together. He was wearing dress whites."

"He's back in his work uniform." Camo Santa nodded toward her own clothing. "And so are you."

"What are you talking about?" She looked down, fully expecting to see her gorgeous gown and bare feet, but what she saw had her taking a step back. She wore her dark brown boots, tailored pants, and mulberry sweater. Just what she'd been wearing the night she first saw Frederick here at Mansfield Perk.

She turned to look at her reflection in the glass door, as if the twinkle lights strung about the room might be playing tricks on her eyes.

But no matter how long she stared at herself, all she saw was the outfit worn to the clinic that day.

"What the…?" Anne ran a hand down the cashmere sleeve of her sweater. Where had her ball gown gone? And when had she put on boots? She was sure she had run across the parking lot barefoot.

"See," Santa said. "If you need more proof, look over there. Your friends are still at your table."

Anne turned from her reflection in the side door and saw Dr. Russell, Henrietta, and Louisa sitting at the table just as they had been that night, holding the very same beverages, wearing the same clothes.

Something must be seriously wrong with her. Anne looked at Camo Santa as if the lunatic might be able to offer a rational explanation. "Am I experiencing some sort of dissociative episode? Are you a hallucination?"

Camo Santa chuckled. "Sometimes, Dr. Elliot, the most powerful moments of our lives take place in an instant, over and gone so quickly that it seems almost as if we never lived them. Yet they changed our whole lives."

"I really don't understand," she admitted, staring at Santa in confusion.

Was he saying that her evening with Frederick Wentworth hadn't been real? All those things he said, the dance, the email…they hadn't happened?

But it all had felt so real. She could still feel the fabric of his dress coat beneath her cheek.

Good Lord, had her mind constructed a fantasy so elaborate that she believed she actually experienced it? Had she been standing at this door all along, imagining what might happen if she turned and faced him?

"I must be going crazy."

"You're perfectly fine, doc," Camo Santa assured her with a warm smile and that infernal twinkle in his eyes. "You'll understand soon enough. I promise."

With that, he took her forearm in his white-gloved hand and turned her back toward the side door of the Mansfield Perk.

The last thing she heard Camo Santa say was "Merry Christmas," and then he was gone.

THE SLEIGH BELLS that hung on the main door of Mansfield Perk jingled loudly, and without looking, Anne knew that Frederick once again stood in the very same room as she did.

Just like the night she'd first seen him, this night apparently.

"This cannot be," Anne breathed. She had been with him at the Nurses' Christmas Ball. He'd held her in his arms. He'd written her that email professing his love.

It had all seemed so real. So perfect.

Perhaps too perfect.

Anne closed her eyes tightly, trying to make sense of things that defied reason and logic.

She was, in fact, back in Mansfield Perk the fateful night of their first meeting.

Frederick was here too. She could sense him, feel him.

Anne turned and faced her past. Or was this her future? She could no longer be sure.

Frederick stood beside Lieutenants Benwick and Harville, just as he had the first time they'd played this scene.

But unlike before, Frederick's eyes searched the room until they landed on Anne. His expression registered no shock at all, as if he'd been expecting to find her standing there all along.

Without a word to his friends, Frederick waded across the sea of tables and across the seven years that separated him from Anne.

She met him half way, and they stood in the center of the room staring at each other in shock. He had been there too...at the ball with her. Somehow, she was sure of it.

"Anne," he breathed. His forehead wrinkled. "I—I don't understand this."

"No," Anne replied, reaching up to touch the pocket of his BDU coat, just to make sure it was real. "Neither do I, but here we are. Again...maybe."

He put his large hand over hers, holding it against his heart.

"And somehow you know how I feel about you," he said, dropping his voice low. "How I have always felt about you."

A tear slipped down Anne's cheek, and she nodded. "My feelings for you have never changed either."

Anne threw her arms around Frederick with careless abandon. Holding him tight, she pressed her lips to his neck.

"All these years, I believed I was content, fulfilled," she said. "And I was, for the most part. But seeing you made me realize that my heart could hold so much more joy."

Frederick tipped Anne's face toward his.

The air around them seemed to shimmer, and every sensation was magnified.

Anne sighed as Frederick's lips brushed hers softly, gently. Anne wrapped a hand around his neck, pulling him more fully against her body. The kiss turned hungry, and she felt his groan vibrate through her own chest.

Reality crashed upon Anne, and she realized they were creating quite a scene.

She pulled away, but Frederick would not let her go far. He rested his forehead against hers.

"I never stopped loving you," he whispered. "I seem to love you even more now than I did seven years ago, though it hardly seems possible."

"I love you too, Frederick, and the years we spent apart…." She tapered off, unsure how to summarize her feelings.

"I know," he said as if he truly understood her unspoken sentiments. "But they brought us to this moment."

"Yes, they did, though I hardly understand exactly how it happened. Did we have some sort of joint hallucination?"

Frederick shrugged and kissed the tip of her nose. "I don't want to question it. But here comes someone who appears to have plenty of questions."

Just as before, Louisa sidled up beside her. This time, Anne stood firmly in Frederick's embrace. He shifted slightly so that they stood side by side, but he never let her go.

"Dr. Elliot! Why didn't you tell me that you knew these sailors?"

Anne frowned. Apparently, Louisa was not part of this bizarre Christmas miracle time jump.

"Yeah, Wentworth." Harville slapped his buddy on the back. "Why didn't you tell us that your Dr. Elliot was here in Charleston?"

"I didn't know she was," he replied, coloring slightly at his friend's admission that he had spoken of her and their past.

"Then it is fortunate," Louisa said, "that we decided to come to Mansfield Perk to celebrate Henrietta finally setting her wedding date with Charles." Her eyes focused on a point over Anne's shoulder. "But more importantly, why don't you introduce me to your shipmates?"

Anne turned her head to find Lieutenant Benwick lingering behind them. She glanced at Frederick, and recalling the unlikely hook-up between the melancholy sailor and bubbly Louisa at the ball, they both smiled.

The introductions were made, and somehow, Louisa managed to wrap herself around Lieutenant Benwick's arm, which did not seem to displease him in the slightest.

"So," Louisa said to Anne. "How do the two of you know each other? I thought Dr. Elliot was a man-hater just like Dr. Russell."

Anne rolled her eyes, but explained briefly that she and Frederick had known each other in the past but had not spoken in seven years.

"And *that* is how you greet each other after a bad breakup and seven years of time?" Louisa asked, incredulous.

"Well, I suppose we've met once before," Anne tried to explain before realizing that the truth was inexplicable. "Briefly."

"In a manner of speaking," Frederick disclaimed, tightening his grasp on Anne as if she might vanish.

He turned her in his arms so that she once again faced him, effectively cutting off her view of Louisa and the other sailors. "I never expected to find you here," he confessed. "And still single."

"And I took a job on a naval base because I could not quite let you go," she whispered for his ears alone. "It was foolish of me, but then there you were. Or here you are."

Confused, she shook her head. "And your email? It said you were staying in Charleston."

She looked at the phone still clutched in her hand as if to confirm his words. The email could not be there, could it?

The ball had never occurred, and neither had her conversation with unsuspecting Henrietta. Frederick had overheard none of her admissions, so the email could not exist. No beautiful words of love for her to cherish for all eternity.

Anne activated the screen.

And there was the message, every glorious word of it.

"Oh!" Anne cried. "Look." She held the phone up for Frederick.

"My message? But how?"

A smile bloomed on her face even as happy tears slid down her cheeks. "Maybe that crazy Santa was right. Maybe we lived all those moments in just one instant."

"Or maybe it was a Christmas miracle."

Frederick cupped her jaw with his free hand and tipped her face up to his.

"My decision to stay in Charleston was made long before the *Kellynch* reached port, but seeing your beautiful face just confirmed that I had made the best choice. This is where I wanted to work before I saw you, but now...I realize this is where my heart lives...has always lived. With you."

ACKNOWLEDGEMENTS

I am indebted to Jane Austen for creating the wonderful characters that inhabit Persuasion. Thank you, Jess, Cecilia, Rebecca, Kimberly, and Melissa, for allowing me to write with you. My deepest thanks go to my editorial team—Jakki Leatherberry, Octavia Becton, Marilyn Whiteley, and Bert Becton. As always, all mistakes in this text belong to me, but I will try to foist them off on someone else.

ABOUT THE AUTHOR

Jennifer Becton worked for more than twelve years in the traditional publishing industry as a freelance writer, editor, and proofreader. Upon discovering the possibilities of the expanding ebook market, she created Whiteley Press, LLC, an independent publishing house, and she has since published in two genres: historical fiction and thrillers.

You can connect with Jennifer on her website: www.BectonLiterary.com or on Twitter at @JenniferBecton.

MISCHIEF AND
Mistletoe

MELISSA BUELL

To Jess—

"Hey, what do you think about writing an Austen Christmas story with me?" You, my friend, are the best writing co-conspirator ever.

To Chris—
All I want for Christmas is you. And some chocolate. And books. But mostly, you.

"If adventures will not befall a young lady in her own village, she must seek them abroad."

—Jane Austen, *Northanger Abbey*

CATHERINE MORLAND SWUNG a teal silk gown from the metal hanging rack. "Tada!" she cried. "If I trim it down a lot, it's perfect."

Mrs. Morland glanced over her shoulder and nodded. "Excellent find, sweetheart. Are you ready to call it a day?" She opened her mom bag and pulled out four packages of gummy fruit snacks. "The natives are getting restless."

Cate rolled her eyes and laid the gown on top of the other dresses draped over the basket of the cart. "Maybe if you didn't give them sugar, they wouldn't be so crazy."

"We both know that without treats, we wouldn't

have lasted ten minutes in the store," Mrs. Morland replied as she tossed the foil baggies to Catherine's four youngest brothers.

"Can't we go wait with Charlie in the van?" Tommy whined, pulling on his mother's sleeve.

"Catie is going to check out now and I'll take you out to the van," Mrs. Morland said as she unbuckled Bryce from the child seat in the shopping cart. "Pay for my things, and I'll pay you back once we get home."

Cate nodded as she pulled her dark blonde hair back into a ponytail. As soon as her mom and brothers were out of eyeshot, she crossed the aisle to the used books area. She scanned the shelves quickly, pleased to see that this thrift shop actually alphabetized by author last name. No matter that all fiction genres were thrown together. She had dealt with worse, such as the estate sale on Pine Avenue with three bedrooms full of books that turned out to only be non-fiction titles mixed with the occasional National Geographic.

"Yes, an Allan Duprie. Haven't read this one yet." She slid the book off the shelf. The cover showed a pale girl in an Edwardian gown creeping into a graveyard. *Fifty cents.* She flicked open the first page. "And at twenty five cents, it's sold." Cate eased down the row of books, passing up books that she had already read and owned copies of. "Mom would kill me if I brought home another Regency romance. Oh. My. Word. I don't believe it." She reached out with shaking hands for the maroon hardcover book. Her index finger traced over the title imprinted on the front. "The Mystery of the Mirror? Are you kidding me?"

Her mind whirred as she paused before opening the front page. *It's going to be at least five hundred dollars. No, more than that. How is it even here? It's not a Reader's Digest version. How much money do I have on me? I should just put it back. But, I'll always wonder how much it cost.* She bit her lower lip and closed her eyes as she opened the cover. She peeked at the light pencil mark and then stared down at the book. "This can't be right."

She kept a firm grip on the book with her left hand as she pushed the cart with her right. As she approached the register, she willed her heart to stop beating so wildly.

The clerk at the register gave her a tired smile. "Welcome to Thrift Barn. How can I help you?"

"Can you please tell me the price for this book?" Catherine asked as she handed over the book.

"We list the prices inside," the clerk answered as she showed the price on the inside page. "It's two dollars." Seeing the look on Catherine's face, she added, "It's because it's a hardback. The paperbacks are only a quarter."

Feeling faint, Catherine managed to nod. "I'll take it. Oh, and everything else in the cart, please."

CATE DUCKED UNDER the low doorway into her attic room and sat down at her sewing project table. She spread the new dresses she had purchased in front of her.

"This blue is perfect," she murmured as she ran her hand over the satin skirt.

She rechecked the latest order from her Sew-Easy shop on her battered laptop. One navy blue dress, tea length fit and flare with 3/4 sleeves for Ellie Dashwood. Cate had the other two Dashwood dresses made and hanging in her sewing closet. The scarlet red chiffon gown she had purchased at an estate sale two months ago had been perfect to make over into an asymmetrical halter dress for Marianne Dashwood. The hand beading had taken several hours to complete but it was worth the effort. The dress for the youngest sister started as an emerald green velvet choir dress that Cate bought for a dollar at a yard sale. Taking in the sides was easy as was lowering the neckline a little so it wouldn't choke the poor girl.

The order was due in four days and Cate had resolved that if she had not found the right dress by tonight, she would have to go purchase new material from the discount fabric shop ten miles away. She knew that material would be at least fifteen dollars per yard and she needed a lot of yardage to pull off the gown she knew she wanted for Ellie Dashwood. Not everyone could look at the navy blue bridesmaid dress with the bubble sleeves and huge butt bow and think, "That would be a lovely Christmas ball gown."

But that was Cate's talent and she worked slavishly to perfect it.

She picked up the seam ripper and proceeded to pick apart the skirt, bodice, sleeves, and untold yardage of tulle and netting from the underskirt. The Disney musicals station from Pandora played in the background, giving her energy to keep working. She made paper patterns when the request came in and transferred those to muslin patterns. She draped each one on her dressmaker's form and sent the photos she took to Ellie. Ellie loved her dress. Marianne requested that the dress be a little shorter and tighter than the pattern. Maggie only asked if it was possible to have pockets added to the gown. Cate was happy to fix each issue as best she could.

Cate checked the clock on the wall, relieved to see she had an hour before Mom would expect her to help with dinner. She pinned the muslin pattern to the material and cut out the rich silk material with her Geiger scissors, a gift from Mrs. Allen. The sweet woman was both the Morland family's landlady and neighbor. Since the Allens were childless, Mrs. Allen had practically adopted Cate. Mrs. Morland appreciated another feminine presence in her tomboy daughter's life.

Being homeschooled and at home with her brothers all day long felt like a punishment at times. Being able to head next door to Mrs. Allen's quiet house was a balm to Cate's soul. It was at Mrs. Allen's house that Cate first took an interest in sewing.

Mrs. Allen hosted a sewing day for the ladies from

church when Cate was twelve years old. Mr. Morland took a morning off from sermon preparation to watch the younger Morland boys with James' help. At fifteen, he was responsible and even changed the occasional diaper.

While most of the ladies chatted over coffee, Cate was an attentive pupil as Mrs. Allen demonstrated how to cut out an easy pattern for a baby blanket.

"Seeing as how your mother has so many little ones at home, this blanket making will come in handy," Mrs. Stuart joked.

Cate scowled at the older lady but pulled her face back into a smile when she saw her mother looking sternly at her. *Everyone thinks they can make comments about how many children we have in our family. We all know we have a lot of children. Our house is bursting at the seams and we never have enough money for all the things we want.* She caught herself before she could go on. Mom had instilled in her the belief that she must be grateful for even the little they did have. *We've never gone hungry. We've never been cold. My clothes are hand-me-downs from the older girls at church but at least I have clothes.*

She looked down at her blouse. "Mrs. Allen," she said quietly. "Is it possible for me to learn how to sew something to cover up this bleach stain?"

Mrs. Allen's eyes were kind as they looked at Cate's shirt. "I know you can, honey. And I'm going to help you." She leaned closer over the sewing table. "I've offered to your parents to take you shopping, you know. But your father, he is a proud man in the best way. He doesn't want to accept charity."

"I know," Cate mumbled. This was another lesson taught to the Morland children. *We have to work for what we have. It makes you appreciate it more.*

Cate began to babysit for church families on Friday and Saturday evenings to save up money to buy fabric. She went shopping with Mom one day to buy new shoes for the little boys. One of the ladies at church shared that a new consignment store had opened in town. Mom was thrilled at the deals she found on slightly worn shoes. Cate was thrilled to find a church dress, new with tags attached, in the exact aquamarine shade she had been looking for. The only problem was the dress was a size too large. Mom assured her that Mrs. Allen could help her tailor it. Cate made her first thrifty sewing purchase and her future was sealed.

Whenever she found an elaborate gown for less than ten dollars, she bought it. She never knew how she might use it but she knew that she'd find a use for it one way or another. Ladies at church found out about her sewing and redesigning skills and enlisted her help. She made prom dresses, costumes for plays, and formal evening gowns. Mrs. Allen began to drop hints about a future career in fashion design. Mom and Dad weren't completely sold on the idea until a neighbor asked Cate to make her a wedding dress using her mother's wedding dress. Mistaking Cate's hesitation, the neighbor offered her $500. Cate agreed and the money went into the savings account for fashion design school.

The dress was beautiful after Cate removed the

yards of lace that trimmed the bodice and skirt, slimmed down the sleeves, and removed two of the four petticoats. The bride was thrilled, the mother was excited to see her daughter wear her gown, and Mr. Morland was happy to see Cate working diligently.

MRS. ALLEN RANG the bell after dinner and Mrs. Morland invited her inside for coffee and pie.

"The pie is a day old but the coffee is fresh," Mrs. Morland apologized as they sat down in the kitchen.

Cate looked up from where she was drying the dishes. "Hello, Mrs. Allen."

"Good evening, honey. Why don't you come sit down for a minute? I have something exciting to tell you," Mrs. Allen said with a mischievous smile.

After hanging up the towel, Cate sat down opposite Mrs. Allen at the long dinner table. *It seems like she has news. I hope it is good news!*

"As you know, my husband and I are patrons of the arts. One of the causes dear to our hearts is the annual Dickens' Christmas Festival up in Santa Barbara. One of the committee members has asked me, as a Platinum Sponsor, if I would like to have a part in designing the costumes for this year's festival. Naturally, I thought of you. Can I hire you to be the designer for the festival?"

"I-I…" Cate stuttered as she stared at Mrs. Allen. "Me? Design for the whole festival? Isn't it kind of a big deal?"

"It does bring in ten thousand visitors to Santa Barbara," Mrs. Allen said thoughtfully. "That revenue is appreciated by the community, of course. The costumes have an important part in all of it to get everyone into the spirit of the festival. There are write ups about the festival in all the local papers and occasionally national ones, if it's a slow news week."

"What about the costumes that were used previously?" Mrs. Morland asked as she passed out the plates of pie.

"The last ones were made back in the 80s and have strained their last seam, unfortunately. They have been patched beyond belief. It's time for fresh costumes and a fresh face to make those costumes. What do you say, Catie?" Mrs. Allen asked.

"It's a dream come true," she gushed. "I've always wanted to make a whole set of clothes that coordinate. It's almost like a fashion line but set in 1890. Which is fantastic, don't get me wrong," she rushed to say. "Wow. Thank you, Mrs. Allen. This is such an amazing opportunity."

"And you'll be paid, honey. That money will help pay for school, of course." Mrs. Allen winked.

"I can use that money to buy new material?" Cate asked, her mind whirling with ideas of what she would do with fresh yardage.

"The material will be purchased separately. You don't have to spend any of your own money, dear."

Mrs. Allen turned to Mrs. Morland with a smile. "Isn't she a sweet little thing?"

Mrs. Morland nodded her head. "She's sweet but very naïve, I'm afraid. Too much time at home with only her family or her nose in a book. I don't know what will happen to her up in Santa Barbara."

"Mom, I'm eighteen years old! I'm officially an adult. You won't have to worry about me." Even as Cate said it, she felt despair washing over her. This wonderful opportunity would be gone forever because her mom thought her too young.

Mrs. Allen's laugh filled the room. "I'm sorry, friends. Of course I won't have Cate go alone. Norm and I always stay at our condo in Santa Barbara during the festival. We'll be there earlier this year because of the planning I'm in charge of. We want Cate to stay with us. We have plenty of space and a car service is available to drive you if Norm or I aren't available. We'll return home for Thanksgiving, of course but then head back to Santa Barbara."

Mrs. Morland rubbed her forehead. "I'll speak to Jim about this. This would be a wonderful prospect for Catherine." She turned toward her daughter. "But what will I do without you?"

"You can hire one of the neighbor girls to come watch the boys or help around here a few days a week," Cate suggested weakly.

"I don't mean with the chores and laundry, silly. I meant what would I do without you, my sweet girl?" Mrs. Morland's eyes filled with tears. "I'll be the only female in this testosterone charged house. I do hope you'll return quickly and help me regain my sanity."

"Is that a yes?" Mrs. Allen asked as Cate leaped up from her chair.

"Final approval from Jim, of course but I think it'll be fine. I just needed a minute to wrap my head around it. Think of it," Mrs. Morland said as Cate squeezed her around the waist. "My little girl a designer in her own right. Who would have thought the girl with grass stained pants and perpetually dirty hands would grow up into one so lovely?"

"Thanks. I think," Cate said with a wry smile. "I need to pack! And ship off the last orders I've finished. Oh, and begin sketching out some ideas for costumes. There's so much to do!"

She started out of the kitchen and turned around to face Mrs. Allen. "Thank you so much, Mrs. Allen. You're like my fairy godmother." She gave the older woman a hug.

Mrs. Allen beamed at her. "You know I love you like you're my own daughter, honey. I'm happy to do this for you. Go on with you. We leave for Santa Barbara in three days."

CATE STARED OUT the back window of the Allens' hired car. The palm trees waving in the gentle breeze, the sapphire blue ocean surging onto the sandy beach, and the sun shining in the bright blue sky seemed like a scene from a movie. *This is more than I thought it would be. Soon I'll be standing out there, toes in the sand, the coolness of the ocean washing over me. It's like when Leona meets Mr. Rowland on the banks of the Adriatic where the Danae shipwrecked and Leona sees the ghostly apparition of the ship's captain. She wonders—*

"We're almost there," Mrs. Allen said next to her, jiggling Cate's elbow. "The condo is a block away."

"Thank you," Cate said, slipping out of her daydream. She would have to be careful not be too consumed by her bookish thoughts. Not everyone understood the way that her family did. Her mother tolerated it, it amused her father, and her brothers thought she was just a bit crazy. No one else knew how much time she spent with her book friends, both while reading and in her own imagination. She preferred to keep it that way.

"Norm, where are we eating tonight?" Mrs. Allen called to the front seat.

Mr. Allen turned around in the passenger seat. "I thought we'd take Cate out to The Pump Room. I think she'll appreciate the history of the building. She's got an old soul." He winked good-naturedly at Cate.

"The Pump Room sounds wonderful. What can you tell me about it? Any tales associated with it?" Cate asked, leaning forward.

"Now that you mention, there might be a ghost story. I'll have to ask around for the details. I believe it's part of the Haunted Santa Barbara Tour," Mr. Allen answered.

"Hush now, Norm. Don't frighten the poor child. She won't sleep a wink a night for fear of ghosts," Mrs. Allen admonished her husband.

"I'm not afraid of ghosts," Cate assured her. "I've read plenty of books about ghosts but most of them have plausible explanations at the end."

"Sort of like Scooby-Doo," the driver chuckled.

"Like who?" Cate asked.

"Popular TV show for kids. You've never seen it?" the driver asked over his shoulder.

"I was homeschooled," Cate said ruefully. "We didn't watch a lot of TV. Mostly PBS shows. Very educational."

"Her father's a pastor," Mr. Allen added. "You know how everyone keeps track of what the pastor's kids are watching and doing. Isn't that right, Catie?"

"That's right," Cate said quietly. *And that's the reason I've never had a boyfriend. No one wants to date the pastor's only daughter. But…no one in Santa Barbara knows who I am! Maybe I'll finally have the chance to meet someone who likes me for me and doesn't worry about my father's profession.* She felt much lighter suddenly. *So many dreams are coming true just by being here in Santa Barbara. Maybe I do have a fairy godmother after all.*

THE HIGH CEILINGS and tall columns gave the room a lofty feeling while the 18th century portraits hanging on the walls gave an air of sophistication. Sconces burned low on the walls while candles lit each table. Overall, the effect was timeless and striking while also assuming a haunted feeling. *Or maybe that's just me,* Cate thought with a smile. She glanced up and gasped at the huge chandelier hanging in the middle of the room.

"Stunning, isn't it?" Mrs. Allen asked. "It was imported from an estate in England. Most of the furnishings here are antiques. The original owner wanted as much authenticity as he could get."

"But they don't serve curative waters," Mr. Allen said. "Unless scotch and water is considered curative…"

Cate knew well enough not to spin a circle, taking in all the sights like a tourist. She tried to take a casual glance around while Mr. Allen spoke to the maître d. A portrait on the wall of the foyer caught her eye and she edged closer to it.

"Lovely, isn't she?" a voice spoke from behind her.

"Yes," Cate murmured as she took in the sight of the young woman with a regal bearing wearing a gown belonging to the 18th century. "I believe it's Marie Antoinette."

"It's a reproduction of a portrait painted by Martin van Meytens. Marie Antoinette was only—"

"Twelve years old," Cate interrupted. "Two years before she was married by proxy to Louis, then Dauphin of France. Did you know that they made her have oral surgery to fix her teeth before she was allowed to marry him?" She stopped suddenly, embarrassed at her outburst.

The speaker came to stand by Cate's side. She looked over at him furtively. Her mother had hammered it into her head not to seem flirtatious and all the heroines in her novels had not presumed to flirt with men they just met. Well, except for Amelie and look how that turned out for her. A few side glances told her that he was several inches taller than she, possessed a frame that was in good shape, short brown hair, and lips that curved naturally into a smile.

The young man turned toward her and held out his hand. "Hello, I'm Henry. It's good to meet someone so well versed in history."

Cate faced him and slipped her hand into his, a shiver running down her spine as she looked up into his chocolate brown eyes. "I'm Cate. Well, Catherine, actually. But everyone calls me Cate. Or Catie at times. I'll stop talking now."

Henry chuckled. "It's fine. So, is it your first time at The Pump Room?"

"Yes, I'm here with Mr. and Mrs. Allen, friends from home." Cate motioned to where they stood chatting with another couple across the foyer.

"You know Mr. Norm Allen?" Henry asked, surprise coloring his voice.

"They are members at my father's church and have been friends of our family for many years. Do you know them?" Cate replied.

"I know *of* them. I suppose everyone near Santa Barbara knows of Norm Allen. His company brought many jobs to the area. They give out scholarships to local kids as well. I believe they are benefactors of many facets of the arts in town."

"I know they are involved with the Dickens' Festival," Cate answered. "I'll be helping this year with the costumes."

"Indeed," Henry said, his eyes twinkling. "I hear it's a wonderful event. Many volunteers have signed up."

"Cate, our table is ready," Mrs. Allen called out. Her eyes flitted over to Henry and lit up.

"Hello, ma'am. I'm Henry Tilney," Henry said as he crossed the foyer.

"Nice to meet you, Mr. Tilney," Mrs. Allen said as she shook his hand. "Are you local to Santa Barbara?"

"I am and my family still lives here. I moved away a few years ago for college but I'm hoping to return closer to home," Henry replied.

"Norm, meet Mr. Tilney," Mrs. Allen said, touching her husband's elbow.

"Tilney," Mr. Allen said, a look of concentration in his eyes. "Why is that familiar to me?"

"My brother Frederick used to work for you down at the docks," Henry said.

"And your first name, son?" Mr. Allen asked.

"Henry, sir."

"That's it. Henry Tilney, scholarship winner. I never forget the scholarship kids. It's good to meet you." Mr. Allen gripped Henry's hand and shook it heartily. "How's your education going? Finished your BA and now working on your MDiv at Master's?"

"I'm surprised that you remember that," Henry

said, his eyes wide. "You awarded that scholarship six years ago."

"We keep track of our award recipients. It's important to me to know that my wealth is making a difference for someone else." Mr. Allen grinned. "When is graduation?"

"In May, sir," Henry replied. "Should I send you an invitation?"

"Please do. And now I'm afraid we must be seated before Pierre has a coronary. Would you care to dine with us, Mr. Tilney?" Mr. Allen asked.

"Thank you but I can't. I am meeting my father for dinner. I happened to get here early." He caught Cate's eye. "I'm very glad that I did."

She gave him a shy smile, happy that she hadn't fully scared him away with her outburst earlier. "It was nice to meet you," she said before following the Allens to their table. *Perhaps we'll meet again. I should find a way to slip him a note. But he might think that too forward. Well, fate or providence brought us together once. Maybe it will happen again.*

CATE GATHERED HER backpack and canvas tote bags from the trunk of the hired car. She turned to face the Theatre Royal and breathed deeply. This was it. She had to be brave and walk in there like she knew she was the best designer they could have hired.

Confidence was key, wasn't it? *I just hope no one asks how old I am! That would blow it. But they can't fire me if Mrs. Allen is the one who hired me, right?*

She squared her shoulders and marched for the front doors. A sign on the glass window read, "Dickens' Christmas Festival Staff Meeting. Closed to the public." *That's me, I'm staff!*

Cate managed to open the heavy glass door with her elbow and stuck her booted foot into the crack of the door. She flung it open and swung her heavy bags inside before the door could catch on them. She followed the "Festival Meeting" placard to a room on the left side of the foyer. At the check-in table inside the room sat Henry Tilney who grinned when he caught her eye.

"You!" she gasped, her heart beating wildly.

"Me," he answered with a wink. "I had a feeling I would see you again."

Her mind raced back to their conversation the evening before. She narrowed her eyes at him. *"Many volunteers?"*

"You didn't happen to ask if I was one of them," Henry said with a sly smile. "Would you like to check in?"

She shuffled the bags to free up her right hand to sign the clipboard. "Am I the first one here?"

"Besides the theatre manager and the festival director, yes. Bonus points to the new girl for being early."

Is he flirting with me or being friendly? I wish Mom and I had talked more about the difference between the two. Usually in books the hero fixes a smoldering gaze at the heroine and she falls for him. I don't see any smoldering in Henry's eyes. He's simply attentive. And funny. And looks very handsome in that dark green sweater.

"Cate?" Henry asked, clearly repeating himself.

"I'm sorry, what?" She shook her head to clear it.

"Would you like to stash your bags under the table? They seem a bit unwieldy."

"They are. Yes, I'll just keep my backpack with me. Everything else can wait until I meet with the costume department." At Henry's lifted eyebrows, she proceeded to ask, "I do have a costume department, right?"

"I've been helping out for several years now and usually it's staffed by volunteers. Basically, anyone that could rope his grandma into bringing her sewing machine for a few hours of work. Sorry," Henry said. "You didn't know that?"

"Mrs. Allen implied that the festival is a big deal in the community. I assumed that meant it would be well-staffed. My mistake." Her mind filled with the thoughts of all the sketches she had created for elaborate costumes for the festival. They could only be accomplished with many helpers in the few weeks before the festival began. She didn't know anyone in town that she could beg to volunteer.

"I don't know if it will make you feel better but I started a pot of coffee. It should be ready now. It's not as good as Mansfield Perk but pretty good for this single guy, if I do say so myself." Henry pointed to a side table filled with coffee things, pastries, and fruit.

"What's Mansfield Perk?" Cate asked as she pulled

a paper cup from the stack, filled it with rich, dark coffee and went on to find the right balance of sugar and cream.

"Only the best coffee place in California. Perfectly roasted coffee, great service, and they let you stay for hours to write. For a poor MDiv student, paying a few dollars for a cup of coffee and a quiet place to sit and study is huge." Henry also poured a cup of coffee but drank it black.

"What seminary are you attending?" Cate asked after she had mixed her coffee properly.

"I'm impressed you know that it's called a seminary," Henry replied as he walked back to his seat at the table.

"I'm a PK. We know these things." Cate sat at the other chair at the check-in table.

"Ah. I can see that." He watched her over his cup.

"What do you mean by that?" Cate blew on the top of her coffee to cool it.

"You are very knowledgeable about French art and history but seem a bit naïve about the world. It's not a bad thing," Henry assured her. "It's refreshing to find a girl like you in the world."

"My mom called me naïve earlier this week. I'm thinking it's not quite the compliment you both are making it," Cate complained. "And you never answered my question."

"Question? Oh, the seminary. I'm attending The Master's College. It's about an hour and a half from here. Close enough that I can come home occasionally but not so close that my father can assume I'll be home every evening."

"Is your relationship better with your mother?" Cate asked.

Henry's face grew melancholy. "My mother passed away five years ago, I'm sorry to say. Her death was felt heavily by us all but most especially my little sister Eleanor. Thirteen is very young to lose your mother. I try to spend time with Eleanor so she's not lonely but it's not the same as our mom, obviously."

"And your father isn't at home with your sister?" Cate asked, grieved at the family's loss of a beloved mother.

"Good morning, Henry!" a voice boomed in the room. "Always good to see your handsome face."

Cate turned to see a middle-aged woman with a puff of white hair glide into the room. Her black pantsuit was accented by a scarlet red scarf around her neck and matching red heels.

"Hello, Miss Aggie," Henry said as he rose. "I'm happy to be here."

"And who is this fetching creature sitting with you?" Miss Aggie stood in front of Cate with a keen look in her eye. "Your girlfriend?"

"No," Cate choked out. "We only met last night. I'm the costume designer. Cate. Er, Catherine Morland. I know the Allens?"

"Is that a question or a statement, dear child?" Miss Aggie asked.

Cate straightened her shoulders. *Confidence.* "I know the Allens. Mrs. Allen hired me to be the designer."

"And your clothes? Where did you buy them?"

Miss Aggie looked Cate up and down.

"I-I didn't buy them. I made them, ma'am," Cate replied, feeling her face flush.

"Then Beth knew what she was doing when she hired you." Miss Aggie paced around Cate. "Perfect fit, perfect shade for your coloring, great use of material." She peered more closely at Cate's dress. "What is that material?"

"I believe it's shot silk. It used to be a prom dress," Cate said, running her hands down the sides of the short dress.

Miss Aggie's eyebrows rose. "Used to be? I'm not sure I understand."

"My talent with sewing is also hooked with my talent for thrifting," Cate explained. "It's much cheaper to buy a piece of clothing already made and use the material from it to make something new. If I were to purchase shot silk new at the fabric store, it would be at least $50 a yard. I bought this dress for three dollars."

"Impressive," Miss Aggie murmured. "Can you do that with our costumes?"

"Remake clothes into costumes? Yes, of course. But it takes time to find the right clothes to make into new items. It took me several months to find the right shade of blue—"

"Our budget changed and I'm afraid that costumes had to take a big cut. If you're able to use your thrifting power, that should save us. I was quite worried about what to do. I'm not worried anymore."

She smiled at Cate and then Henry. "I need to make some phone calls. Hopefully everyone else shows up in the next ten minutes or we'll start without them." She spun on her red heels and flounced out of the room.

"Who was that?" Cate asked in awe.

"You just met Miss Aggie, the festival director. She has the reputation of being tough as nails but I think she likes you."

"She obviously likes you," Cate said, smiling at Henry. "What did you do?"

"Stepped in three years ago when the Ghost of Christmas Past didn't show up for the performance. I only forgot one line. She decided I was good to have around."

"And how is your stage career now?" Cate asked as she pulled her sketch book from a tote bag.

"Never acted since then," Henry said. "And I'm happy to keep it that way."

"You don't like everyone looking at you? I think that will make it hard to be a pastor. People look at you every Sunday when you're preaching."

"It's not the looking that bothers me." Henry paused until she looked up at him. "It's the acting. I hate falseness. Being someone I'm not. That's what I disliked. Everyone told how much they admired me for 'being' the Ghost. But I wasn't really the Ghost." He rubbed his hand over his face. "Does that make any sense?"

A warm tingle spread through Cate. "Perfect sense.

Honesty is to be prized." *He's the ideal hero. Honest, humble, kind, handsome. And single!*

THE HOURS FOLLOWING the first meeting were a blur of faces, names, and sounds to Cate. Everyone she met was excited that she was on board with making new costumes. One of the actors even offered to burn the old costumes to make room in the costume closet. Cate finally understood when Miss Aggie showed her the costumes in the storage area.

"What are these?" Cate asked in horror as she took in the plaid mini-skirts and shorts on the first rack.

Miss Aggie winced. "They were the last designer's attempt at doing a 'modern' take on A Christmas Carol. Obviously, that designer is no longer employed."

"I can see why." Cate shook her hair back over her shoulders. "I'll look through here and see if there is any material that can be salvaged." She picked at a mini-skirt. "Maybe this can turn into a muff or a scarf."

"Here's the key for the closet. It will also open the work room next door. It's set up with sewing machines and tables. They aren't the newest machines but they'll do. Feel free to poke around. Any sewing supplies you can find, you can use. I'll show you where the petty cash is so you can go shopping. You must turn in your receipts. I think that's all for now. See you later, honey," Miss Aggie called as she stepped from the room.

"Bye," Cate replied as she stepped further into the storage closet. She slipped in her ear buds and started her "Happy Taylor Swift" playlist. "Everything Has Changed" was the first song on the list. Henry's face sprang into her mind as the song filled her ears. *I do want to know him better. And they are the beautiful kind of butterflies.* She knew she was grinning like a fool in a dusty room full of moth-eaten clothing but she didn't care.

She emerged an hour later with treasures in hand: an unused bolt of dark red velvet, a bag of wigs, and a dark green cape.

"It's not much, but it is a start," she said as she opened the door to the sewing room.

The morning sun shone onto the long work tables and Cate jumped up and down excitedly. "It's just like a real sewing room!" She set her finds down on the nearest table and bent to look more closely at the machines.

The four machines were probably twenty years old but looked to be in excellent condition. Cate had brought along her Elna that she had saved up to buy but she looked forward to learning to use these new machines. *I hope I can find some volunteers who already know how to use these machines. Maybe Mrs. Allen has friends she can contact. But do rich ladies sew? Not everyone is like Mrs. Allen…Maybe they pay a maid to sew for them for charity projects.*

"Excuse me?" a voice called out.

Cate turned to see a stunning young lady standing the doorway. Her black hair was carefully curled and pinned back at the sides and her white dress, though simple, was obviously couture. Her red wedge espadrilles matched her small purse hanging from her shoulder. Overall, she seemed the very picture of Santa Barbara sophistication.

"Can I help you?" Cate asked, stepping forward.

"I'm Isabella. I'm here for my fitting." She grinned, showing her straight white teeth. "I'm playing Fan."

"Fittings! Yes, this is the right place. I wasn't expecting anyone quite yet. Please forgive me. I need to run downstairs and get my things," Cate apologized. "I'll be right back."

"No worries," Isabella replied, settling down on a stool. "Take your time." She took out her phone from her bag and began to tap on it.

Cate rushed down the stairs to pick up her bags from below the check-in table. *I thought the schedule said that fittings were this afternoon. I must have made a mistake.*

"Can I give you a hand?" a familiar voice asked from behind her.

"James?" Cate cried out as she spun to see her older brother walking toward her. "Why are you here? I mean, it's wonderful to see you but...why aren't you at school?"

"Furlough for the professors means no class for us this week," James replied as he hugged her.

"Us?" Cate asked.

"I brought my roommate, John Thorpe, with me.

Mom and Dad said you were here in Santa Barbara working on the festival. John's sister and mom are part of the festival, too. He's going to stay with them while they're here in town," James explained as he lifted two of the heavier bags from the floor.

"And where will you stay?" Cate asked as they entered the foyer of the theatre.

"The Allens offered to let me stay with them, if that is okay with you."

"Of course it's okay! I haven't seen you in months. I want to know everything that's happening in your life. What are you reading right now? Is your English class good?" Cate asked excitedly.

A young man with dark hair emerged from the opposing hallway and smiled at Cate flirtatiously. "Hello there. You must be Catherine."

"Cate, this is my roommate, John," James said.

John reached out and took the bag from her hand. "I feel like I know you already," John said, looking down into her eyes.

"Nice to meet you," Cate said as she glanced away. "If you'll follow me upstairs, that would be great."

Whereas Henry's gaze had sent tingles through her, John's look had given her a scary shiver down her spine. *He's like Heathcliff. Dark and brooding. But he smiled at me. And he's James' friend. It's nothing.*

The men set the bags down on the work table with the rest of the items Cate had found. Isabella stood up from the stool when they entered the room.

"You're James," she stated, holding out her hand.

"I am," he replied, staring at her. "And you are?"

He finally thought to shake her hand but seemed to forget to let it go.

"James, this is my sister, Isabella," John said with a satisfied smirk.

Cate stood silent, glancing back and forth at the siblings. *I can see the resemblance. This is an odd coincidence, though.* She looked down at her clipboard with the schedule of costume fittings on it. *One o'clock is the first fitting. I thought so! Why is Isabella so early? And so insistent that she was on time?*

"I'll be taping up the schedule in the hallway and getting a few things from the storage closet," Cate announced, breaking the spell that Isabella had on James.

James dropped Isabella's hand abruptly. "Let me help you."

Cate gave James the key to the closet and told him to pick up all the men's shoes he could find. "I don't have the budget to buy all new shoes. We'll see what we can do with those."

"We?" James asked. "Are you roping me into this now?"

"If you're here, I'm putting you to work," Cate said impishly. "And maybe you'll get to see more of Isabella," she teased.

"She is pretty, isn't she?" James asked, a dreamy smile appearing on his face.

Cate rolled her eyes. "Get to work, minion. I have a lot to do." She found a cork board on the wall in the hallway and pinned the fitting schedule and the rehearsal schedule onto it. As she walked back to the sewing room, she heard Isabella and John talking.

"You're late," Isabella hissed at John.

"You said eleven. I got here at eleven," John answered. "It's not my fault you weren't downstairs when we got here."

Cate froze in the doorway. Neither one heard her approach. *Do I back up quietly or boldly walk in like I didn't hear anything? This is awkward.* She continued to walk into the room with a smile pasted on her face. The Thorpes both stopped speaking immediately.

"James is working in the storage closet," Cate said. "I'd love for more help, John."

He looked down at his watch and shrugged. "I'm sorry but I have to go. Maybe another day. It was nice to meet you. Say hello to the Allens for me." He flashed a grin at her.

"I will." Cate turned to her sewing box and took out her measuring tape. "I'll start your fitting now, Isabella. You're two hours early. That's why I wasn't ready."

Isabella looked up, the picture of innocence. "Oh, I am so sorry! I must have misread the schedule. But it's better to be early, right?"

"Right," Cate agreed, anxious to begin her work. "Let's get started then."

CATE GLANCED DOWN at her watch for the tenth time in two minutes. "Why isn't he here?" she fumed.

She had scheduled for the Allens' hired car to pick her from the Fabulous Finds Thrift Shoppe at 2:00. It was now 2:30 and the car was nowhere in sight. Her team of sewing volunteers was due to arrive at the theatre at 4:30 to begin working on cutting out the patterns she had made. *If only I had my cell phone,* she thought once again. *Why did I leave it at the condo? I could call the Allens and ask them to pick me up. Or call James. He has a phone. And a car. Maybe the store will let me use their phone. If the car isn't here in five minutes, I'll ask.*

A drive-thru burger restaurant shared the parking lot with the thrift store. Cate could smell the charbroiled burgers and her stomach growled. *Did I eat lunch? I know I ate a muffin this morning but have I eaten since then?* She glanced down at the three large bags of clothes she had purchased. *It's going to look lame to drag these bags with me to the restaurant. I'll look homeless.*

A dark blue sedan pulled into the lot and parked near the restaurant. Cate startled when she realized who the driver was.

"Henry?" she called out as she stood up from the bench in front of the thrift store.

The driver turned his head and smiled in recognition. "Hi, Cate. What are you doing here?"

A passenger emerged from the front seat. Cate's heart sank when she saw how pretty the other girl was. Her light blonde hair was back in a ponytail and she looked sweet and friendly. *He must have a girlfriend. I guess I misunderstood.*

"Cate, this is my sister, Eleanor," Henry said. "I picked her up today to bring her as one of the sewing volunteers. Is that okay?"

"That's fantastic! You're going to the theatre? I scheduled a car to pick me up but it still isn't here. Could you possibly take me with you? I have to get these costumes there," Cate explained hurriedly. *Sister! Not girlfriend. Yes!*

"Of course we can," Eleanor answered with a smile. "I'm so glad I finally get to meet you."

"I'm happy to meet you, too! And the fact that you are a sewing volunteer is so fantastic," Cate said.

"Do you mind if we pick up some food before we head over to the theatre? I skipped lunch earlier," Henry said, picking up two of the clothing bags. "Studying for exams."

"You read my mind," Cate replied with a sweet smile.

MRS. ALLEN SIGHED in the back seat next to Cate. "Honey, I don't know how you got so much done in so little time. All the ladies in the Sewing Guild said that you where flitting here and there because everyone was calling you over. You've worked a miracle with those costumes, let me tell you. This will be the best festival we've ever performed."

"Thank you, Mrs. Allen," Cate said, feeling her face heat up from the praise. "I couldn't have done without all of my helpers. Eleanor, especially. The girl is incredibly fast with a machine. She might say she doesn't have designing skills but her sewing skills easily beat mine."

"She is quite good but I say that your sewing skills are spectacular," Mrs. Allen answered, patting Cate's knee. "Eleanor's brother Henry was around a bit, wasn't he?"

"He said that he volunteers every year," Cate said absently, looking at the window as Orange County came into view.

"That's right. His mother was involved, too. Until she died, of course. Poor thing. She died so quickly. I remember receiving that email from someone in the Guild. Your little friend, Eleanor, must have been only twelve or so when it happened. It is very sad to think of a girl living without her mother."

Cate felt tears well up in the back of her eyes. She had been away from her mother for only two weeks but it felt much longer than that. How much had Eleanor suffered in these past five years? *At least Henry is around. That's better than nothing.*

"I overheard your brother inviting his roommate home for Thanksgiving. Is he coming?" Mrs. Allen asked.

"I believe both John and Isabella are coming for dinner," Cate said. She had mixed feelings about this invitation. She would enjoy getting to know Isabella better. She seemed to always be at the center of events with the theatre. Everyone wanted to be her friend but Isabella chose to spend time with Cate. Since

James was helping Cate, Isabella and James were constantly chatting about friends they had in common. *I'm glad that James seems to like her but I don't really like how much John hangs around. He never helps like James does. He just…lurks. He's a lurker. Is that a thing? Like Quasimodo. But John doesn't have a hunchback. He still gives me the creeps, though.*

"I know that being home for five days is quite a short trip," Mrs. Allen said apologetically. "But I'm sure you know that we have to be back in time for final fittings next week and the opening of the festival on December 5. At least you'll be home to help your mother with all of the baking today."

Cate smiled to herself. Baking Day on the Wednesday before Thanksgiving was always a special day for her and her mom. Dad would take the little boys to a park or a ball game or a cheap movie so the house would be empty. Cate would help Mom chop, mix, cut all the ingredients for the three different pies they made as well as all the side dishes for Thanksgiving Dinner the next day. She could almost smell the cinnamon and apples as she thought about it.

"There is a possibility that Mr. Allen may have to travel for work and miss the opening of the festival," Mrs. Allen said, looking up from her phone. "He texted me from the front seat, silly man."

"I want to make sure you don't forget it," Mr. Allen called back. "This way I know that I told you."

"Will you be traveling with him?" Cate asked, suddenly aware that she might not have a place to stay when they returned to Santa Barbara.

"It depends on how long he'll be gone. If it's longer than two weeks, yes. I don't want him to be lonely at Christmastime," Mrs. Allen said. "Oh, but you can stay at our condo, honey. That would still be fine with us."

I don't know if it will be fine with my parents, Cate thought. *Will they not let me go back to Santa Barbara?*

EVEN THOUGH CATE was swamped with the costuming project, she still took on sewing projects from her Sew-Easy site while she was in Santa Barbara. She had her standard ten dress designs that she offered on Sew-Easy. Each had a different name taken from either her favorite literary characters or favorite classic movies. The most popular costume dress was the Katie Scarlett, a Southern belle inspired gown. The Audrey was reminiscent of what Audrey Hepburn might have worn to a fancy dinner. Cate's favorite latest "Audrey" creation was a deep blue dress with a full skirt and nipped in waist for a sweet doctor named Anne.

Every once in a while, an order would arrive that would cause Cate to stretch her imagination. A recent order was for an Emma Woodhouse who requested a yellow gown. When Cate warned Emma that not everyone could wear yellow, Emma had replied that she worked as a beekeeper. Cate shrugged and set off to find a beautiful golden gown that would please Emma. Pleased customers meant more money for her savings account and her tuition payment was due shortly.

Cate sat in her attic room the Saturday after Thanksgiving staring at the keyboard for a full minute before she ventured to open her email. Mrs. Allen had reported to Mrs. Morland the possibility of not remaining in Santa Barbara until the festival ended. Cate's parents were very uneasy with the idea of her staying alone in their condo. Mrs. Morland had sighed and said, "If only there was a family you could stay with, Catie. That would let me sleep at night."

"Maybe my friend Eleanor Tilney could invite me to her house," Cate said, thinking out loud.

Mrs. Allen told the Morlands how admired General Tilney was in Santa Barbara society and that Henry had been faithful in driving his sister Eleanor to the theatre to help out a few days a week.

"Does your friend not drive?" Mr. Morland asked with a twinkle in his eye.

"I've never asked her," Cate said. "I think Henry likes to drive."

"Mmmhmm. I'm sure that's it," Mr. Morland replied, stroking his graying beard. "And this Henry. Does he live at home?"

"No, he's on campus at The Master's College," Cate reported. "Working on his MDiv, Dad. I think you'd like him."

"Why don't you call or email Eleanor?" Mrs. Morland said. "See if Dad or I could speak to her father about you possibly staying there. I hope they have enough room at their house."

Mr. and Mrs. Allen burst out laughing at that. Everyone stared at them until they quieted. "I thought you knew, dear," Mrs. Allen said, wiping her eyes. "They live at Northanger Estate."

Cate sat perfectly still. "Northanger Estate as in where they filmed *The Mystery of the Mirror*?" she had screeched. "As in my favorite book and movie in the entire world?"

"That would be the one," Mr. Allen said. "I believe they have plenty of room for you."

Immediately, Cate had called up the volunteer information sheet on her phone and located Eleanor's email address. She wrote a gushy email, erased it, and wrote another email that was strictly factual. That seemed too dreary. She finally settled on something in between and sent it off with fingers crossed.

Now, two days later, she had a response.

Dear Cate,

Thank you for emailing me. I'm glad your Thanksgiving Dinner was great. Ours was quiet, as usual. My brother Frederick showed up for dessert, so that was a surprise. I spoke to my father about you staying with us. He had already been thinking of offering for you to stay with us during your time in Santa Barbara. You and I could drive together to the theatre, if that would suit you. I hate to burden Henry with the driving when I know he needs to study. (He doesn't see it as a burden, though.) Please let me know if the Allens are leaving town. Even if they do stay, you are welcome to come stay with us. I'd love to show you around other parts of Santa Barbara.

See you soon,

Eleanor

"I can stay at Belcourt Castle? I mean, Northanger Estate," Cate corrected, pulling up the fan site online.

There were many web pages for *The Mystery of the Mirror*, mostly dedicated to the movie made three years ago with Jay Engel starring as the brooding Duke Beau d'Riche. Cate had to admit he had the smoldering good looks the Duke was endowed in the book with but the thing that caught her attention in the movie was the setting. She was sure that the mansion they had filmed the movie in was in France. She had included traveling there on her "dream board" for vacation taped inside her bedroom closet door. And now she found out that it was not only two hours away but she could stay there!

She clattered down the stairs to find her parents and give them the good news. Another one of her dreams was coming true.

CATE TAPED UP the FINAL FITTING sign to the sewing room door. "Last fitting for all cast members," she yelled down the stairs. "If it doesn't fit now, it never will!"

Isabella came slowly up the stairs, speaking to the man next to her. She touched his shoulder lightly and threw back her head in laughter. He steadied her as she faltered on the step and she leaned into him. Cate watched with wide eyes.

I thought she and James were officially official now! She came to our house for Thanksgiving Dinner. That's a big deal, right? Who is this man? I don't like this at all.

Isabella stopped abruptly when she saw Cate standing in the hallway. Her face paled slightly but then she smiled. "Catie, do you know Frederick?"

Hairs stood up on the back of Cate's neck as Frederick lifted his eyes to look at her. If ever a man looked like a pirate, it would be him. Rakish good looks, a gleam in his eyes, a sly grin. He raised his eyebrows at her. "Hello there," he purred at her. "I hear you know my family."

"Frederick Tilney?" Cate gasped.

"The one and only," he agreed, sweeping her a low bow with a chuckle. "I'm in town for Thanksgiving and decided to see how the old town is doing. And meeting new friends, too." He smiled back at Isabella.

"Are you staying at Northanger Estate?" Cate asked, feeling her throat close up.

"That drafty old barn?" he scoffed. "Never. I have a hotel room. I'm only here for two more nights."

"You will be here for opening night tomorrow, won't you?" Isabella asked with wide eyes.

"You bet," Frederick said. "Catch you later, Bella." He nodded at Cate and gave her a wink.

She shivered in distaste as he made his way back down the stairs. "That guy…"

"I know, right?" Isabella whispered in her ear. "I can't help but fall all over myself when he's around. I mean, have you seen him? Totally hot."

"I have to go in for fittings," Cate said uncomfortably.

"What's your problem?" Isabella asked, following her into the room.

Cate shook her head. "I don't have a problem. You do. I thought you were dating my brother and then I see you with Frederick Tilney…"

"I'm not with Frederick. I'm just showing him around the theatre. Giving him someone to hang out with. Jimmy understands." Isabella looked into a mirror and applied more lip gloss.

"Who is Jimmy?" Cate asked. "Oh, you mean James? No one calls him Jimmy."

"I do," Isabella said breezily. "I think I need you to take in my costume a bit. It's too big in the waist."

"It's fine. There are other costumes that need to be fitted better," Cate replied, crossing the room. A headache pounded over her right eye. She didn't know how to take Isabella's words. She was used to things being black and white, truth and lie. Somehow here in Santa Barbara, there were many gray areas. And most of them appeared when Isabella was around.

OPENING NIGHT FOUND Cate backstage zipping up costumes, ironing petticoats that had somehow gotten wrinkled overnight, and assuring the actors they had all the pieces to their elaborate costumes. She was proud of the work that she and the team had pulled off in such a short time. They had reworked old dresses and coats to look like something that would have been seen while Charles Dickens was alive and writing the play. The elaborate gowns of the ladies were mostly cobbled together from several different dresses that miraculously came together into a cohesive piece.

She watched the show from the wings, jumping up to help when the occasional costume mishap arose. The time she spent with the cast and crew over the last few weeks had created a bond she hoped would continue. *Maybe they'll have me back to work on another show sometime. Perhaps in the summer?*

The ghost of Marley on stage was delivering one of Cate's favorite lines. She mouthed the words with him. "No space of regret can make amends for one life's opportunity misused." *I never want to miss one of life's opportunities. I need to be open to all possibilities.*

Cate could see the front three rows of the audience from where she sat. Eleanor and Henry sat with an older man in the middle of the second row. *Neither Henry nor Frederick look much like their father. He looks rather stern. But he did offer for me to stay with them starting this evening. He must be kind inside.*

Her bags were packed backstage. As soon as all the costumes were put away, she was headed off to

Northanger Estate with the Tilneys. *I probably won't be able to sleep tonight. I wonder if they have any props left from the movie at their house?* Cate had packed her newly purchased copy of *The Mystery of the Mirror* in her suitcase to show Eleanor. *But I also promised Mom I wouldn't freak out about being at my dream house. Maybe I'll save the book for later.*

THE PORCH LIGHT shown dimly above the enormous double door. Cate took in the sight of the three story mansion, her breath catching in her throat. *Charisse beheld the crumbling edifice, knowing that once she entered, her life would forever be changed. The man she loved —*

"It is a grand house, isn't it?" General Tilney asked as he unlocked the forbidding door. "Though not as grand as the Allens' house, eh?"

"The Allens' house is nothing like this," Cate murmured as she hoisted her backpack over her shoulder.

The general looked pleased. "Well, be it ever so humble, we call it home."

Humble? I think our house and the Allens' house would fit inside Northanger Estate and there would be room left over!

Sconces shone on the walls, giving the entryway a creepy feeling. Cate smiled when she recognized the coat of arms hanging on the wall near her. *That was in the movie. So was that table. And that urn.*

"Do you have many people interested in touring your house?" Cate asked. "Because of the movie?"

Eleanor looked panicked for a moment but General Tilney waved his hand. "We used to have a few nosy folks poking around. I got rid of them quickly. No one will be bothering you while you're here, Miss Morland."

"Oh, please, call me Cate. Miss Morland is much too formal," Cate protested.

Henry entered the hall with her suitcase and the rest of her bags. "Which room did you have for her, Eleanor?"

"The Blue Room," Eleanor said. "It was Father's suggestion."

"The third floor it is," Henry said, leading the way up the staircase.

General Tilney walked beside Cate. "I thought you'd enjoy having your own suite of rooms, Miss, er, Cate. You're probably used to that with the Allens."

"I had my own bedroom and bathroom at their condo here in town," Cate said, running her hand over the carved wooden banister. "It was quite lovely."

"And have you stayed with the Allens for very long?" the general asked.

"No, it's only been for about three weeks. I've known them my whole life, however. They live next door to my parents."

"I believe they don't have any children. Is that right?" he persisted.

"That's right. Mrs. Allen tells me I'm like the daughter she never had. She's been quite kind to me. I owe a lot to them," Cate acknowledged. She stared up in wonder at the paintings hanging on the wall on the third floor. *I think that's a Monet. And that's a Renoir. And they're probably not reproductions.*

General Tilney smiled widely at her. "It's an honor to have you at our home. Please let us know if we can do anything for you. Henry and I will leave you now. Eleanor will help you get settled."

"Thank you, sir," Cate said, feeling the ridiculous urge to curtsey to him.

"I'm glad you're staying here," Henry said as he passed her to go downstairs. "You'll be very close. For Eleanor's sake, you know."

"Good night, Henry," Cate replied. *Is it my imagination or did his cheeks seem red? Eleanor might have insight into Henry. I'll have to ask her later.*

The Blue Room was the same room that Charisse in the movie version of *The Mystery of the Mirror* slept in. Cate knew the minute she stepped in the room. The carved bed was the same, the heavy cabinet in the corner was the same, and the window was in the right place.

"I know this room," she murmured. "Monsieur Mauvais is lurking in the closet and Charisse doesn't know he's there. She's talking to the mirror and Mauvais answers back. Charisse thinks the mirror is actually speaking to her and it drives her mad."

Eleanor looked furtively at the doorway. "Don't let my father hear you talk about the movie or the book, please. He hates that we used our home for that movie."

"How could he hate it?" Cate asked aghast. "It was so well made. It followed the book very closely."

"The reasons for why he chose to allow them to use our house are—"

"Eleanor, don't stay too long," General Tilney's voice carried up the stairs. "I'm sure our guest is tired."

"I'll see you in the morning," Eleanor said, giving Cate a quick hug.

"Good night," Cate said, feeling frustrated at the story being cut off. Instead of dwelling on it, she closed the door and unpacked her suitcase. The attached bathroom had a claw foot bathtub, a luxury that Cate had always wanted to try. *Tomorrow. I'm too tired to take a bath tonight.*

She changed into her snowman flannel pajamas and crawled under the heavy coverlet, reveling in the smooth sheets. *These must have an unbelievable thread count.* She snuggled into her pillow and closed her eyes. She dropped off to sleep quickly. A buzzing sound woke her and she sat straight up in bed, heart pounding. *Where am I?*

Her phone glowed on the bedside table next to her. She reached over and saw a text from Isabella.

- Hey. Is he at the house 2? -

Cate typed back, blinking her blurry eyes.

- Who are you talking about? -

A minute passed and then a reply came.

- Frederick. Is he at the house? -

Cate scowled at the phone. *Why is she asking where her 'friend' is at 2:35 a.m.? Why is she pulling me into it? I'm going back to sleep.*

   - I don't know where Frederick is. Going
   back to sleep now. Turning my phone off. -

She dropped the phone on the nightstand and closed her eyes again. Unfortunately, she was now awake. She leaned up on one elbow and surveyed the room. *I can't believe I'm in the same room that Charisse was in when she discovered who killed her parents.* A chill ran through her veins. *I never thought about how creepy that is. I can't get back to sleep now.*

Cate threw on her robe and crept from the room, glad to see that a nightlight glowed in the socket in the hall. *Maybe I can get some milk in the kitchen. That always makes people sleep in books.*

She made her way down the stairs and stood in the entryway for a minute, trying to decide which hall to go down. *I guess I'll find it sooner or later, if I don't get lost. They never showed the kitchen in the movie. It's probably too modern.*

After two false starts, she finally found her way to the kitchen. She shrieked when a shadow stepped out of another doorway into the kitchen.

"Cate, it's okay," Henry assured her, turning on the light. "It's just me."

"Sorry," she muttered. "I'm just spooking myself. I'm not used to big, dark houses."

"Except in movies?" Henry teased, moving around to the refrigerator.

"Did Eleanor tell you about that?" Cate asked, shaking her head. "I'm so sorry. I'm not really a huge movie fan. It's only that book. And that movie."

"Don't worry," Henry said, taking a gallon of milk from the fridge. "I won't tell my father. Would you like some milk? It helps me sleep."

"I'd love some milk." She paused. "But can I have a few ice cubes in mine? I know that's odd—"

"But it keeps the milk cold until you're done drinking it," Henry said, a smile lighting up his tired eyes. "I drink it the same way."

They sat and talked for an hour, the moonlight shining through the kitchen window. Henry was impressed about her playing baseball with her brothers. She laughed at his story of his brother teaching him how to drive. Henry walked her back up to the third floor and bowed to her. "Farewell, mademoiselle. Until the sun rises."

"You *have* seen the movie!" Cate exclaimed. "That's Duke Beau d'Riche's line to Charisse the night before he dies."

"Makes people think he dies," Henry corrected. "And you call yourself a fan." He grinned at her and then headed back downstairs.

"I think I'm in love," she whispered as she floated off to her room. Henry dancing with her on the set of "A Christmas Carol" and whispering the Duke's lines filled her dreams the rest of the night.

THE FOLLOWING MONDAY, Cate and Eleanor stayed at Northanger Estate all day. Eleanor was eager to help with Cate's Sew-Easy orders that were piling up. While Eleanor went upstairs to find another pair of scissors, the doorbell rang.

The general had left earlier that morning to attend a conference of some sort for retired Navy personnel. Eleanor seemed much happier now that her father was gone. He was always polite and kind to Cate but seemed to demand immediate obedience from his children. Eleanor explained that ever since her mother passed away and Frederick ran away from home, her father had changed.

"I know he loves us in his way," she said while they were driving home from a thrift store the previous evening. "He wants the best for Henry and me."

Cate left the sitting room and answered the front door herself. John Thorpe stood on the doorstep, smiling down at her.

"Hey, Catie. Looking hot, as usual," John drawled. "I'm supposed to pick up my sister here. May I come in?" He brushed past Cate.

"Why would Isabella be here?" Cate said, confused.

"She said she was spending the day with the Tilneys. Everyone knows the Tilneys live here. What's going on here? Is this their maid's sweatshop?" John laughed at his own joke.

Cate ignored him as she knelt back down in front of the dressmaker's dummy and continued hemming the dress.

"What are you doing?" John asked, shock evident on his face.

"Sewing," she replied as well as she could around a mouth full of pins.

"You are on your hands and knees. Working with your hands. Don't you have an assistant to do that sort of thing for you?"

She slowly rose and plucked the pins from her mouth with a shaking hand. "I don't know why you think I'd have an assistant. I am a seamstress and a designer. This is what I do."

"For charity work. To look good in town." John laughed. "A little hobby."

"It's not a hobby. I sell what I make. It's my job. It's my calling." *It would be very wrong to stick him with these pins. Keep telling yourself that, Catherine.*

He narrowed his eyes. "The first night you were at The Pump Room, my sister said you were wearing vintage Chanel. And my sister knows clothes."

"I had no idea you were at The Pump Room that night," Cate said, growing more angry. "I knew you were a lurker. It was vintage Chanel. I bought it from an estate sale from an elderly gentleman who was getting rid of his sister's clothing."

John blanched. "You wear used clothing?"

"What do you think vintage is? You talk about driving vintage cars!"

"Not the same thing," he sniffed. "I was under the impression that you were quite wealthy."

"I don't know who gave you that impression," Cate replied in bewilderment.

"You said your family had an estate in Fullerton near the Allens—"

"We live on a property owned by the Allens. My father is a pastor. I'm one of seven children. We are not rich."

"But Mrs. Allen said you're like a daughter to her. Surely you'll inherit the Allens' property," John protested.

"That has never been discussed with me," Cate said hotly, putting her hands on her hips. "And it's none of your business. I think you need to leave."

"Gladly," John sneered at her. "I don't need to play up to the poor little pastor's daughter."

Cate pulled the heavy door open. "I've always felt you were not a nice guy and I was right!"

"That's all you got?" John laughed as he stepped outside. "Have fun back at the poorhouse. I can see why my sister is dumping your brother."

"I hope I never see you again!" Cate yelled as she slammed the door.

She turned to see Eleanor standing on the bottom step, eyes wide. "What just happened?"

"I think John Thorpe thinks he broke up with me?" Cate said. "What's wrong with men?"

"I thought you liked Henry?" Eleanor ventured.

"I did! I do," Cate amended. "I have liked him and I still like him. I don't know how he feels about me. As you can see, I don't know much about real life relationships. The heroes in books aren't so complicated."

"With real thoughts and emotions?" teased Eleanor as they walked back to the sitting room.

"Yes, those," Cate sighed as she got back to work.

CATE RUMMAGED IN the bottom of her purse to stem the flow of her dripping nose. Towards the bottom of her thrifted vintage bag was a familiar brown napkin. She wiped her nose with the wrinkled Mansfield Perk napkin even as her eyes filled with tears again.

The last time she had been to the coffee shop had been last week with Henry and Eleanor. On Henry's recommendation, she had ordered the Peppermint Twist Mocha and she hadn't been disappointed. The fact that he knew her tastes after only knowing him for four weeks should have been a shock but it felt like they had know each other forever. That's what made leaving Northanger Estate so much worse.

She sat at the bus stop bench, staring once again at the schedule she pulled up on her phone. She hadn't charged her phone last night and only had 32% battery life left. *I don't know how far I can go with that,* she thought desperately. *I hope the bus is on time.* She pulled her dark blue crocheted beanie further down on her blond curls as she pulled her thoughts together.

All had been going well at Northanger until General Tilney returned home late Wednesday evening. The front door had banged shut and Eleanor and Cate looked at each other in alarm.

"Eleanor!" her father yelled. "Where are you?"

She ran into the entryway from the second floor television room. "Right here. What's the matter? Is it Henry? Frederick?"

Cate stepped into the doorway, heart pounding. *Was Henry ill? Had he been in a car accident?* He had come by for dinner earlier that evening but left an hour ago to get back in time to study for tomorrow's classes.

"Plans have changed. I've afraid Miss Morland needs to go home," General Tilney said tersely.

"But what plans—"

"Do not question me, Eleanor. Tell your friend she must leave."

Cate took the stairs up to her room, willing herself not to cry. "I'll call Dad and he can drive up to get me tomorrow. If the van will make it that far. I hope Mom doesn't have to make the drive. Maybe I can hire the car service the Allens used. But how much does it cost?" She pulled her suitcase from the bottom of the closet. *The Mystery of the Mirror* still sat at the bottom of the suitcase. "I never got to tour the whole house. Maybe Eleanor can show me around in the morning, if her father isn't in too big of a rush to leave."

Eleanor appeared at Cate's door, clearly distraught. "You obviously heard. I'm so sorry, Cate. Please believe me. I don't want you to leave Santa Barbara."

"It's fine. Plans change," Cate said. "I don't have to be at the festival this weekend. Any of the volunteers can handle any costume trouble. My main job has been done. I'm just sorry that I didn't get to spend more time with you. We never got to decorate your house for Christmas. Maybe in the morning we can —"

"I guess you didn't hear that part. We have to leave very early in the morning so I need to ask you to leave right now." Eleanor looked to be in anguish.

"Oh. Yes, I missed that. I'll get my stuff now," Cate replied woodenly.

What did I do? Did the general know that I was asking about why he let them film here but won't talk about it? Or that I asked how his wife died? Does he not like the fact that I have a crush on Henry? Did he hear us talking late that first night I was here? Does he look down on my sewing job? It could be any of those things! And I can't ask Eleanor. It would break her heart to answer.

So now Cate sat at the bus stop that Eleanor had dropped her at, reliving the time she had spent at Northanger Estate. *If only, if only, if only. That's all I can think about. If I had spent more time avoiding mischief and asking questions, I wouldn't be in this mess. I could be helping Eleanor decorate Northanger for Christmas. Now I have to go home and answer Mom and Dad's questions and I don't have answers.*

The bus arrived on time and Cate hauled her suitcase and bags inside.

MRS. MORLAND KEPT Cate busy in the two weeks since she had returned home. She had cleaned the house, helped pick out a tree, decorated the house, helped sew costumes for the Christmas pageant, and prepared food for the Christmas Eve Feast. Each year, the Morlands invited the whole church to their home for a potluck feast. The house and yard would be filled with church members of all ages and someone always led carols around the piano in the family room. It was usually one of Cate's favorite days of the year but not this year.

"Still glum?" Mr. Morland whispered to his wife over coffee on Christmas Eve afternoon. "I could hear her music playing earlier upstairs. 'Blue Christmas' on repeat is not a good sign."

Mrs. Morland nodded thoughtfully. "I thought that once she was home and away from the excitement of the city and the glamour, she'd be our old Catie again. She still helps me and plays with the boys, of course. But there's a particular sadness I can't make disappear with busyness. She's been staying up in her room listening to sad Christmas songs and sketching new ideas for gowns when I don't have anything else for her. Maybe she's in love."

Mr. Morland's jaw dropped. "In love? With who? Not with that college boy, Henry, surely. Isn't it too soon for that?"

"You know that I was half in love with you when we went on our first date," Mrs. Morland answered with a kiss on his cheek. "Girls tend to fall in love quite fast. First loves fall even faster."

"Poor Catie," Mr. Morland said quietly. "Maybe I should take down that mistletoe on the porch."

"No, you don't," replied his wife. "It's a tradition to have the Morland mistletoe. Cate will have to grin and bear it when she sees others kissing. We need to be getting on with things. Guests will be arriving in a few hours."

Mr. Morland took out the kitchen trash bag his wife handed him. On his way back inside, he found a young man looking at a slip of paper in his hand standing near the driveway.

"Can I help you?" he called out.

"I hope so, sir," the man replied, walking up the driveway. "I'm looking for Catherine Morland. Does she live here?"

"Would you happen to be Henry?" Mr. Morland asked, a wide grin on his face.

"Yes, Henry Tilney. And you must be Mr. Morland. Is Cate home?" Henry asked anxiously.

"She is but I think you and I can talk together first. My wife just made some coffee. Would you care for a cup? And some delicious chocolate pixie cookies?"

"OH, I WON'T ask for much this Christmas, I won't even wish for snow, And I'm just gonna keep on waiting, Underneath the mistletoe—"

Cate clicked Pandora closed on her laptop. "No, I won't be waiting under the mistletoe." Cate scowled. "And we never have snow in Fullerton anyway. Wishing doesn't do any good."

Cate sighed as she watched the clock strike six. "Time to go downstairs and pretend to be merry," she complained to her reflection.

Her hunter green velvet dress was a new style she had designed, the Jane. The high waist and box neckline made her look more mature. She glanced down at her phone once more but there still wasn't a text or email from Eleanor or Henry. *I've been written off by the Tilney family forever. So much for the most wonderful time of the year. Bah, humbug.*

She emerged from the narrow stairwell to see the house already filling up with party guests. She found her mom in the kitchen ladling wassail into mugs.

"Can I help you?" Cate asked automatically.

"Sure, sweetie. Run on out to the garage and get the other tray of cheese from the fridge. It seems to be going fast."

Cate smiled at guests as she made her way to the front door. Stepping outside, she stood still at the sight of Henry Tilney sitting on the bench on the porch. He smiled up at her, a mug of wassail in his hand.

"Merry Christmas, Cate," he said, his eyes twinkling. "Care to go for a walk?"

"I have to get cheese for my mother," she answered, still staring at him.

"That was an excuse to get you outside," Mrs. Morland said from behind her, handing Cate her coat. "I don't need you for a good long while." She closed the front door.

"Do you like to walk and look at Christmas lights?" Henry asked again, standing up.

"Yes, it's my favorite Christmas activity. How did you know?" Cate asked as she slipped on her coat and started down the driveway.

"I had coffee with your dad and mom this afternoon. And met your brothers," he added. "I sampled all of your mom's Christmas cookies. It seems you were up in your room the whole time. Your brothers said your new favorite Pandora station is Melancholy Mistletoe."

"If I knew you were down here, I'd have been down immediately," she replied, her cheeks heating up. "I mean, not that I was desperate to see you—"

Henry stopped walking and turned to face her. "I didn't know what happened to you. When I came home that weekend, my father said that you left for home without a word. I thought you must have been angry at me or I misread something. I headed back to school and finished my exams. I don't know how well I did because I kept thinking about you."

Cate felt the familiar tingle return to her stomach. "I was thinking about you, too."

"Eleanor finally told me the truth this morning about my father making you leave. My father had forbidden her to talk about it but she said she didn't want me to have a terrible Christmas. I drove straight here." He gently reached out and held her hand. "I would have been here much sooner if I had known what had happened."

"Thank you," Cate said, blinking back tears. "I owe your sister big time." She looked up at the lights twined around the neighbor's tall trees on the edge of the yard. "'He had never dreamed of any walk, that anything, could give him so much happiness.' That's one of my favorite lines in 'A Christmas Carol'."

Henry started walking again but didn't drop her hand. "I know that we all seem to kow-tow to my father and I suppose that's true. He was just so broken up after my mom died that I don't want him to get upset again."

"That makes sense, I guess," Cate replied, squeezing his hand. "You know, I made some really good gingerbread this morning. If you want a piece, we should head back to my house."

As they walked back, Henry told her about Frederick arriving home with Isabella, announcing to

General Tilney that they would be getting married. The general had said, "Well, at least one of my children will marry into money." Eleanor had put the pieces together and asked her father if he had spoken to John Thorpe. It turned out that John Thorpe had boasted to General Tilney at The Pump Room that Cate was set to inherit from the Allens. After that time, General Tilney sought to have Henry and Cate spend more time together. Once Cate had set John straight, John made sure to tell the general the truth when he saw him at The Pump Room bar the evening that General Tilney came home from the conference.

"No wonder he was so angry!" Cate exclaimed as they stepped onto the porch. "If he thought I was a rich heiress…Oh well. I'm glad it's worked out."

Henry paused and looked up. "You know, while I was sitting out here, I kept looking at that and wondering why it was there."

"What?" Cate asked. Her face warmed as she noticed the mistletoe. "Oh, it's tradition. My dad likes to say that the couple who kisses for the first time under the mistletoe is destined to stay together. It's Morland family tradition to hang the mistletoe in various places around the house. We're all a bit mischievous that way."

"Mischief and mistletoe. I like that," Henry smiled, his eyes gleaming in the glow of the white twinkle lights. "I don't know exactly where life will take us but I'd like to give this a shot. Us a shot." Henry looked earnestly into Cate's eyes. "I don't know about your dad's theory about mistletoe and destiny but… what do you think?"

Cate's kiss under the mistletoe answered that question.

The End

ABOUT THE AUTHOR

Melissa Buell lives in Southern California with her husband and kids. She's an English teacher by day, author by night. She loves to read, bake, and take photographs. She has been known to thrift clothes into costumes and dress up for Jane Austen parties.

You can connect with Melissa on her website www.authormelissabuell.com or on Twitter @Melissa_Buell.

A Tale of Three Christmases

Rebecca M. Fleming

PROLOGUE

MAGGIE FLUFFED THE pillows in the corner, arranging the biggest ones just so, before burrowing into the pile and wrapping a quilt around herself. At seventeen, she knew she was too old for running to the treehouse, but sometimes a girl just had to hide. Even from here, she could hear Marianne's high-pitched wailing. *She can't even cry without drama,* Maggie thought, wishing she'd grabbed her iPod when she escaped. *It's not like she's the only one who got her heart broken.* Pulling the quilt tighter around her shoulders, Maggie leaned her head against the wall and stared out the treehouse door, tracing the familiar lines of home with her eyes. *I'm going to miss this place as much as I'm going to miss Daddy*, she thought, feeling the familiar burn of tears.

Norland Park was a sprawling, old-fashioned country house, hugged by deep porches with windows glinting gold in the setting sun. It was a house that looked old, and was—members of the Dashwood family had lived on the grounds for generations, ever since some great-great-great relative sailed across the pond from England and settled in the rolling hills of northwest Georgia. The house had no distinct style, as various generations made additions and renovations, at one point demolishing and rebuilding the whole thing. It was a house that demanded attention, but also welcomed company. Maggie knew every nook and cranny of the stately home, and very nearly every inch of the extensive grounds. Norland was the only home she'd ever known, and now in a cruel twist of fate, Maggie, her two sisters, and their mother, would be forced to find a new place to call home.

Even though she was the youngest, and the others tried to keep the details from her, over the last few weeks Maggie had overheard enough whispered conversations to know her father's death meant everything was about to change—in a big way. Because of an obscure family tradition, with roots back in England, the Norland estate only passed to male heirs. Even in twenty-first century America there was no way around the clause—it had been worked into the deed itself. As a result, Norland Park and all its splendor would soon fall into the hands of Maggie's half-brother John, and his wife Francesca.

John assured his stepmother that she and the girls were welcome to stay at Norland as long as they needed; he would not turn them out. Maggie almost idolized John when she was little, and believed he meant what he said, but doubted Franny would be so generous. *If she has her way,* she thought now, *we'd be gone before the moon rises tonight.* There was no love lost between the Dashwood girls and their "big sister"—Francesca had swept into their lives with the unwelcome force and bluster of a nor'easter. The only daughter of a stock market millionaire, Francesca Ferrars craved the respectability an Old Family Name gives to wealth, and when John Dashwood stumbled into her path—she pounced. Maggie still had nightmares about the wedding, some ten years before, the day her mysterious big brother disappeared from family circles.

And now, it's all hers. Every stick and stone of Norland is Franny's. I have no Daddy and no home.

CHRISTMAS CHAOTIC

"**HOW ARE WE** supposed to have Christmas without Daddy?" Marianne wailed, dropping dramatically onto the leather sofa. "Not just Christmas, but a party! Heartless Francesca and her Yankee family."

Maggie stiffened, biting back a snarky response, as Ellie, the oldest of the three Dashwood girls, drew a deep breath.

"We've been over this, Marianne," she said in the soothing voice so often used with their high-strung sister. "Christmas will happen whether people die or not, and with the holiday comes certain expectations. Traditions that must be upheld. Whether we like them or not, these things do happen."

"But Francesca acts as if nothing horrible has happened, as if someone made her Queen of the World and we're all her servants. Christmas minions or some such ilk. I won't have it. I will not be cheerful.

I will not be 'sparkling and vivacious.' And I will. Not. Sing." Hurling herself off the sofa, Marianne punctuating the last words with forceful stamps of her high heel-clad foot. "And you can't make me, Elinor," she cried before leaving the room as abruptly as she'd entered.

"It's going to be a long few weeks isn't it, Ellie?" Maggie asked, moving to perch on the arm of her sister's chair. "If she's this wound up before the 'Yankee family' even arrives, what will she do when Franny's brothers get here?"

Ellie closed her eyes and sighed. "I can only imagine. And it is not a happy imagining. What about you, Magpie? How are you holding up against Francesca's holiday onslaught?"

Maggie wrinkled her nose at the childish nickname, making Ellie chuckle. "Okay I guess. It does seem weird to be getting ready for a party, when we just had a funeral. But at the same time," she hesitated, glancing sideways at Ellie.

"It's okay, Maggie," Ellie assured her, slipping an arm around her shoulders.

"I think I'm sorta glad. I mean," she took a deep breath, "Christmas was Daddy's favorite holiday, and he always loved hosting a big bash, you know? So even though Franny is making it this posh, Yankee thing, it's almost like Daddy's still here and just having a little fun."

Ellie smiled. "I know exactly what you mean. I think Daddy would be rather amused at Francesca's plans, and he'd definitely be teasing her into a frenzy.

Not," she warned with a raised eyebrow, "that I am suggesting you should."

Maggie grinned, "Who me?"

"Yes you, Magpie, love of my life. You are more than capable of teasing a saint to distraction, and Francesca is no saint. Mind your manners—you're a lady, so act like one."

"Yes, ma'am," Maggie sighed. "Sometimes, Ellie, you sound like *such* a librarian!" With a shriek and giggle, she jumped off the chair arm and darted out the door, as Ellie tossed a pillow at her retreating back.

A slow rain fell, rendering escape to the treehouse impossible. Maggie found herself wandering the house aimlessly, trying to find a quiet spot to curl up and lose herself in a book, but everywhere she tried to settle, the solitude was penetrated by the animated, shrill voice of Marianne or Franny, sometimes both. In a moment of desperation, she ducked through a door leading to the old servants' stairs, and began to climb. *Nobody will come to the attic*, she thought, *especially not Franny—she might get spiderwebs on her precious shoes.*

The attic was expansive, shadowy, and mostly forgotten. Dormer windows offered little light on a day like this, but Maggie didn't mind. The attic, like the treehouse, was her private domain, and countless hours had been spent prowling and poking in dusty corners. Over the years she created a few special hideaways for herself, depending on mood or atmosphere, and today she migrated toward the broad chimney. With fires burning below, the chimney radiated an inviting circle of warmth. Maggie pulled a blanket from her stash in a nearby trunk, and curled up in the old wingback chair tucked right next to the chimney with a sigh. *This is better,* she mused, opening her book and prepared to spend the whole afternoon in that very spot.

It was too gloomy to read, situated so far from the windows, but Maggie's stash had more than just blankets. Wrapping the blanket around her shoulders, Maggie got up to kneel by the trunk. Moving aside another blanket and tossing a pillow into the chair behind her, Maggie rocked back on her heels and paused. *That's funny*, she mused, *the flashlight and camping lantern should be right — hello, what's this?* As another pillow shifted, something shiny caught Maggie's eye.

Moving the pillow out of her way, Maggie's eyes widened at what she uncovered. The glimmer of shininess that caught her attention turned out to be mirrored glass and silver inlay on the cover of a dark wooden box. Lifting the box out, she was surprised at its weight. Roughly the size of one of her father's law books, the box felt twice as heavy. *Do glass and silver weigh* that *much?* she wondered, running her fingers over the design. The pieces were cool and smooth to the touch, mesmerizing. Unable to decipher the image, she turned the box slowly, hoping each new angle would make a picture fall in place.

"Oh," she gasped suddenly. "It's Norland." Her own voice, though barely a whisper, startled her. Glancing quickly around the attic, noticing the camp lantern further back in the corner, revealed now with the box in her lap, Maggie felt a tingle of excitement. Setting the lantern on the chair behind, letting the light shine down on her, she allowed herself a brief study of the embellished cover, its fragmented portrait of her beloved home. *It really is beautiful,* she observed before curiosity took over, prompting her to run her fingers along the edges, seeking for a way to open the cover and reveal the contents. Finally, she brushed against a small embedded latch and with the softest of clicks the lid opened a fraction of an inch. Raising the lid slowly, carefully, Maggie smiled at what she found inside.

In keeping with the understated elegance of its exterior, the interior of the box was simply lined with deep, rich blue velvet. Resting inside, nearly filling the space, was a thick, leatherbound volume tied with a satiny blue ribbon. Tucked under the bow were an old-fashioned fountain pen and an envelope reading "Margaret Dashwood" in a familiar script. Carefully drawing the envelope from the ribbon, she smiled as she ran her fingers along the letters. *Of course Daddy knew about my hideaway, knew I would need to retreat, but when did he have a chance to stash this little surprise?* she wondered. Lifting the flap, she drew out a Christmas card. Seeing her father's post-production addition of conversation balloons above the family of snowmen on vacation made Maggie giggle. Opening the card, she was surprised to see it filled with his neat, blocky print. As she began reading, tears stung her eyes and she unconsciously drew the box closer to her chest.

My Magpie,

Merry Christmas. My guess is that Christmas is a few weeks away, and you have resorted to hiding from Marianne—not to mention Francesca. I am sorry I had to leave you to fend for yourself. We were always a team. (By the way, I give you leave to tease Franny —just don't let Ellie catch you. She never understood our delight in tormenting her).

You may be wondering about this box, and its contents. I found the box years ago, when you were just a wee girl, among some junk in the barn. After cleaning it up, I kept it a secret, even from your mother, waiting until...Well, I figured the time would come. And it did, my Magpie.

Of all my children, you have roots sunk deepest in the fertile Norland soil. You've roamed these grounds, inside and out, since you could waddle, and leaving will hit you the hardest. I'm sorry for that too; I wish my ancestors had known that sometimes daughters love the land even more than sons. This box is yours, a small piece of Norland to keep with you, and—I hope—help ease the pain of starting over.

As for the journal inside—Margaret, you have a gift. A way of seeing the world, and teasing out the little details that make up life's ultimate stories. I want you to keep writing, write down everything you hear and see. But for this journal, I have specific instructions:

You may only write in this book during the weeks leading up to Christmas and extending to New Year's Eve. What you write during that time is up to you, it can be caricatures of your extended family (ahem), a record of what has changed, or whatever whimsical idea tickles your fancy at the moment. But only during the Christmas holidays.

Additionally, you may only use this journal for three Christmases. This year, next year, and the year after that. I refrain from explaining my reasons, but trust me. I have them.

Lastly, call me sentimental, but I hope you choose to use the fountain pen when you write. Obviously you can use whatever you like or have handy, but the pen is included in the gift. It was mine, a graduation present, I intended to give to you when you graduate. You know what they say about the best laid plans, so I tuck it in here. The important thing is, you have it.

Look after your mother, Magpie. Ellie will undoubtedly take over the practical concerns of this next chapter, but she will need your support. Keep Momma smiling. Help her settle into the new adventure by maintaining your sense of humor. As for Marianne...Oh, Marianne. Perhaps the best help is just to be. Avoid getting caught up in the storms, and there will be plenty, but do not shut her out. She can't help herself, poor girl. My hope is that one day, she'll find herself and learn that love bears all things.

Take care of yourself too. You are strong and fierce, my little one, but it is okay to lean on others. I love you, so very much, and wish I could be spending this and every Christmas with you.

With infinite love, Daddy

Maggie could barely read the words through her tears; when she got to the end, she buried her face in her arms and cried. She had refused to indulge in a good cry since the funeral. Marianne was holding her own in that department well enough for the whole family. Now, reading her father's words, Maggie gave in to the sweet release of grieving, really grieving. She mourned the upcoming loss of Norland as much as she did his death, and he had known she would. At last she could cry no more, and her heart felt lighter somehow, as if a small flicker of excitement or anticipation were kindling to life. Wiping her eyes and nose on her shirttail, *Franny will love that*, Maggie untied the ribbon and thumbed through the journal pages.

The leather was soft and pliable, smooth as velvet in her hands and the color of a rich caramel latte. Though the deckle edged pages were crisp and white, there was a hint of the comforting 'old book' smell Maggie found so enticing. A bright purple ribbon marked the first page, where her father had written a reminder: "For Christmases only, Magpie." She smiled, knowing it would be very hard to resist writing in the book every day. *But I must make it last three years—three Christmases.* As perplexing as she found his limitations, her father's instructions presented an intriguing challenge.

Today is for looking only, she thought, gently placing the journal, pen and card back in the box. *And this is staying safely hidden in my trunk. I can't have Franny, or anyone, finding it.* She tugged a pillow over the box and fluffed a blanket to disguise any suspicious lumps, laughing at herself. *It's not like anyone comes up here but me.* Happy with the look of things, Maggie shut the trunk and moved the camp lantern to sit on top, crawling into the chair and rewrapping the blanket around herself. Unable to concentrate on her book, she soaked up the quiet sounds of Norland until it was time to join the family for dinner. With a secret project of sorts, surviving Franny's Christmas plans suddenly seemed more doable.

FROM HER HIDEAWAY in the treehouse, Maggie could see everything—even hear some of it—without being seen. Franny's brothers were due to arrive any moment, and Maggie wanted to see the kerfuffle without getting involved herself. She had, technically, met the Ferrars boys at Franny and John's wedding, but since her seven year old self spent most of that weekend hiding from all the strangers, her memories were hazy at best. Franny had been particularly agitated at breakfast that morning, fretting about their imminent arrival and hoping they would be suitably impressed with her new domain.

The sudden slamming of a door startled Maggie, and she glanced up to see Ellie storming toward one of the outbuildings near the treehouse. *That's funny,* she thought. *Ellie never slams doors. I wonder whether Franny or Marianne provoked that?* Just as she decided to climb down and see what upset her sister, a tall, lanky man came around the corner, running directly into a very distracted Ellie. As the two attempted— and failed—to regain balance, landing in a tangled pile of arms, legs and a very smooshed hat, Maggie decided her overhead view was best after all.

"I am so sorry!" Ellie's voice was much higher

pitched than usual. "I had no idea anyone was out here, and I had to get away—wait, what are you doing out here? Who are you? I'm sorry. That was rude. I don't know what's wrong with me today. I promise I'm not this rude," she stopped to take a deep breath. Maggie was able to see the guy's grin from her treehouse perch, and his deep laughter had a friendly warmth. *Can laughs be warm? His is warm—it makes me feel warm fuzzies inside,* she wondered absently.

"You must allow me to apologize, m'lady. The fault was entirely mine," his voice tinged with laughter. "I should not have been skulking around corners, avoiding my inevitable destiny. Will you permit me to assist you up, or shall we stay here until someone comes looking for us?" As he spoke, he disentangled himself and moved to sit across from Ellie with a comically innocent expression.

"I, ah, should probably, um," Ellie floundered. "Do I know you?" she suddenly asked, cocking her head to one side. "Oh my word, you're —"

"Edward Ferrars, at your service," he interrupted with a surprisingly formal bow for one sitting in the dirt. "Please don't hold it against me," he added flashing another grin.

Ellie groaned, burying her face in hands, muffling her voice. "Of all people to run into and make a fool of myself, it would be Francesca's brother. I think I am going to die in approximately three-point-seven seconds."

"I wish you wouldn't," he replied in a voice equal parts soothing and teasing. "I think you must be one of the Dashwood girls, and I know my Christmas holiday just got a lot more interesting."

Maggie giggled in spite of herself, quickly holding a pillow to her face to muffle the sound, as Ellie raised her head to meet Edward's frank, open look. "Mmm," she murmured. "I can't decide if that makes me feel better or worse, thank you very much. Yes, I am 'one of the Dashwood girls.' I'm Elinor—Ellie. I must express sincere apologies for my appalling lack of grace and manners." She paused, and Maggie wished she could see her sister's face. "And I should warn you," she continued, her voice eerily steady, "if you tell anyone what you have witnessed here, I will make your life miserable. I am a Librarian, with unending information at my disposal, and I am not afraid to use it."

The expression on Edward's face shifted from teasing to concern to surprise to delight in quick succession, and Maggie laughed out loud in spite of herself.

"Margaret," Ellie sighed, "get down here. Immediately."

As Edward looked around for the mysteriously invisible laughing Margaret, she sighed and climbed down. Jumping the last few ladder rungs, she landed with a soft plop and arched one eyebrow quizzically. "Yes, Ellie?"

"Oh! Another one!" Edward cut in, before Ellie had a chance to scold her. "And a tree-dwelling Dashwood at that," he added, standing and offering a hand to assist Ellie. "I would introduce myself, but I gather you have been snooping the whole time, eh?"

Maggie grinned. "Well, I was technically here first and y'all crashed my party. Why did you come slinking around the corner like that anyway? Weren't you supposed to be arriving in the normal way—by car, at the front door?" She gave him a searching glance, taking in the dusty boots and untucked shirt tail peeking from beneath his heavy sweater.

"Ah, yes, I," he stammered slightly. Suddenly realizing he still held Ellie's hand, he dropped it and took a step backwards—tripping on his forgotten hat. Losing his balance, again, he flailed wildly and caught hold of Ellie as he fell, bringing her down on top of him with an "oomph."

"Oh crud," he muttered, "I am definitely not making a good impression, am I?"

"Well, that would depend on what kind of impression you wanted to make," Maggie answered with a laugh, moving to help them up. She stopped mid-reach when a sudden giggle took her by surprise. "Ellie?" she asked, a note of concern in her voice.

Edward tilted his head, trying to see Ellie's face. "Ell? Are you okay?" His eyes widened when Ellie's only response was to laugh harder, and bury her face in his shoulder. Instinctively he wrapped his arms tighter around her, as an answering laugh escaped him.

Maggie watched the two in stunned silence, before breathing a soft "Wow."

Finally, Ellie's giggles stopped and she breathed a deep sigh, visibly relaxing in Edward's arms. Maggie only had time to raise her eyebrows in reply to Edward's quick wink before Ellie realized where she was and abruptly rolled off his chest onto the grass, headbutting Edward's chin in the process.

"Oof," Edward grunted softly, as he sat up and rubbed his chin.

"Oh crap," Ellie groaned. "Maggie, help me up," she added, waving one hand in Maggie's general direction and covering her face with the other. "What is wrong with me today?"

Edward shook his head at Maggie before gently turning Ellie's face toward him, moving her hand to look her in the eyes. "Hey," he said, his voice low and soft, so Maggie could barely hear the words, running his thumb across her cheek, brushing away a surprising tear. "Correct me if I'm wrong, but your daddy just died, my sister has taken over your home, and strangers will be spending Christmas with you. If that's not a *carte blanche* for having a bad day now and again, I don't know what is. And Ellie," he paused, "I'll give you twenty bucks if you tell Franny to go eat tinsel when she comments on our dishevelment."

Ellie smiled, raising her hand to brush away a stray leaf before resting lightly on his shoulder. "Thank you," her voice soft. "But if you think I'm going to tell Francesca that for a mere twenty dollars, you're insane," she winked as she tweaked his ear. Edward made a grab for her, but she sprang up and away, pushing Maggie between them as a shield.

"Oh good grief," Maggie sighed. "I can't decide if y'all are adorable or ridiculous. This whole family is more than a little ridiculous, in my personal opinion, so maybe you are adorably ridiculous. Are you sure you've only just met?"

"Hmm, well, there was that weekend of Wedding Infamy," Edward tapped his chin thoughtfully. "But I don't remember any ear-tweaking librarians, just a couple skinny, gawky teenagers more interested in their dog than entertaining the debonair Ferrars brothers."

"Funny," Ellie remarked, with one eyebrow arched, "I remember a pair of weasel-y brothers, too caught up in being brooding, mysterious college boys to bother being polite to their sister's new family."

"We were obnoxious, weren't we?" Edward pulled a face. "I hope I have outgrown that phase, and we can be friends this time? Though I should warn you that Rob is still very much a weasel."

Maggie snickered, and Ellie tried to hide her smile. "Mmm," she murmured. "We shall see. What do you say we start by tidying up a bit before —"

"Edward!" Francesca's shriek cut through the yard.

"Too late," Edward muttered, bending to pick up his now very flattened hat.

"Edward Alexander Ferrars! What in thunder are you doing back there? How did you get here? Robert hasn't arrived yet. Come inside this instant and explain yourself!" Francesca stood with her hands on her hips at the top of the porch steps.

Exchanging guiltily amused smiles, Edward, Ellie and Maggie moved toward the house. Maggie fought back a laugh as Franny grew more agitated the closer they got. With a sideways glance so full of mischief even Ellie choked on a laugh, Edward stopped at the foot of the steps. Leaning on the post, he crossed his legs nonchalantly.

"Franny," he drawled, "I do believe your feathers have ruffled. Whatever is the matter, ma'am?"

Franny sputtered, looking between her brother and the Dashwoods with something akin to horror. "Look at you! You're a mess! What have you been doing?" She raised a hand. "No, don't answer that. I don't think I want to know. Edward, you are a Ferrars. And you are a guest at Norland. Behave. With. The. Proper. Dignity." After spitting out the last word, she turned sharply on her heel and stalked into the house, leaving the others in a stunned silence.

"That went over nicely," Edward remarked drily, before offering Maggie and Ellie each an elbow. "Shall we go beard the dragon in her den, ladies?"

The next two weeks flew by. Robert Ferrars was every bit as weasely as Edward promised, arriving three days after he was supposed to, and quickly providing further evidence for Maggie's theory that Edward must have been adopted. *There is no way he shares the same gene pool as Franny and Robert*, she thought regularly. Regardless of where he came from, Maggie was simply glad he came. Edward's friendship was genuine and his company pleasant, even if his delivery was bluntly awkward at times. *Even Marianne likes him*, Maggie noted one day, as her notoriously fastidious sister laughed over Edward's bungling attempts to join family singalongs. *He's completely tone deaf, and she likes him.*

Whenever she could, Maggie would escape to her attic hideaway. The journal beckoned her, and she loved the idea of still being connected to her father in some way. *I know he can't actually read it, doesn't know what's going on*, she thought a few days before Christmas, running her fingers over the soft leather cover, *but he knew I would need to tell the stories, to talk things over the way we used to on coffee dates to Mansfield Perk.* It was hard sometimes to remember to leave pages blank, for next year. The empty pages begged her to fill them with everything from conversations to sketches of the personalities gathered under Norland's roof.

That first day when Edward ran into Ellie and tripped on his own hat? We should have seen it coming: he's all arms and legs, bumping into people—or furniture, sometimes the door—and getting tangled up. He is rather coltish, or maybe like an exuberant puppy, trying to grow into himself. He's so good humored about it. He knows he's a totally spastic klutz, and you can't help but laugh with him. Well, Franny doesn't laugh, but at least she stopped shrieking every time he knocked something over. Now she just grits her teeth and mutters things.

The one she should be muttering about is

Robert. He's such a creeper, and gets worse and worse the longer he's here. I caught him slinking about the hallway where our rooms are the other day, looking extra sketch. He didn't even have the decency to look guilty when I came around the corner and saw him. He looked annoyed. I must remember to tell Ellie we should probably all use the keyed locks with him around. Too bad John can't kick him out for being a weirdo.

I can't decide if I like John or not. Horrible, I know. I have all these memories of him from when I was little, in the Pre-Franny Era, and even though he didn't come to Norland often, he was wonderful. Rather like Edward, actually, but not so klutzy. Ellie looked at me like I was delusional when I mentioned it, so possibly my subconscious has a selective filter. However he was then, he is very different now; more withdrawn, maybe a little lost. Sometimes I think he really wants to be a big brother to us, but he either doesn't know how or he isn't allowed. I'm fairly certain Franny wears the pants in their relationship. And we all know how she feels about the Dashwoods lingering in the home. (Does she forget she is a Dashwood too, I wonder?)

Edward has a crush on Ellie, I've decided.

They really do make a cute couple: the professor and the librarian. Nerds. They're adorable. He makes her laugh, and brings out a mischievous streak we'd all forgotten. In turn, her friendship and support, her ability to listen and understand his weird academic passions, have made him more sure of himself. I hope they're able to explore the potential, but Franny saw them talking the other day and got a queer look on her face. They are always talking, about everything and anything. One day, I found them in the treehouse; Ellie was telling him how we used to keep bees and that beeswax candles are her favorite smell in the world, because they remind her of summers. Whenever Ellie talks, Edward focuses intently on what she's saying—you can tell he's really listening. He listens to all of us, of course, but with Ellie it's something deeper.

John was able to gently persuade Franny that perhaps a Christmas dinner for family and a few close friends would be in better taste than a party, considering the recent death of our father. She relented, and the evening was surprisingly not horrible. Christmas itself was quiet, and restful actually. Edward gave Ellie a necklace with an enameled beehive charm (he said he ordered it from With Love;

I looked them up online, and it's the sweetest florist and gift shop in Oregon. Makes me want to visit just to meet the owner and poke around the place), which made Franny's eyebrows skyrocket. I think she finally figured out her brother might have a serious interest in the eldest Miss Dashwood. Since then, we've all been kept busy with errands and sorting through belongings. It wasn't until tonight, New Year's Eve, that things came to a head.

Marianne made a comment about Edward and Ellie, and Franny lost all pretense of composure. It quickly turned into a screaming match, Franny vehemently declaring her brother would never connect himself to the Dashwoods, that their father had plans for him to marry a wealthy heiress and create a dynasty. Marianne felt the need to point out that marrying a Dashwood had been quite good enough for her, and why not let Edward make up his own mind. It was shocking. Edward and Ellie both were bright red, and John looked as if he wished to run away. Momma ended everything with a quiet announcement: "We're leaving," and left the room.

I guess our time at Norland is really over

now. But where do we go? Where will I be next Christmas?

Christmas Cursed

SOMEHOW, ANOTHER HOLIDAY season had arrived, with Christmas just around the corner. Maggie hoped they could stay home and celebrate in their snug little house, but Franny had been planning a grand "Southern Christmas Soiree" since the first week of football season. Apparently, she had designs to out-dazzle last year's fete, which was "necessarily subdued coming so soon after the death of the family patriarch," with hopes to firmly entrench herself in Society. Maggie had her doubts, but if she had to suffer through another of Franny's parties, at least it would be at Norland. *And Edward is sure to be there.*

The promise of seeing Edward and Ellie together again made her smile. In spite of good intentions, Edward was not able to visit them in Barton as often as hoped, and his last visit had been particularly awkward. Outgoing, teasing and comfortable among the 'Dashwood Belles' as he dubbed them, Edward had been oddly tense and withdrawn, often starting to speak before abruptly stopping himself and leaving the room. *But with Marianne being so emotional and dramatic about Wills leaving, I think* life *was awkward.* Maggie sighed. The last few months had been as emotionally tense as the months after Daddy died—worse if you asked Marianne. Maggie tried to avoid her sister as much as possible since Wills skipped town; instead of getting over his sudden departure, Marianne was spiraling deeper and deeper into emotional denial. *If that's what having a boyfriend does to you,* Maggie mused during an afternoon ramble through the winter woods, *I'd rather not have one. Ever. There's plenty of things to do without a boy.*

Giving in to the temptation to climb a lovely gnarled old apple tree, Maggie began to mentally compose her first Christmas entry. *Only being able to write at Christmas is quite cumbersome,* she thought. *A whole year has gone by, and so much has happened! I should catch a ride into town with Ellie tomorrow, spend some quality time with the comforts of Mansfield Perk. It's going to take a rather large drink to get the Marianne-Wills saga explained in a way that makes sense and still captures the intensity.*

The next morning, Ellie dropped Maggie at Mansfield Perk on her way to work, with promises to collect her at lunch. After getting a chocolate chip muffin and the largest hot chocolate they served, Maggie found a table by the window, soaking up the sun, with a view of the whole shop. *There is the best people watching here*, she thought, noting several college students frantically cramming for approaching exams. Settling in, she pulled the journal from her oversized purse. Sipping her cocoa, she browsed through last year's entries, chuckling to remember some of Franny's meltdowns and surprised at how many pages she used for the first Christmas.

She sighed a little, reading the last entry—written on New Year's Eve, per Daddy's instructions. *Poor Franny tries so hard. I wonder if she'll ever figure out that things go smoother when you don't force them. Just let it happen—regardless of how it will happen.* Almost a year later, and Maggie could still hear Franny and Marianne shrieking at each other, and Mother's quiet "We're leaving" silencing the room. *It all seems so silly now,* she thought. *I hope things go better this Christmas, though with Marianne sulking about Wills I probably shouldn't hold my breath.* Turning the page, Maggie blinked in surprise. Where her ribbon marked a clean page, the start of the second Christmas's story, a green envelope rested. Certain she would have noticed it last December, Maggie wondered who had been poking among her things. Drawing the card out of the envelope, she gasped.

Merry Christmas, Magpie!

You're starting to write your second Christmas, and I hope this year is better than last. I have a hunch Francesca is having an elaborate bash, and you're all spending Christmas at Norland. Enjoy the homecoming, my girl, and don't let Franny's overzealousness for Proper Society ruin Christmas. Try not to let Marianne steal your cheer either—that girl loves an excuse for melodrama, and a morbid anniversary is prime drama potential. Especially if Franny tries to make her sing in public. I rather wish I could see that showdown.

Your special task this Christmas is to make Ellie relax and laugh, I feel certain she has taken on great responsibility this year. She is capable of great love, though I think it scares her sometimes. Also, hug your mother often. It will be hard for her to be a guest at Norland, during Christmas.

Don't hide in the treehouse too often, mind your very best manners—you are, after all, an adult now. 18. A true lady. So grown up, my little one, and still so very young. Revel in your youth, and cherish this Christmas.

With infinite love, Daddy

Maggie read the card twice, but there was no denying her father's hand. *How on earth did that happen?* she wondered, flipping through the journal. Nothing else lurked in the pages, and she opened to the blank page once more. *Impossible, and yet...I have the card in my hand.* Propping the mysterious card open against the window, she took up her pen to write.

The strangest things happen in this family. This year has been no less strange, and I hardly know where to begin. When Momma made her announcement New Year's Eve, the resolve, the very quietness of her tone, shocked us all. Imagine our greater surprise a few days later when she relented and gave us the rest of the news! Her aunt, hearing about Daddy's death through the wonder of the Southern Grapevine, phoned with the news that we could move into her little house in Barton. Apparently Aunt Jenn is a widow herself, and when her husband—a Middleton, of the Barton Middletons you know—died, he left her a small fortune. Including a rather substantial estate outside of Barton with not one, but two houses. Turns out Aunt Jenn lives in the big house, and said we could have "the cottage." (Spoiler alert: It's nowhere near as big as Norland, but it is definitely not a cottage.)

We made the move to Barton mid-January, and settled nicely. The house is cozy and neat, with delightful nooks and the best window seats. Barton and the outlying country is beautiful. Expansive and green, and the trees! It feels a lot like Norland, only wilder. Freer. Less gentrified. Marianne calls it barbaric. But she liked it well enough when she and Wills were an item—she met Wills because of the wildwood surrounding our new home, and she's not forgiven the trees yet. It's not the trees' fault that Marianne got lost, in the middle of a tantrum-induced walk, right as a March storm broke. If Wills hadn't been having his own Byronic fit, she might have wandered all afternoon and into the evening, but he found her and was able to escort her home. From that point on? They were disgustingly inseparable.

Marianne, I believe, truly fell in love. Or what she thinks is love. She has so many dramatic, overwrought ideas, sometimes I wonder whether she even knows the rest of the world operates differently from the tricked out version in her head. To say she fell head-over-heels for Wills would be an understatement. I think we all had a crush on him at first, even Momma and definitely Aunt Jenn. Who wouldn't? Willoughby Allenham has movie-star looks. Dark, broodingly dark, eyes; wavy, just too long hair that curls against his collar and falls across those eyes; a devilish grin and the deepest dimple you've ever seen. The only flaw marring his perfect looks? A scar, faintly visible, tracing the line of his jaw on one side. His dark perfection was a stunning pairing with Marianne's golden beauty—the way a church steeple stands stark against a steel grey sky before a storm. They were too perfect for each other.

Things got intense, Marianne fell harder and harder, and we started to get a little creeped out by Wills's broodiness. (By we, I mean Ellie and myself. Momma listened to our concerns, but didn't want to make Marianne unhappy). One temperamental artist in a relationship is more than enough, and lo and behold! We soon learned Wills is a cellist with the Atlanta Symphony, showing much promise and with an illustrious future ahead of him. He said he was taking a leave of absence from symphonic duties before embarking on a tour—mysteriously vague about details, this only added to Marianne's enchantment. And when he learned she sings like an angel? You could literally hear the wheels spinning. I believe he honestly thought they could take their show on the road and find fame and fortune.

And then, he left. With barely a goodbye, and no explanation, after nearly eight months of an intense and tempestuous relationship, he vanished. To say Marianne did not take it well is vast understatement. Her emotional distress, and general agitation, has been even worse than when Daddy died. She lost herself so entirely in Wills and the idea of their coupling, she's floundering. The only thing to spark her interest, even a little, was Aunt Jenn's gift of new dresses for Franny's Christmas shindig.

Though you wouldn't guess to look at her, Aunt Jenn really is a fairy godmother. When she first told us we were having custom dresses made, Marianne went wild. All her emotions funneled into sketches and designs for one stunning dress after another. After chatting with the designer and mastermind behind Cate's Creations, we were instructed to send only our measurements, our color of choice, and specific hemline and neckline details. I was dubious at first, we all were, but when the dresses came, we were dazzled. Cate must be a magician. We sent her the barest of guidelines, as requested:

Marianne: Red; Halter; Asymmetrical layers with beads

Ellie: Navy; Ballet neck; 3/4 sleeves; Tea length fit-and-flare

Me: Dark Emerald; Knee-length; Surprise me

Somehow, from those few descriptions, she created dresses that perfectly reflect our personalities and preferences. It's amazing. From now on, anytime I need a special dress, I am only wearing one of Cate's Creations. Even Marianne was pleased, and the rich red Cate picked brings roses back to her cheeks. I hope the dress is the start of a Christmas miracle and she can shake free of the whole Wills debacle.

PAUSING IN THE arched doorway to survey the scene, Maggie had to admit Francesca had outdone herself. When the Dashwood women arrived a few days before, they were sternly informed no one was to go into either the formal dining room or the adjacent 'drawing room' until the night of the party. Maggie attempted to peek several times, but was never able to catch more than a whiff of fresh paint. Apparently Franny set screens in front of all the doors, and covered the windows, to preserve her surprise. *She certainly had something worth hiding*, Maggie marveled now, eyes wide. *This is a winter wonderland if there ever was one!*

From her place in the doorway, Maggie could count half a dozen Christmas trees glittering and shining in the light of who knew how many candles. The bulbs in the antique chandelier, a family heirloom acquired on some long ago trip to Europe, had been replaced with the flickering kind. Looking closer, Maggie realized not all of the candles were really candles; wall sconces and standing candelabra lamps were also fitted out with the flame-like bulbs. Every metal surface was polished to a high sheen, and glass was everywhere—colored, mirrored, crystal— reflecting and refracting the light. *There are real candles in there somewhere*, she thought, wrinkling her nose at the scent of vanilla hanging heavily in the air. *You can't even smell the trees. I bet they're fakes.* Regardless of their origin, the trees were spectacular, decorated in what Maggie could only define as "classic Franny."

The whole wonderland had a very "classic Franny" feel, but a bit more tastefully executed than some of her previous demonstrations, Maggie noted with some relief. *There's no denying this is beautiful. I wonder if she hired a decorator.* The color palette was overwhelmingly creamy, antique whites with deep green and gold accents. There was a surprising lack of red, and Maggie idly wondered how Franny would react when she saw Marianne's dress. Greenery twined with thin gold ribbons was everywhere, in many places sprinkled with tiny gold Christmas balls, and massive pots of white poinsettias were artfully tucked in corners. The abundance of twinkling light and glass elements gave the space a sense of sparkling, as if the air were somehow alive and dressed for the party too. *It might not be our Christmas, but it is definitely a Norland-worthy Christmas,* Maggie decided, stepping into the room.

The furniture had been rearranged to accommodate decorations and soon-to-arrive guests. The double set of French doors between the dining and drawing rooms were propped open, tiny fairy lights woven in the greenery flanking the door frames. Moving further into the dining room, Maggie realized not only had the table been shifted closer to the wall, but nearly all of the furniture from the drawing room had been removed. The space felt almost vast, in spite of the mini Christmas forest, and the rugs had been pulled up too—revealing a highly polished wooden floor, perfect for a spontaneous dance. A sudden flurry of notes made her jump, and she turned to see several members of a strings group warming up in the corner by the bank of windows. *Oh boy,* Maggie thought, *this could get interesting. Very interesting indeed.* Since Wills's disappearance, Marianne adamantly refused to listen to classical, instrumental, or any other string-heavy music that reminded her of Wills. *And everything reminds her of Wills.*

"As you can see, the architecture and design of Norland lend so naturally to entertaining, we barely had to do anything to prepare for tonight's gala." Franny's voice entered the room ahead of her, and

Maggie rolled her eyes at the "Southern diva" tone she was using. *Edward sure labeled that right,* she thought, turning to see who she was talking to. Stifling a giggle, Maggie was happy to be mostly hidden from view by one of the larger trees. Slipping a little further into its shadow, she watched as Franny continued to pontificate to the Steele sisters.

Anne and Lucie arrived the day before, and Maggie had yet to deduce their connection to the Dashwoods or Norland, even a Ferrars connection was suspect. Though Lucie had taken a queer interest in Ellie, spending most of the previous evening trying to lure her into confidential girltalk over Franny's spiked eggnog, the Steeles seemed to want little to do with anyone. *Except Franny,* Maggie noted with a quirked mouth. *I wonder what they're up to, because nobody is that fascinated by Franny's prattling.* Fortunately, Franny's lecture on the importance of tasteful decor was interrupted when Robert and Edward walked in, arguing about something or other, in their usual style. The effect their entrance had on Lucie was instant and intriguing, and Maggie wondered if she had stumbled upon her answer.

"Edward, Robert," Franny snapped. "Manners. We have company present, and a larger party expected soon. Schoolboy antics are strictly forbidden tonight, do you understand?"

"Perhaps the Christmas spirit has made them restive," Lucie purred. "I, for one, am all aflutter with anticipation for tonight's revelry. I have never been to a true Southern Christmas soiree, you know." As she spoke, Lucie cast coy glances at the Ferrars men. Maggie rolled her eyes again and decided the time was right to make an appearance.

"Maggie!" Edward smiled, opening his arms to hug her. "You look beautiful tonight. Very festive as well," he added, giving the tinsel garland in her hair a light tweak.

Maggie returned the hug, then stepped back and gave a quick spin. "We discovered a fairy godmother in Barton," she laughed. "When did you get here? I was beginning to think you weren't going to make it in time."

Edward blushed. "I was delayed by a University matter," he mumbled. "Unpleasant business, definitely not acceptable party conversation."

"The important thing is you made it," Maggie replied, squeezing his arm. "Have you seen the others, do they know you're here?"

Before he could reply, Marianne swept into the room. "Edward! I'm so glad you're here, we were worried you were going to miss Christmas! Wait until you see Ellie; you won't believe how pretty she is tonight." As she spoke, Marianne seemed to float to Edward, air-kissing him on both cheeks, and smiling broadly. Maggie knew she was overcompensating for post-Wills doldrums, but wagered the others would not. A sharp hiss cut through the air, and Maggie glanced at Lucie in surprise. The younger Steele sister quickly schooled her features back to simpering, as Franny found her voice.

"Marianne, that dress is—"

"Red, Franny. My dress is red," Marianne interrupted, spreading her arms. "That is, I believe, a color commonly found in Christmas decorations."

"I was going to say highly inappropriate," Franny replied evenly, one eyebrow arched. "This is a Christmas dinner soiree, a very dignified and respectable affair. And I don't think I need to remind you the stateliness of the home demands a certain refinement of character, carriage and dress. I would suggest you go upstairs and find something more suitable."

Marianne's eyes glinted dangerously, and Maggie started backing slowly to the door, wondering if she could find Ellie in time to prevent a screaming match. Before she made her escape, Edward stepped forward, placing one hand on either woman's shoulder. "Ladies, ladies, ladies," he began, a small smile on his face and diplomacy in his tone. "It's Christmas Eve Eve, Santa is watching, and red is an acceptable color for Christmas, Franny. If the design is a bit, ah, flamboyant, we must remember that Marianne is a musician, and has a creative, expressive spirit. Now, can we all be family and host a good party?"

"Oh, Edward," Franny sighed, pulling a face before reluctantly nodding her head. "Okay, fine. I still question the appropriateness of that dress, but you make a little sense. And thankfully you didn't come in black, Marianne. I'm glad you seem to have put your mourning behind you."

"Mourning? Did you wear actual mourning for

your father?" asked Lucie, cocking her head and blinking.

"Oh no, dear," Franny said, in an almost-whisper. "She has been mourning a lover, it was a nasty breakup."

"You poor thing," Lucie cooed, "I hate to think about suffering a breakup, and so close to Christmas! I feel so sorry for girls who find themselves in that place."

Ellie, walking in with Mrs. Dashwood at that moment, startled as if she'd been struck. Maggie cast a quizzical glance her way, but Ellie merely smiled and commented on the decorations. Lucie chimed in with more gushing, and Maggie worried Franny might begin pontificating again, but John wandered in, mentioning the first guest had pulled in the drive. Franny gave frantic instructions on where to stand, or not stand, for greeting the guests as they arrived, with an especially piercing glance at the Dashwood sisters when she added "And interact, pleasantly!"

The evening went smoothly, much to Maggie's delight, though she frequently caught strange glances being exchanged between Lucie and Ellie, Lucie and Robert, and Ellie and Edward. There was a strained quality to their interactions, but Maggie was able to detect nothing truly amiss despite her close attention. *Franny may have succeeded in pulling off a successful party*, she thought after dinner, as everyone moved back into the drawing room space. *No catastrophes, and everyone appears to be having a genuinely good time. Even John is relaxed and more like the big brother I remember from ages ago.* Sipping a flute of sparkling cider, Maggie turned to find an out of the way spot to people watch, and found herself face-to-face with Wills.

"Oh," she gasped, as his face drained of color. Before she could fully process this development, Marianne's voice sliced across the party noise.

"Wills! Oh, Wills!" The desperateness in Marianne's voice tore at Maggie's heart, but it triggered a steely resolve in Wills. He clenched his jaw as Marianne joined them. "Wills, you're here! Oh, I didn't think you'd come, why didn't you tell me you could make it? Surprises are wonderful, but I'd rather have known. And where have you been during dinner?" Finally taking a breath, she beamed at him, a hopeful expectancy flushing her cheeks.

"I have been here the whole time, ma'am," Wills replied stiffly. Formally. "I am here in the employ of your hostess and sister-in-law, as a musician."

Marianne staggered back, and Maggie quickly wrapped her arm around her sister's waist. "I don't understand," she began.

"There is nothing to understand. I am here to play mood music, and Mrs. Dashwood is paying for my services. That is all."

"But, Wills—Willoughby," Marianne's hopeful smile was fading fast. "I don't understand," she whispered.

"Marianne," John stood at her elbow, surprisingly protective. "Are you okay? What's going on?"

"That's Wills," Maggie spoke softly. "The one who

broke Marianne's heart when he disappeared without a trace last month."

"John, make him answer me," Marianne's voice wavered, her eyes filling with tears.

"I think we should take this somewhere private," he said instead, giving Wills a look that brooked no argument. "The three of us, and your mother, are going to my office. Now." Beckoning Momma, John ushered them out of the room, leaving Maggie to field questions and smooth over their absence. She quickly told Ellie and Edward what happened, and the sisters exchanged worried glances.

"Poor Marianne," Lucie murmured, causing both to jump. "And in the middle of such a merry party too. I call that very bad luck. Don't you?" She turned and gave Edward a piercing look. As he blushed and shuffled his feet, Lucie continued. "Fortunately, there are still men who keep their promises." Maggie squinted at Lucie, wondering about the strange tone in her voice, as if she were trying to relay a message—or threat.

"Maggie," Ellie said softly, "let's go, Marianne will need our support, whatever is happening."

Long after the party ended, and everyone went home, Maggie stole away to her attic hideaway, journal in hand. Finding everything as she left it, almost a year ago, she sighed in relief and sank into the old chair.

That was a Christmas party like no other. Franny wanted to make an impression on society? She succeeded, though perhaps not quite the way she intended. There were weird undercurrents all night, before the party even started. It was only a matter of time before everything exploded, but I don't think anyone foresaw how that would happen.

Marianne and Wills are definitely, irrevocably over. Ellie and I slipped into John's office just as Wills was starting his "defense," if you can call it that. Apparently, his leave of absence from the symphony was a forced leave, while he was investigated for a number of nasty side jobs. Fraud, embezzlement and extortion, nice friendly charges. It would seem the very charming Wills conducted affairs with a number of women in positions of power, using them to curry favors and access funds. One of them discovered his unsavory scheme and outed him, thus the investigation. His departure from Barton was a result of being informed he was facing charges and needed a lawyer. All his assets frozen, he was forced to resort to playing small gigs, like Franny's. Thankfully, Francesca and John truly did not know Wills was the devil who broke Marianne's heart, but it was still a dicey situation. Marianne is more distraught than ever, and swears she will never be involved with men or music again. Oy.

Just as John kicked Wills out, there was a bone-chilling screech from the dining room, quickly followed by the sound of shattering glass and garbled shouting. In the minute it took to get from John's office back to the party, Franny managed to topple a Christmas tree, throw a candlestick through the French door (she has very bad aim, fortunately), and generally scandalize her guests. John quickly swept Franny into his office, and Ellie and I did our best to send everyone home with reassurances and Christmas wishes. Robert conveniently disappeared, Anne Steele looked traumatized, Lucie looked like the cat who ate the canary, and Edward looked even more miserable than Franny. It took some time, and not a little whisky, before we were able to get answers out of anyone. The answers were shocking indeed, and I understood why Franny reacted so. I should like to throw something myself—and my aim is much more accurate.

Lucie took advantage of the Dashwoods being preoccupied neatly out of the way to propose a toast to "the first of many Ferrars Christmases, and a lifetime as Mrs. Edward Ferrars." Chaos and calamity ensued. Nobody saw it coming, nobody had an inkling. Nobody wanted to believe it. When pressed for answers, Lucie merely smirked and said they had been engaged for several months (that would explain the awkwardness when he visited last month, if true), and involved far longer. Edward said nothing, only looked more and more miserable, meeting Ellie's confused glance with so much raw pain in his eyes it made me want to cry.

Lucie's weird overtures toward Ellie make sense now, the veiled threat in her sugary words. She must have known Edward has special feelings for Ellie, must have known this Christmas could have been something special for them. I'd suspect Franny as mastermind behind the plan, except for her total shock and distress. There is some queerness afoot, something isn't ringing true. I just can't prove it. And I shan't have a chance to investigate further, because Momma decided we're returning to Barton. Tomorrow. It looks like I'll get to celebrate Christmas at home, after all.

My consolation is the Steele sisters have been kicked out. John, wonderful John, has come into his own tonight and informed Lucie that while he cannot control what Edward does or does not do with his life, he would not tolerate such rude, ungracious behavior from guests. "Norland is a resting place, and you have disturbed the peace enough." I love that. I think Norland is working magic on John, restoring him to his former goodness. Maybe John can find the answers; I hope.

This Christmas is officially cursed. It has to be. Leaving Norland and spending Christmas at home seemed like a good idea. And this morning, gathered around the tree, handing out gifts, everything did feel right. Almost. Marianne's eyes were swollen from crying, and Ellie has been more quiet than usual since Lucie's bombshell. But still. It was good. Until Ellie opened a beautifully wrapped box that appeared under the tree. Her name was printed on the label, but no one else's. As she carefully lifted the lid, a sweet, familiar scent wafted on the air. Beeswax candles. Inside, a small card with the elegant logo of With Love rested on a ribbon-tied bundle of long tapers. Ellie blinked away tears, and handed me the card. It was from Edward, and only said "I'm sorry. I hope to have answers soon, for everything. I hope these can brighten your days, and remind you of happier ones. I'm sorry, Ellie, so sorry."

Once Ellie started crying, Marianne teared

up again. Then the phone rang. Aunt Jenn called to let us know before we saw it on the news: Wills eloped with the socialite daughter of a wealthy and prominent senator. Apparently his new family could help clear his name, and reinstate his income. Christmas was officially a lost cause.

There are so many mysteries, so many questions unanswered—and unasked, and so many hearts broken. Christmas should be happy, not sad. The new year looks bleak. I don't think I shall write again until next December. There will only be disturbing things to record in the days to come, and next year...Next year, we are due a good Christmas!

CHRISTMAS CHARMED

CHRISTMAS MUSIC PLAYED softly in the background, and Maggie hummed along to Michael Buble's crooning as she wiped down tables and pushed in chairs. After spending so much time there as a patron, Ellie convinced her to apply when Mansfield Perk advertised an open position, and Maggie had been an official barista-of-all-trades since June. She found she enjoyed the work, and being paid to learn the ins and outs of drinks while getting to know the other people who appreciated the shop's cozy atmosphere felt incredibly lucky. As much as she loved establishing relationships with the regulars however, her favorite customers were the travelers, the passers-through.

Maggie, now a Creative Writing student at the local college, let her imagination run wild creating stories about the people here one day and gone the next, sipping their drinks and living mysterious lives. She often scribbled first impressions or hurried thoughts on napkins, stuffed in her apron pocket, to be smoothed out and explored in her writing journal later. One day she hoped to compile her character sketches into a series of short stories to serve as entrance portfolio for an MFA program—a dream she kept tucked close to her heart, out of the public spotlight. Today though, her thoughts kept drifting to another journal.

Only one section left, she mused, straightening the creamer station. *I wonder why only three Christmases were allowed? Why not every Christmas? And how do I even begin to end this?* Her father's last gift had been a lifesaver, there when she needed it most, and a way to work through the ups and downs of Dashwood family drama. Even as she dreaded having to set down her pen and close the journal, saying another 'goodbye,' Maggie found herself anticipating the release of sharing a year's worth of family news. *But not tonight,* she remembered. *We're going to Ellie and Edward's to decorate the tree!* The promise of an evening spent in her sister's home, with family, tinsel and festive treats galore, made Maggie smile. *And their story is the happiest Dashwood news of the whole year, I'm going to enjoy revisiting that in the writing.*

"Why are you smiling like the cat that ate the canary, Miss Magpie," asked a familiar voice.

"Brandon!" Maggie looked up in surprise, her smile broadening. "When did you get back? We didn't expect you until Christmas Eve!"

Brandon grabbed her hand and twirled her in for a

hug. "I finished the job early, and couldn't stay away from the Dashwood girls a minute longer. My life was getting boring, I needed entertaining, and y'all are always good for a laugh." He winked.

"Right," she laughed. "You can't fool me, you missed Marianne. Have you seen her yet? Does she know you're here? Are you coming to Ellie and Edward's tonight? Please say yes!"

With a laugh of his own, Brandon set his hands on her shoulders. "Easy, Magpie. Take a breath, girl. You got me: I was pining for Marianne. Aching and wasting away to nothing. No, she doesn't know I'm here yet—and yes, I'm coming tonight. And don't tell her, it's a surprise."

"Eee!" Maggie squealed, before clapping her hand over her mouth. "Brandon, are you going to—"

"Maggie," he interrupted with a raised eyebrow. "Hush. I need to pick up a dozen of those amazing muffins y'all sell; I promised Ellie I'd bring something and we all know I can't cook to save my life."

As she boxed up the muffins, Maggie tried to coax more information from Brandon, but he just smiled and told her to wait and see. "Okay, be that way," she sighed dramatically, handing over the box and taking his money.

"Oh, I will," he said with another wink, turning to go. "See you tonight, Magpie. And don't be late! I'd hate for you to miss anything exciting."

Maggie couldn't help laughing as she watched him leave. *He is the best thing to ever happen to Marianne,* she thought.

Later that evening, after everyone had eaten way too many savory treats, and the finishing touches were being placed on the tree, Maggie curled up in a corner of the sofa with a mug of cocoa, surveying the scene. The old farmhouse was drafty and neglected when Edward bought it in the spring. He and Brandon did all the renovations themselves, working through the hot Georgia summer to get the house ready for Ellie. While the men focused on structural and practical aspects like patching holes, stripping floors and busting out walls to expand rooms and add closets, Ellie made the house a home. *It's beautiful,* Maggie thought now, *not as elegant as Norland perhaps, but it's homey and cozy. It's so Ellie.*

The large room downstairs where they gathered now was as warm and welcoming as her sister and brother-in-law. Edward made sure Ellie always had beeswax candles from With Love, and tonight their soft honeyed fragrance brought to mind childhood memories. Watching the two of them now, heads bent together as they tried to untangle ornament hooks, Maggie knew this Christmas would be the best yet. Her gaze wandered to their mother, and she smiled at the look of utter contentment on her face. *I know just how she feels,* Maggie mused. *This is what peace feels like.* The smile deepened as her eyes found Marianne and Brandon. *He must be teasing her about something, look how she blushes!*

Even though he was a relative newcomer to both the area and the family circle, Brandon Delaford slipped into place as if he'd been born a Dashwood.

His unassuming manner and genuine desire to be of help in any way quickly won their friendship. A skilled builder, it was some months into their acquaintance before the Dashwoods learned their new friend was in fact a much sought after architect. The discovery only cemented their regard, and as they grew closer it became apparent Brandon had a special appreciation for one of the Miss Dashwoods.

After the fiasco with Wills, Maggie thought her sister might actually follow through on her declaration to never even look at another guy. To the relief of everyone, Marianne 'found her way out of the black depths of brokenness,' with a little gentle prodding from Brandon and his guitar. It had been a slow process, and the healing tempered Marianne's spirit even as she learned to laugh—and love—again. The over-the-top dramatics once so annoying to Maggie had given way to a simple embracing of life, the good and the bad, a change that brought all three sisters closer together. Now, watching her sister laugh at Brandon's teasing, Maggie knew everything was turning out just as it should. *Maybe that last entry won't be so hard to write after all*, she thought. When Brandon pulled out his guitar and began to strum as Marianne softly sang Christmas carols, Maggie hoped for many more nights like this—cozy and familiar, surrounded by the people she loved and the love they shared. And she knew that life for the Dashwoods was finally headed toward a happily ever after.

Much later that night, Maggie stole away to the attic, thankful once more their house in Barton had an actual attic with dormer windows. Maggie convinced her mother to let her commandeer one of those dormers in the spring, creating a cozy nook where she could work on homework, read or just soak in the silence. She sat for a moment, her favorite quilt wrapped around her shoulders, looking at the leather book in her hands. It was even softer now, after two Christmas seasons, and its comforting weight in her hands settled her restive mind. "Okay, Daddy," she whispered. "The last Christmas awaits."

Tugging on the ribbon marker, and opening the journal, Maggie smiled when a blue envelope fell into her lap. *I don't know how it happens, but I love that it does*, she thought. *Some things, you just don't ask questions about.* Drawing out the card, she wondered what message awaited her this year.

Merry Christmas again, Magpie.

Your third and final Christmas for scribbling in this journal has arrived and, if I know you, there are only a few pages left. I can picture you so clearly, hunched over the journal, scribbling furiously, with the slightest of furrows to your brow. You get so lost in your writing, the whole world could fall away and you would never notice. I love that dedication and intensity in you, my Magpie. But don't let it take over.

By now, I feel certain you have all settled into a new routine, a happy new way of living. I hope Ellie has found love with someone who looks out for her, and that Marianne has learned to walk in grace and not just gracefully. And you...You are now 19. A wonderful age, on the very brink of a new decade.

I have one final instruction for you, Margaret: Live. Embrace the adventures given to you. Write the words that must be written, but do not forget to live in the world. Take care of you now, Maggie. Your sisters, your mother, they're going to be okay. It's your turn to fly, and I pray you soar.

I love you to infinity, and beyond, my little Magpie.

Daddy

Blinking back tears, Maggie slipped the card between the pages of the book and closed it gently. *Oh, Daddy.* Turning off the little lamp, she leaned her head back against the wall and looked out the window into the night. *December stars are always brightest,* she mused, searching out her beloved winter constellations. *And Daddy knew me well. It is so easy to hide behind the writing, to lose myself in the story.*

Some time later, Maggie turned the lamp back on and opened to her final pages.

Every year, there's a new story to tell. This year at last it is a happy story, a happy ending.

Our happiness began early, surprisingly, when John worked with Edward to unravel Lucie's claims and procure his freedom without making a scene in the public eye. She had been a student of his one semester, and was attempting to coerce him into marriage or else face charges of harassment and discrimination. I don't know what evidence she had, or thought she had, but her scheme was destined to fail. (I think she knew that, somehow, and that's why she kept making digs at Ellie, even after Christmas. Misery wanted company, perhaps?) Turns out she ultimately wanted an additional monthly allowance, conspiring with Robert, the mastermind behind the plan and now her husband, in her attempts to blackmail Edward. Yup. Weasely Robert Ferrars. Talk about brotherly love. Franny was furious, banning Robert and Lucie from Norland indefinitely. She even decided that Ellie was a good match for her brainy brother, and helped smooth their transition from cute friends to an adorable couple. In a moment of true grace, she and John offered the grounds of Norland for the wedding in September. It was beautiful, and Ellie is blissfully happy. At last.

I have a hunch Marianne will follow her down the aisle soon, Brandon is head over heels in love and I feel certain he is going to propose before New Year's. To see her happy and in love—really in love, and not a dramatic pretense of love—has been our delight. She returned to music as well (also thanks to Brandon), and I expect her new sound will take her far. Certainly farther than Wills will ever make it—hard to be a renowned cellist from a federal penitentiary.

I will always miss Norland, especially at Christmas, but life in Barton is everything I could hope for. I am surrounded by family and friends; the world is full of promise and hope. I've taken time to hide and heal, and now I emerge ready to conquer anything. Daddy knew exactly what he was doing, and I trust him in this as ever.
Here's to loving, laughing, and most importantly: living.

This is [definitely not] the end.

ACKNOWLEDGEMENTS

I count myself incredibly privileged to be part of this awesome group; Jessica, Melissa, Kimberly, Cecilia and Jennifer have been wonderful to work (and laugh) with – and tell amazing stories. Thanks for letting me join the fun, ladies!

Thanks also to Steven, my beta reading guinea pig, even though this is not your genre of choice. Your commentary made me laugh out loud sometimes, and was tremendously helpful.

And, of course, the biggest "Thank you!" of all goes to Jane, for writing it first and letting me fall in love with these characters over and over again.

About the Author

Rebecca M. Fleming is a dreamer, writer, quarterback fangirl, lover of all things Austen and the next Elven Queen of Middle Earth. A fervent believer in fairy tales and the power of Love, she often describes her purpose as "the distributor of tough love and fairy dust," and is determined to tell all the stories.

You can connect with Rebecca on her website: http://fairyjane.blogspot.com, or on Twitter at @FairyJanePress. You can also email her at fairyjanepress@gmail.com.

WITH LOVE, FROM
Emma

CECILIA GRAY

Chapter One

A LONE HONEYBEE buzzes by my face, and I swear its furry, yellow-and-black-striped abdomen brushes my nose. The furious hum of beating wings zips past my left ear as it slingshots around my head in a daring hello. I crane my neck to watch it soar over the other guests, dart between the strings of a double bass in the middle of Gershwin's "Someone to Watch Over Me," and fly over the gazebo into the woods.

It's the day before Christmas and we're smack in the middle of a Heartfield, Oregon, winter, but I'm not surprised to see the little bee. While there is a light dusting of snow covering the open meadow behind the community center, since yesterday the snowfall has stopped and the sun has burst out from behind the clouds in grand fashion. It knows today is an important day for my best friend and it better put in an appearance.

With my blond hair spun into a beehive knot and my shoulders bare in a strapless, gold, Cate's Creations sundress, I'm getting a bit of an unseasonal tan. The warm spell is enough to shake awake clusters of dormant bees, including the ones in my backyard, wood-framed hives. They'll take any opportunity to break free and do their business. And by business, I mean *business*—like the kind you do in the bathroom.

Bees are about business of all kinds, and the queen bee keeps business rolling.

Everyone assumes she has it easy. That she shakes her pheromones and fifty thousand drone and worker bees flock to her attention. Sure, hives are dormant for winter, but once spring chases the chill away, the queen needs to make sure that the worker bees gather pollen and the nurse bees take care of the larvae and the drone bees, otherwise lazy creatures, are up for mating. All while laying two thousand eggs a day. Can you imagine?

All that work. None of the credit that goes to the noble worker bee or the beleaguered drone bee. *Queen* bee. As if all she does is be waited on, hand and foot.

I know all about being a queen bee.

To the untrained eye, my best friend's wedding seems like the logical culmination of a series of unrelated, natural events. Kismet, harmony, inevitable wedded bliss. The guests seated around me in white fold-out chairs seem to believe it.

"Taylor and West are *perfect* for each other. What a darling set of soul mates." That's Taylor's aunt—

bride's side, front row, wearing a linen hat with a brim wide enough to blot out the sun.

"Taylor's such a cool girl. She and West...It's just meant to be." That's West's law school buddy— groom's side, mid-row.

They all talk as if some celestial Cupid had been involved.

Cupid wishes.

Taylor met West at a bar on a boring Wednesday night in January. She had intended to stay home. I was the one who had dragged her by her perky blond ponytail and set her down on that barstool. I was the one who had encouraged her to give out her number when West asked for it, even though she felt he was— and I quote—*kinda beige*. Taylor is a Lindy Hop instructor, from a family of dancers and movement instructors, and her gauge for beige is way, way off.

When West stopped by my flower and gift shop, With Love, before their first date, I'm the one who'd recommended a bouquet of snapdragons, which are tied to legends of mystery and deception and danger, so he would seem—quoting again—*less beige once she got to know him*. Through dates and fights and special occasions, I was there with tissues and encouraging words and gift ideas and a shoulder to lean on.

Now, here I am—bride's side, sixth row, aisle seat —on a beautiful late afternoon, getting ready to watch my friend marry the man I handpicked for her, a man who is wearing something not at all beige. I chose his black, cutaway tuxedo coat with notched lapels, a perfect match for Taylor's gown: a cream, tea-length, cap-sleeved dress that makes her look like the 1920s bombshell she is at heart.

Even though everyone around me is acting like Taylor and West were a forgone conclusion, their tunes were different when they first began dating. West's friends and family thought Taylor was too flighty and short (short!) for their button-upped guy. Taylor's family and friends thought West would be too stuffy and staid for their fun-loving girl.

I knew differently. Taylor and West are old souls from different eras, bridged by love. They're so much happier together than they ever could have been apart or with someone else. Obviously.

"Oh, Emma, hello, I didn't see you sneak in," Taylor's aunt says, her body now swiveled around and angled at me, much like a hunter's rifle. Five rows between us but she somehow latches those keen green eyes right into the hooks of my soul. "What are your Christmas plans, dear? Do you need a place to go?"

My smile wants to collapse, but I flash a perfect row of white teeth. "No, ma'am, thank you for asking."

She purses her lips sympathetically. "Well, if you change your mind..." She swivels away but not fast enough. I catch her muttering beneath her breath. "Pretty girl like that should be married by now."

I let my smile fall once she's turned all the way around. Really, as if I need to be married. Since losing my parents, I've had plenty of offers for places to celebrate Christmas. I've grown up in Heartfield my whole life. I have cousins and friends and more friends.

True, this year is a little light on invitations, but mostly because so many have children. I'm just at that age—twenty-seven—where family logistics are more complicated for my married girlfriends and my relatives. Throw in in-laws and children and dogs, and well, I don't want to be a bother. Seeing everyone the day after Christmas is fine with me, too.

One day, I'll have my own family, and no one will give me that stupid, pitying look ever again. Today's just not that day.

I'm attending Taylor's wedding on my own. A lot of guests seem to be arriving with someone on their arm...or a lot of someones on their arms and tugging their pant legs and crawling all over them. They take up seats around me in twos and fours and even a party of ten. Taylor's family seems to have embraced her big band theme, judging by their sleek silk teal, cream and gold dresses, smart striped suits, and thick hairbands with jeweled accents.

The chair to my left is empty, so I slip my clutch off my lap and set it down on the seat. A glance at the slim, gold watch on my wrist tells me there's another fifteen minutes before the start of the ceremony. I turn my attention to the white gazebo ahead.

West unbuttons and buttons his cuffs for what must be the fifth time. Why aren't his groomsmen calming him down?

He has two—both partners in his law firm—who wear smart, black suits with white roses at the lapels.

Elton and Frank. Or Elvis and Married-So-Who-Cares, as Taylor dubbed them in a not-so-veiled attempt to matchmake me.

Ha. As if the student could become the master!

Taylor's two bridesmaids, her aunt's daughters, wait patiently for the bride's arrival on the other side of the gazebo. Their slate-gray, knee-length dresses have fringe accents at the hem, a design straight out of the Roaring Twenties. I'd like to take a comb to one of them, Harriet, whose hair is frizzy in the wind. Taylor's mother and aunt had been pretty insistent on them serving as bridesmaids, which is why I'm here as a guest and not part of the wedding party.

Not that I mind. My hands are already full with the flower arrangements. With the entire town, including the community center, already decked out for Christmas, it was hard to find a way to incorporate the wedding theme into the existing holiday cheer. I had the community center pull the plug on all its green and red Christmas lights so only bright white lights remained running along the gazebo and roof. I then designed a climbing trellis of Indian plum, a native winter plant whose clusters of delicate, white petals shower down from its stems.

Any minute now, the five-piece band will strike up an upbeat cover of "Wedding March," and Taylor will walk proudly down the aisle clutching a bouquet of candy-colored Grevillea blossoms that I hand-harvested from the evergreen bush at Taylor's home. Its red, pink, and apricot petals are echoed in the sugar flowers that the baker piped around the edges of the three-tiered wedding cake.

No coincidence. Queen bee shenanigans and all.

"Move over, love."

I don't even lift my head to see who is casting his shadow over me. I would know Lance Knightley's voice underwater with my ears plugged and Taylor's Lindy Hop band playing Metallica. Some girls might find it smooth or confident. *Sex-on-a-stick*, if you're Taylor's aunt. *Whiskey going down right*, if you're Taylor. *Clive Owen after a cigarette and without an accent*, if you're West and horrible at metaphors, which he is. I suppose they're right. There's nothing wrong with Lance's voice—just what he says sometimes.

"Maybe that seat is taken," I say.

He picks up my clutch and steps over me, his leg brushing my knee. I pull down the edges of my dress and swipe at the sensitive skin. Lance sits down anyway and holds my clutch out to me. I take it and finally turn to look at him.

He looks nice. Of course. He wears suits like it's a living. This charcoal one stretches across his shoulders. Something about his open collar and the dark tangle of curls at the base of his neck and ears make me stare longer than I mean to.

Too bad the rest of the female population finds him just as easy on the eyes, if the number and frequency of hotties usually buzzing around him are any indication.

Lance owns Heartfield's newest bar, which has been open one year to the day. Our stores would be neighbors on Main Street except for my favorite coffee shop, Mansfield Perk, which sits between us. But because of the proximity, I see him every day.

He arrives at five o'clock, an hour before I close up shop. He parks his black Bugatti with orange stripes in the same spot in front of Mansfield Perk and leaps out in a suit looking almost perfect except for one thing gone awry.

Sometimes it's an open button, sometimes a mismatched sock, sometimes a missing cufflink. Like the universe is trying to help us out and mess him up a little. But whatever wardrobe malfunction he has upon arrival is always fixed by the time I walk into bar an hour or two later. Today, however, he looks perfect to begin with.

"Shouldn't you be on the groom's side?" I ask.

"I don't take sides in love, Emma."

I do not like the pitch in my stomach when he says my name. "Your date doesn't need a seat?"

"Don't need a date." He stretches his arm across the back of my chair. "I have you."

"Ha. You wouldn't know what to do with me if you did."

He turns his head so we're nose to nose. His eyes—which, I kid you not, are the clear gold of creamed honey—seem to sparkle as he asks, "Is that a dare?"

I pull back my head because being this close to his mouth isn't doing my blood pressure any favors. Lance is always doing or saying something flirtatious one minute, but the next minute he has a waif draped over him for free drinks. "Having me is one thing. Keeping me is another."

His eyes crinkle at the corners. He turns to glance down the aisle, then sits facing forward. His arm is still draped across my chair, but I can't hold myself up in my seat the whole ceremony so I let out my breath and lean back. Big mistake in the strapless number. His arm heats my bare skin, and he rests his palm on my shoulder, his thumb lazily tracing the curve of my neck.

"Have I met the bridesmaids before?"

See what I mean? He's already got his eye on the bridesmaids.

"Probably not. They're Taylor's cousins. They live in Portland." I tell him their names, but then add, "The tall one is married," with a bit too much satisfaction.

He studies the motley crew standing on either side of the gazebo, but the insistent stroke of his thumb is making me warm and dizzy. I need to think of something else. Anything else. Maybe Harriet and how her hair really just needs a little gel. Maybe if I adjusted her wide headband forward. She's really quite pretty. She's...

"I think I see a matchmaking opportunity," I say as I'm struck with a brilliant idea.

His eyes dart from the bridesmaids to the groomsmen. "Uh, no. No way."

This is a game we play. Lance thinks owning a bar makes him some kind of expert on human behavior, but I tell him he usually sees people at their worst, when they're drunk or depressed or desperate. I see people at their best, when they're reaching out for connection. This has sparked many will-they-won't-they debates between us, and I'm pleased to say that my record of predicting who will hook up is yet undefeated. Despite this, he refuses to admit I'm the one in charge of our town's relationship status.

The same thing happened to queen bees. They've been around for millions of years—tens of millions of years—but everyone assumed there was a *king* bee keeping things in line. Even Shakespeare makes a reference to a king bee. It wasn't until the 1500s that beekeepers realized a woman was in charge. Typical.

I don't have tens of millions of years, though, so Lance better figure it out soon.

"Our lady in question is..." He squints, as if he can't recall the name I gave him a second ago.

"Surprise, surprise, Lance can't remember the name of a girl."

"I know your name, love. Do I need to know anyone else's?"

It's hard to swallow all of a sudden, and I flinch away. He calls me "love" all the time, but he probably calls everyone love. It's a pretty complicated nickname all around. My mom used to call me love. *Let me braid your hair, love. Let's go to the beach, love. Love, do you want a story?* I wonder sometimes if it would have been better if she'd died when I was younger so I didn't have so many memories of her, so it wouldn't hurt so much, so maybe I wouldn't know what I was missing.

Lance squeezes me against him and drops a kiss in my hair. He doesn't know exactly what made me upset, but he's keenly attuned to my moods. Whatever else I say about Lance, he's a great listener and the best person to be around when you're sad. Maybe he's used to people's sob stories from running a bar, but he always says the right thing or doesn't say anything at all. He never tells me it will be okay or get easier. He just understands. He just is *there*.

After a few moments, I let out a deep breath. "Well, do you accept? Harriet and Elton?"

His eyes bug out of his head. "Elton?"

"You didn't think I meant Frank, did you? He's married."

"You did see Elton's last girlfriend, right? And I mean, in her swimsuit calendar."

"The relationship didn't last more than a month. Maybe Elton cares about more than just a pretty face."

"He also prefers a nice body."

I swivel away on a groan. Elton is hot in that Elvis way. He's the entertainment lawyer in the firm and manages a few local bands, as well as half the celebrities in the Pacific Northwest, including the morning news crews and that chef with all the cookbooks and shows. But he's still a guy, and every guy, whether they admit it or not, is looking for a real connection.

"I think there's something there," I insist.

"Careful, Emma," he says. "Don't let your principles get in the way of a wager."

"Says the man who has never won."

"Do you want to make it interesting?" he asks.

I turn back and arch my brow. "What could be more interesting than winning?"

"The winner can claim a favor from the loser. *Any* favor," he adds before I can ask for parameters.

I tug at my lip, not sure if I like the sound of that. "It can't be *anything*."

"Why do you care if you're going to win?"

He does have a point. Any favor? I could make Lance do anything? My mind hits the gutter pretty fast.

"All right," he relents. "Anything as long as it's legal."

Still a lot of gutter territory left. I stick out my hand. "Deal."

He glances down at my fingers, and his eyes crinkle. "That's not how you seal a deal, Emma."

Before I know it, he dips his head to try and kiss me.

You see, I've kissed Lance before.

He just doesn't remember.

LAST DECEMBER, THE week before Christmas, Lance Knightley moved into his retail space on Main Street. Before his grand opening, everyone else had managed to meet him, including the owners of Mansfield Perk, the art gallery custodian, and even our local patrol officer. I'd gotten a daily glance of him as he parked his fancy car and ran into the bar, with a stack of ledgers under his arm, a smartphone pressed to his ear and a cup of coffee held to his lips.

The retail season had kicked in, so I was too busy to introduce myself. December twenty-third, I'd spent all afternoon filling orders, and before I knew it, darkness had fallen and it was long past dinner. I started my walk home but heard bells, chiming, and laughter from his bar. Above the door was a huge sign: *Grand Opening*.

I figured I'd finally give it a shot and introduce myself.

I walked through the front door and took off my scarf. Eartha Kitt's breathy "Santa Baby" blasted through the speakers, and the bar was packed, one end to another.

Then he appeared in front of me and pointed over my head. I didn't look away at first because he was unexpectedly gorgeous up close. Sunken cheekbones, perfect pout. When I finally glanced up, I saw the mistletoe.

The kiss caught me by surprise. His lips were warm and tasted like mint and champagne. His arm twined into my hair. Our hips were flush. He pulled back with a cocky grin and rubbed his thumb over his lip, studying me with hooded eyes. Then he turned and walked away, a slight lean to his body, as if he'd had a bit too much to drink.

I made my way to the bar on unsteady legs. Then I watched him plant a kiss on everybody who walked in through the door—young, old, man, woman, even a reindeer. Worst yet, when he stopped by the shop the next day, it was to introduce himself as Lance Knightley, as if we were meeting for the first time.

I went along with it.

BEFORE LANCE CAN press his lips on mine, I pull back, grab the hand between us, and spit in his palm.

He grimaces. "Really, Emma?"

I spit in my palm and shake on it. "That's how we seal a deal where I come from."

He leans over to wipe his hand against the snow-tinged grass at our feet. I do the same. When he sits back, he leaves his arm around my chair, his thumb tracing the curve of my shoulder.

I hold my breath and hope it's a short ceremony.

CHAPTER TWO

AS WEST AND Taylor are declared husband and wife, he spins Taylor around, dips her so her head is practically by her knees, and plants a big kiss on her mouth. The crowd goes wild, and the band strikes up "Let's Fall in Love." I fish into my clutch for a tissue and dab my eyes.

They did it. I knew they would, but you know how sometimes when you're in the middle of mundane things, like how he chews with his mouth open or he never takes your side in an argument with his mom? You start to wonder how people even stay together. You forget the magic of it all. That's why we have weddings and birthdays and special occasions for flowers and gifts. To remind ourselves not to get fooled by everyday mundaneness. Love—and what we find in each other—is pretty special.

West lets Taylor up, but then she grabs him by the shoulders, dips him back, and kisses him. We're all on our feet now, wild with clapping. I glance at Lance, and even he is grinning like an idiot.

He leans over and says, "Bet the annual law firm holiday party will have a five-piece band from now on."

"You know it."

"I know Taylor, at least."

Heartfield is a pretty small town. Most of us have grown up in it our whole lives. Lance moved here last year, fresh from Los Angeles, but somehow he feels like part of the community. You'd think he and West were best friends by how he talks. Lance doesn't know how West ate worms on a dare in sixth grade or how Taylor got suspended for streaking during a girl's volleyball match, but somehow he manages to know the important things.

The photographer takes charge. She's adorable with a chic bob and dressed like a French mime, but super-pregnant, so she rests her camera on her belly between shots. "Head into the community center, enjoy some hot cocoa, warm yourselves up. Bridal party? Family? Stay behind for photos by the gazebo, please? Oh, and..." She looks down at a piece of paper in her palm. "Lance Knightley and Emma Gold. Would you stay for photos, too?"

We glance at each other in surprise.

"Chop, chop," the photographer says, "before we lose the light."

It's not dark, but the sun is starting to dip and a

breeze is kicking in. Lance and I fight the crowd, bees against the wind, toward the gazebo.

Taylor grabs me and pulls me into a hug. The tulle of her skirt crushes between us.

"Don't ruin the dress!" I warn her.

"Oh, don't worry about that." She swipes at the air and kisses my cheek. Then she yanks me against her side and says to the photographer, "This girl is the whole reason you're getting a paycheck today."

West clears his throat.

Taylor rolls her eyes. "Not that again."

"Not what again?"

It's their first argument as a married couple, and they are adorable during it.

"Same old," she says. "West thinks *Lance* is the reason we're together."

I lift a brow at West. "Do you now, Mr. What-Flowers-Should-I-Get What-Ring-Will-She-Like Do-You-Think-I-Should-Propose-on-My-Knees?"

West rubs the back of his head sheepishly. Lance leans in to save him from having to take sides. "I did talk him into asking for Taylor's number."

"I'm the one who talked her into giving her number out."

"I'm the one who got him to call."

"I'm the one who got her to answer."

"Get a room," West and Taylor say, then burst out laughing and kiss each other again. The photographer snaps away.

My cheeks flush and I glance around to see if anyone's noticed the awkward moment, but no one else seems to give it any mind. Not even Lance, who has been drawn into a conversation with Frank about whether his bar will be open later tonight. He says yes, but his bartender will be running it until Lance returns to operations for New Year's. A whole week? Maybe he's flying out to see his family in Los Angeles for Christmas. It will be the longest I've gone without seeing him.

The photographer asks us to move into frame. She takes a few more photos, then sweeps us away for the bride and groom's parents and the various configurations of the wedding party.

I feel Lance slip his jacket over my shoulders. I should give it back but it smells nice, and now that it's around me, it is warm and cozy and too difficult to give up.

"Thank you," I say.

He shrugs.

It's not the first time he's given me his jacket.

VALENTINE'S DAY THIS year was rough. Everyone was in love, and that meant everyone was sending flowers. Even with seasonal help, I worked every second of every hour, starting at five in the morning. I set aside dozens of arrangements for those last-minute calls, but I still had more emergency orders that I had expected. With Love had posted closing hours of six o'clock, but as the phone rang into six thirty and seven, I didn't have it in my heart to turn anyone away. These were well-meaning people who just let life get the best of them, so I paid my botany intern (who, thank goodness, had sworn off love for the next five decades by the sound of it) triple time to stay late and help with deliveries, which he normally felt were beneath his stature as a grad student.

By midnight, my knuckles ached from all the cuttings, and I was covered in pollen and petals. Still, I was satisfied knowing that, all over Heartfield, couples were celebrating their love and I was a small part of it.

Having sent my intern home with a big, fat bonus and a small, potted Camellia bush with a few green leaves and a red bud (for gratitude), I made ready to close up shop. I washed out my buckets, returned the leftover stemmed flowers to the fridge, untied my apron, and stretched.

As I stepped outside and locked the shop door, a biting wind made me shiver. I'd been wearing a yellow boatneck tee and black skinny jeans with flats, perfect for the day but totally inappropriate for the midnight chill.

I tucked my arms around me and started the walk home, but I hadn't taken two steps before I saw a figure leaning against the brick wall of Lance's bar. It only took another two steps to realize it was Lance. The man knew how to lean against a wall. Did models take classes in stuff like this, or did it just come naturally to attractive people? His languid length was like something out of a cologne commercial. Maybe he didn't realize he now lived in central Oregon and not Los Angeles.

"I was wondering when you'd close up," he said as I got closer.

"Valentine's is always my latest day of the year, but usually not this late."

"I imagine there are a lot of husbands out there who owe you right now." As I passed him, he kicked away from the wall and fell in step with me. "Would you like a ride home?"

I glanced at his bar, realizing it was closed up.

He grinned ruefully. "Valentine's Day is always my earliest day of the year."

I'm not sure why I hesitated. Since he moved to town, we'd become friendly acquaintances. Taylor and I got drinks at his bar at least once a week. We both sat on the town council, had been to the same dinner parties of mutual friends. Still, we'd never been alone. And I kept remembering that kiss.

If it had been so easily forgettable to him, though, then everything that had happened since was probably just as inconsequential.

"I'm sorry." He took a step back and tucked his hands in his pockets. "I didn't mean to make you feel uncomfortable. I'm always telling the girls in my bar not to take rides from strangers, but here I am—"

"You're not a stranger."

He looked dubious, and I realized he was more uncomfortable than I was. Probably because I'm sure I'd be the first women who'd ever said no to him.

A howling wind cut through the street right then, and I shivered uncontrollably, goose bumps trailing up my arms. He shrugged off his slate-blue suit jacket. I slipped it on.

"Thank you. I didn't mean to be weird. I don't feel uncomfortable around you. It's just late. I'm tired. I didn't mean to come off scared or anything."

Lance didn't look convinced. "I don't want you to do that thing where you're trying to make me feel comfortable. I'm always telling my sisters they don't owe men a damn thing, and I mean it."

Sisters. It all made sense now. He thought of me like a sister. I sighed. Might as well take the ride home.

"You have a big family?"

"See, I'm practically a stranger," he said. "You didn't even know I had sisters. Tons of them. Only guy in a family of four women."

Of course. He probably grew up thinking he was a crown prince. No wonder he was so suave. Still, he was a suave guy with a car that had heating. "Why don't you tell me everything about yourself while you drive me home?"

For such a fancy car, he drove slowly and cautiously, taking full stops at every opportunity. You'd think a cop was following us. *Or that I was his sister*, I thought with a sigh. He probably drove like a hot-riding manic with women he actually wanted to date.

Still, the long drive gave us time to chat. I found out his family still lived in Los Angeles, that he came from a line descended from medieval knights and the recent men of his family were all named for the Knights of the Round Table. So I was wrong. He wasn't raised like a prince; he was raised like a friggin' knight. His father was Gareth, and he was Lance, after Lancelot.

"Did that make you angry?" I asked. "To be named after the knight who has the affair and ruins everything?"

"I hadn't thought of it that way," he admitted. "I figured they named me after the best one."

"I'll bet," I muttered.

He surprised me with a laugh.

He parked in front of my cottage, having arrived in record time—if that record was for the longest time possible it could take. I swear I could have walked it in less. I jumped out, said thank you, and took the half-dozen steps to my front door.

"Emma."

Something about how he said my name vibrated right up my spine. I felt breathless as I turned, walked back to the car and leaned into the driver's door. "Yes?"

I put a lot into that breathless yes. I said yes, but I meant, *yes, you can come in for a drink* and, *yes, you can come in for more.* I'd always wanted my own knight, okay? Me and ten zillion other women, I'm sure.

"You look nice."

Suddenly, *nice* was more than nice. He made it into a new word that had me arching my back. All those promises I'd made myself—that I wouldn't put myself in the position to kiss him again, that he was a player and I wasn't going to be played—faded away. "Thank you. So do you."

His eyes crinkled with amusement. "But as much as I like that jacket on you, can I have it back, love?"

I shrugged it off and tossed it through the open window, swearing not to get caught up in him again.

I PULL HIS jacket tighter around my shoulders as Taylor, during a photo break, walks over to me.

"You have someplace to go tomorrow?" she asks. "You're more than welcome—"

"I'm fine! It's your first Christmas as husband and wife. I'm not going to crash that."

"May as well. All my cousins are," she says dryly.

I'm aware that Lance is looking at me. When Lance looks at you, it's not just looking at you. It's some physical, tangible thing. A caress, a touch—whatever you want to call it. It's a battle not to meet his eyes sometimes because there's always a question or a challenge in them, which means I have to answer or rise to it.

"May I have everyone in front of the gazebo for a group photo?" the photographer asks. "We're going to do candids, so just be yourselves. Let loose!"

Someone (West's uncle?) says, "No farting," and there's a groan as we all move on. There's movement and bodies, and in the chaos, I walk up to Harriet and introduce myself, then ask, "May I?"

I don't wait for an answer or tell her what I want. I tangle my fingers through her bangs to smooth them out. Her mouth opens in a surprised O, giving me a chance to pull the lipstick from my clutch and swipe some on. I tell her she looks great and pull her to stand next to Elton.

Elton really does look like Elvis during his younger days. He's got a shock of black hair that stands twice as high as his forehead, the brown eyes of a vulnerable beagle, and the snarliest upper lip. Unlike the other lawyers in the firm who wear suits and ties, Elton comes to work in dark jeans and two-hundred-dollar T-shirts, but today he's in a suit like the other groomsman and something about it makes him seem more attainable for Harriet.

His eyes light up when he sees us walking toward him. "Emma! My favorite member of the Heartfield City Council."

"Now, now, Elton, no mixing politics and family time. Especially not the day before Christmas."

He grabs his heart, as if in pain, and fakes a grimace.

Elton's been hot on my trail to side with him on a community measure to raze this very meadow for condo developers, but I've made my position pretty clear. Past the cleared green lawn is a gorgeous valley of native wildflowers that keep our bee population—and, by extension, our food population—healthy. Heartfield prides itself on our berry production—boysenberries, salmonberries, and huckleberries being some of our regional specialties—which bring in not only retail dollars, but tourism. Elton can bat his pretty lashes as much as he wants, but I'm not budging.

After Elton fakes my breaking of his heart, he straightens back up.

"Have room for two more in this picture?" I ask.

He holds out his arms. "One under each arm."

Perfect. See, I knew I was right. He's not a snob at all. He's a guy looking to have fun. I just have to show him that Harriet can be fun. I shove her under one arm and take up pose beneath the other. Lance is at my side in a second, his lips a grim line because I'm winning and he knows it. We pose and smile, following the photographer's instructions to be silly or serious.

"So, Emma," Elton says, "Taylor says you're a terrible dancer."

I scowl. "Guilty as charged."

Taylor has already warned me that half the guests will be semi-professional swing and Lindy Hop dancers. As much as she's tried, she's never made me into anything more than a professional bystander. *And I've taught a one-eyed greyhound dog to dance*, she used to say to me, exasperated.

"Guess you and I will be taking up the space by the walls," Elton says.

"Anyone can Lindy Hop." This, from the until-now-silent Harriet, makes me, Elton, and Lance look at her. She clears her throat and adds, "Taylor is used to teaching advanced classes, but I teach a beginner's studio in Portland. I can show you. It's easy, I swear."

Elton smiles and grabs her hand. "My savior! You'll make me into a dancer by the end of the night?"

I smile pointedly at Lance, who just shakes his head.

The photographer reconfigures us, and Lance and I are dismissed while she focuses on the wedding party. I practically skip toward the community center, tightening his jacket around my waist. His jacket that I wore during the candid photographs, as if we're together. I should have given it back.

"Don't be so satisfied," he said. "The night's not over."

"I'm not sure when I will find time to gloat with all the dancing I'll be doing after I master the Lindy Hop *and* win our bet. Multitasking—such a problem!"

He snorts. "You can't think Elton is actually interested in Harriet."

I stop in my tracks and fold my arms over my chest. "Why not? She's nice, fun, and can dance. She's interesting."

"Elton's not interested in interesting."

"Yeah, well, what is he interested in?"

Lance looks at me for a hard moment. "Elton will always want the queen bee."

He can't mean me. Me and Elton? No way. "Do you know how the queen becomes queen?"

The corners of his lips quirk up. "I guess you're going to tell me."

"When a queen lays her eggs, all the bees are the same, but when it comes time to make a new queen, some of the larvae are fed royalactin, which triggers them to become queen. That's all it takes. A little extra nourishment and tenderness and you have a queen."

That's always been the secret to my business. That anyone can feel like a queen, can be a queen, with the right love.

CHAPTER THREE

LANCE AND I enter the community center, which welcomes us with a blast of heat. I take off his jacket, but instead of putting it back on, he rests it over his arm. In the front foyer, a Douglas fir scrapes the ceiling, covered in red and green globes and silver tinsel. At its base are dozens of fake, oversized gifts with sparkly bows.

A pang throbs beneath my breastbone. I put up a tree every year, a little Charlie Brown one that sits on my fireplace mantle and is the size of a bottle of wine.

We skirt around the tree to the reception hall behind the foyer. The band has set up on the stage, and they've been joined by a singer with a sultry voice singing Irving Berlin's "Blue Skies." There are twelve circular tables of five guests spread through the hall. We make the rounds until we find our name tags, side by side, on an otherwise empty tabletop next to the buffet spread. Lance drops his jacket over the back of his chair and pulls out my seat.

I raise an eyebrow but sit down and look at the other cards' names.

"This makes things interesting," I say.

Elton and Frank are supposed to be at our table, as is Harriet. I rearrange the labels so Harriet sits next to me and Elton, with Frank taking up the other seat by Lance.

"That's not playing fair," Lance says.

"All's fair," I reply.

The buffet is farthest away from the band, so we're able to talk without shouting at each other, though we still need to lean in. Which will be perfect for when Harriet and Elton have to converse.

"You look nice, by the way," Lance says. It's what he always says to me, but I know he means it. Just not the way I want him to mean it.

"So do you." That's what I always say.

Taylor's aunt has hawk eyes on us from across the reception hall. Or maybe she just has eyes on Sex-on-a-Stick, as she calls him. He leans over to say something about the band, and I lean closer. Taylor's aunt rears up in her chair to get a better look and knocks over a glass of water, blustering and wiping at her lap, and I realize that, from her vantage point, it looks like we're kissing.

I stifle my laugh.

Lance narrows his eyes. "What are you up to?"

"Just giving Taylor's aunt a reason to gossip."

He glances over his shoulder and smiles knowingly when he sees her. "Naughty minx. How about we give her something more to gossip about?"

His hand curves around my thigh. He pulls me an inch forward so my legs are caught between his and buries his face in my neck. I gasp at the shock and surprise and heat. Part of me wants to pull away, but a stronger part of me wants to grab him and get out of here. I hate that part. She's such a sucker.

"Has she had a heart attack yet?" he asks.

His mouth is close enough to tickle my earlobes with every word, and each parting of his lips sends tremors through my body.

"She's passed out. They're giving her CPR."

He spins around, shocked. Damn. His mouth is gone. I bite my cheek to remind myself this is a good thing.

When he realizes Taylor's aunt has just gone to the restroom to clean herself up, he shakes his finger at me. "You'll pay for that."

Maybe I will, but it would be worth it to have my sanity back. My pulse is barely under control when the bridal party returns from photos. Harriet makes a beeline for our table while the boys make a more leisurely entrance.

"Next to me," I say, patting my chair.

Harriet sits down warily. "You're Taylor's best friend right?" she says. "Emma, the beekeeper?"

I flash my most winning of smiles. "Yes!"

"You probably should have been her bridesmaid."

"I'm happy to be anything she needs," I say. "That's what friends are for."

She eyes me with a curious expression.

"I'm really excited about our dance lessons," I add.

"Oh, good! Taylor said you were hopeless."

I make a mental note to give Taylor a piece of my mind later.

"But I think anyone can learn. I love to teach. I run classes at a retirement home in Portland. You should see some of those guys move." Her eyes light up as she talks about her students. I wish Elton was around to see this, but he's still being social. By the time he makes it to our table with Frank, she's quieted down. There's no time to force a conversation. Everyone is waiting for the grand entrance of Taylor and West.

The couple runs into the room to much fanfare and start off the night with a dance together. Soon, the whole floor is jumping. Ladies twice my age are kicking up their legs higher than I've ever been able to. Harriet is bopping up and down in her seat.

No time like a wedding to help two people fall in love.

I meet Elton's eyes over Harriet's head. "Ready to dance?"

We all push to our feet and join the crowded dance floor. Lance is standing close and I realize it makes perfect sense to partner with him so Harriet can partner with Elton, but my heart's not ready for that. It's still coming down from our near-kiss and my near-mauling of him in front of Taylor's whole family.

"Will you teach both of us how to dance at the same time?" I ask Harriet.

"Do you need a lesson, too?" she asks Lance.

He raises his eyebrow, snatches up a passing woman who must feel like she won the lottery, and spins her away. I take a deep breath and focus on Harriet.

She has us stand on either side of her to show us a simple set of steps where we lean forward and then back. She faces us, like a partner, and shows us how to do it in counterbalance. It's so much easier than anything Taylor has shown me with kicks and flips and somersaults.

"Let me try it on my own," I say and push Harriet into Elton's arms.

They dance a few counts. He's really good at letting her partner him. Within minutes, they're breaking into more complicated moves. Her whole face is flushed and happy.

"Ready for me?"

That voice from behind, his hand on my bare shoulder. My eyes flutter shut, and I sway back.

But no, I will not get sucked into Lance.

I spin around, cross my arms, and force myself back into that push-pull that we've come to know and love. I nod my head over at Harriet and Elton, hand in hand. "I'm ready for you to admit I win. Come on. Admit it. They look great together."

Lance smirks and slips his hand around the curve of my waist. As much as I try to remain stiff, my body doesn't really care what my brain wants. I pretty much melt against him as he leads me around the floor. He doesn't use the moves Harriet taught me but something wholly his own creation. When he turns, I turn. When he steps forward, I step back. It's pretty easy dancing with him. I'm not the only one who notices because another woman cuts in to steal him and her older partner takes me on a twirl. Dancers seem to switch like eye makeup, giving me a moment of relief as I move around the floor with a few of Taylor's cousins and uncles. Before long, I'm back dancing with Elton.

"Harriet's a pretty amazing dancer," I say.

"The whole family's talented."

He's so gracious. He tries a few more moves, and soon I'm warm and fanning my face.

"Need a break?" he asks.

"Yeah, maybe."

He leads me to the foyer with the Christmas tree.

"Thanks," I say. "It was getting warm in there."

"You know, if you want to be alone with me, you just have to ask."

I roll my eyes, but then he kisses me. It's wrong and weird. His lips are cold and brittle. I push him back and step away. "What are you doing?"

Then I catch Harriet watching us from the dance floor, her mouth open in shock. She turns around before I can shake my head or make a gesture to let her know this is all a big mistake. I start to go after her, but Elton grabs my wrist.

I yank it back. "Seriously, don't touch. What were you thinking?"

"I'm sorry." He holds up his hands by his head. "You were flirting with me and trying to get me to dance. I've liked you for a long time and thought you were giving me signals."

My face crinkles in disgust. "Signals? I've been trying to set you up with Harriet."

"Harriet? She doesn't even live here."

"So?"

"So? I'm running for mayor, Emma. I need to stay focused on local issues."

"Dating is a *local issue* for you?"

"Yes," he says, perfectly serious. "Don't you see we'd be perfect together?"

I walk away before he can explain his absurd comment. I have to find Harriet. I'd obviously been trying to set them up, and now she thinks I was scamming Elton for myself, which I would never do to another woman.

I don't see Harriet, but I run into Lance by the chocolate fountain.

He takes one look at my grim face and asks, "What's wrong?"

As much as I hate telling Lance he's right, I have more important things to worry about. "Elton's a jerk. Harriet just saw him kiss me—"

"He *what*?" Lance's body electrifies into a tight wire of tension.

There he goes again, like I'm his little sister who needs protecting. "It's fine. He backed off. But Harriet...I need to find her."

"I'll help you look."

He doesn't tell me I-told-you-so. It probably doesn't even occur to him. Lance isn't like that, which is a relief.

I cast a worried glance Taylor's way. She's gnawing

on a carrot, probably hungry from all the stress and then the dancing. I don't want this drama to ruin her wedding, so I have to get things on track.

Lance and I split up. I go to check the bathroom, but Harriet's not there. When I come back out to the dining hall, she's on the dance floor. Lance is twirling her around. He does the chicken dance around her, making her laugh, while I watch a little awkwardly from the sidelines. It's not the first time I've seen Lance take care of another woman.

ST. PATRICK'S DAY in Heartfield had always been a big to-do, but nothing rivaled the *Law Enforcement Drinks for Free* promotion that Lance ran at his bar this year. Anyone who was anyone was going to be there, and Taylor was dragging me and West, whom she'd officially begun calling her boyfriend instead of "*that guy I'm dating.*"

She popped her peppy face into my shop at 5:59 PM on the dot and said, "We're out of here."

I was already in a mint-green dress that hugged me in all the right places and stopped mid-thigh. It had a dip in the back almost to the butt, but my long, blond hair swung in front of the bare skin so it wasn't too obscene. The front was full coverage, but if you looked closely, you'd realize the green material was sheer, showing the black bra beneath.

It was daring.

Because I was done being single.

I already knew West had his eye on proposing—any idiot could see they should get married—which meant I would officially be the last single in my group of girlfriends.

It wasn't like I tried to be single, but when your work day starts at five in the morning with the arrival of the flower truck and you have to work late every major romantic holiday, you put yourself out of the running.

St. Patrick's Day, though, was fair game. So I pulled off my apron, fluffed up my hair, and grabbed a small, potted plant.

"What's that?" Taylor asked.

"A gift for Lance's bar," I said. Even though I'd seen him at a few town council meetings this month, I'd never really said thank you for the ride home. I was dreading watching him make out with everyone under a *Kiss Me, I'm Irish* sign, but I also knew it would be good for me.

As we walked toward the bar, Taylor was going on about how West wanted her to meet his parents and she was pretty sure they wouldn't like her.

"Everyone likes you," I said. "They'd be dumb not to like you, and West's parents are smart, like Ivy League-smart."

"Exactly, they're Ivy League-smart. And I'm just—"

"Don't say it," I warned her. She thought she was dumb just because she'd never gone to college, but that was a load of crap.

"We're just different," she said instead.

I hugged her around the waist and said, "Different is how species survive. Otherwise it would be all incest and genetic mutations."

"What is wrong with you?" she murmured.

We opened the door to the bar, and a bevy of Irish drunkenness spilled out. Half the cops in town wore ruddy-faced smiles and sang along to the old Irish tunes piping through the speakers.

No Lance on sight. And no kissing signs, which I was more relieved about than I thought I'd be.

Taylor and I proved popular right off the bat. We were brought drinks, danced around, twirled, and regaled with stories. I kept looking for Lance but didn't find him until an hour in, when he walked out of the back office to speak to the bartender.

He smiled when he saw me and said something, but it was too loud to hear. I pointed to my ear, and he gestured to his office. I followed him, eager for relief from the chaos. Loud music and dancing was Taylor's scene, not mine.

"I'm glad you came," he said. His gaze ran over me, but instead of coming back up my eyes, it took another dive down, as heated as I imagined his hands would have been. I jerked the pot I'd brought in front of my chest, as if it would make the dress less see-through, and shoved it toward him.

"A thank you present for getting me home on Valentine's Day."

"I was wondering what this was." He took the pot and held it up. "Clovers?"

"Supposedly, they guarantee one four-leaf clover in the bunch," I said.

"I'll have to let the cops fight over it."

He turned away to set the pot on his desk, and I felt a little calmer with the distance between us. I looked around. It was a neat office, with a desk, a rollaway chair, and a wall full of pictures of another venue—sleek dancers, a wall of tequila bottles.

"Where is this?"

"My family's club in Los Angeles," he said. He was easy to spot in the photos, a head taller than most and a great set of teeth that lit up the camera. The club seemed chic and popular and about twenty times better than anything in Heartfield.

"Why did you leave it and move up here?"

I turned away from the pictures to find he'd come up behind me. I had to lean against the wall just to put a foot between us. He was staring at the photo, thoughtful.

"I wanted something that was my own."

I flinched. I didn't mean to, but he caught it and gave me a funny look.

"You don't agree?" he asked.

"No, I guess I do it's just...My parents left me so little when they died. I'd give anything to have more of them, you know? More of something that was from all of us."

He didn't say the things people usually did after I told them my parents were dead. He didn't ask me how or when. Maybe he knew, like I did, that it didn't matter, that every answer would be just as painful. He didn't tell me he was sorry. He didn't put me in the position of having to make him feel more comfortable with my loss. He didn't use my vulnerability as an excuse to touch me or take advantage of me. He just looked at me with sadness, like he felt it, too. He waited for me to decide what we did next.

Fortunately, before I could make the embarrassing mistake of launching myself at his mouth, the bartender stuck his head in the door. "We got a sloucher."

Lance swore and tore out to the bar. I followed him and saw Taylor with West, making out in the corner. She looked over and gave me a thumbs-up, then pointed to a booth of police officers, clearly the specimens she had scoped out as appropriate for me. I took one look at them, realized I didn't feel any stirring, and sighed. Maybe I wasn't trying hard enough.

Lance's hand fell on my shoulder. "Can you help me?"

He had a girl belted to his side with an arm at her waist. Her head hung over, and she was clearly half-conscious. He started to walk out of the bar, and I followed.

"Does she need to go to the emergency room?"

"No, one of our regulars is a paramedic who checked on her and says she just needs to sleep it off, but the cabs are all busy tonight and I can't spare anyone on staff."

"Oh, well, I don't have a car," I said.

"I know. I'm going to take her home, but I need you to come with me." She slouched further against him, burying her head in his neck. Far from enjoying the attention, he reared away so she leaned the other direction.

"Why?" I asked. "I don't know her."

"She's out of it, and I'm going to be taking her to the address on her driver's license. I don't know what or who I'm going to find when I get there."

"You need a character witness," I said, finally understanding. "Yes, of course. Let's go."

It took a while to maneuver her into the backseat of his Bugatti. His driving to her house was fast, smooth, with quick turns and gear shifts. Luckily, the girl's roommates were home and awake, and they took her in.

Lance seemed relieved as we got back in the car and went back to the bar, now slow as molasses. "Best possible scenario," he said.

"Do you have to deal with that a lot?"

"Not as much here as in Los Angeles. She's just my second."

I looked out the window at the casual pace of the buildings we passed. It was like we were in a golf cart.

"I didn't get a chance to tell you earlier," he said. "You look nice. Again."

I smiled. "You, too." My phone started beeping, and I glanced down. "Oh, crap, I didn't tell Taylor I was leaving."

"Is she worried?"

"Yeah, let me let her know we're on our way back."

"That's a good friend you have there."

"Thanks, but she's mostly freaking out I'm not

getting hit on by the guy she's handpicked for me."

"Oh?" He was earnestly curious.

"Yeah, one of the cops in the corner...I don't know. I mean, maybe he won't even be interested. It seems like he's out with his friends."

"He'll be interested," he said flatly. He turned to me and grinned. "And if not, I'm happy to put in a good word for you."

ONE DANCE BETWEEN Lance and Harriet turns into two and then three. Harriet looks like she's having a great time, which makes me realize that I'm not. The room feels too stuffy. The back of my dress is sticky against my skin. I haven't eaten, but my appetite is gone.

I walk over to Harriet, and she smiles at me, so everything must be okay between us. The relief is palpable beneath my breastbone. I guess she didn't really have a chance to care much about Elton, and I realize I've been freaking out over nothing.

"Lance is such a great dancer," Harriet says.

I nod and join in with the steps. Lance spins me once, then spins her.

She laughs—a little loud, it seems—and rests her hand at his elbow. "You're a natural!"

It shouldn't bother me, but it does. He's good. So what? Does she have to give him a medal, too?

Harriet quickly picks up another partner, the ten-year-old son of one of the guests. She shows him the moves, leaving me and Lance to dance on our own. He takes my hand. We go through some steps.

"I can hear you counting it out, love," he says, smiling.

"That's because I am," I mumble.

I wish I looked as graceful as Harriet and Lance do together. I've never been much of a dancer. The queen bee doesn't dance, either. She leaves that to her worker bees. They have a dance called the waggle to communicate with each other about where to find pollen. There are over a hundred moves in a waggle. If a bee can learn them, why can't I learn a simple eight-count?

Harriet spins the boy off to his mother and comes back to us, grinning. Lance watches her with an unreadable look in his eyes.

"Just lean into it," Harriet says, guiding me.

I step on Lance's foot and mumble my apologies.

"No, like this," she offers. Great, now she's pitying me. She's so smooth while I feel like I'm learning to manage an extra limb. This time I bump into his chin.

"Forget it," I say, pulling away.

Lance pulls me back. "Emma, wait."

Harriet's pity is one thing? Lance's? No way. I can't take it. The song comes to end, just as I yell, "I don't want to dance with you! Just leave me alone!"

I feel sick and confused as heads swivel toward me. I turn and head for the exit.

CHAPTER FOUR

TAYLOR FINDS ME sitting beneath the Christmas tree, my chin resting on my raised knees. "What's up, buttercup?"

I bury my face in my hands on a groan. "I'm so sorry. I don't know what happened!"

"Well, in case you missed it, one of the guests had a crazy outburst at this guy she's been mooning after for a year."

"I do not *moon*." I give her a glare, but then my face collapses. "I'm so embarrassed. I feel awful. On your wedding day! I don't know what happened. First, Elton tried to kiss me."

"He what?" She sits down and scoots next to me, beside two silver packages with satiny blue bows.

I recap what happened and then say, "Harriet was nice, but for some reason, it just made me feel worse. I felt stupid and clumsy, and I hate feeling stupid and clumsy. Are you trying not to *laugh*?"

She giggles.

"I guess you're not trying that hard," I mutter.

"Emma, listen to yourself. You *like* Lance."

"We've been through this," I say. "I don't like Lance. I can't like Lance. I'm like his sister. And, anyway, Lance is a drunken man-whore."

She gasps.

"Okay, that's unfair and not true," I amend. "But he is not interested in me. As West would say, let's look at the evidence." I hold up a finger. "One, he doesn't even remember our kiss. Two, the night he drove me home, he didn't try to come in, even though I was putting out all the signals. Three, he offered to help set me with up with another guy. Four...Do I even need four? We've been alone a lot. He's never made a move, not once."

"I know, and I agree. I've heard all this before," she says. "But that doesn't change the fact that you have feelings for him, feelings you've never admitted to yourself, and until you do, there is always going to be awkwardness between you two."

Oh god. Could she be right? Do I have the dreaded *feelings* for Lance? I wish it was as easy as she thought it should be. "Come on, let's get you back inside. Rumor has it there's a wedding."

She lets me tug her to her feet, but as she goes on ahead, I linger in the foyer.

I told Lance to leave me alone, and based on the horrified look on his face, I'm worried he will.

I've told him to leave me alone before, but he didn't.

MOTHER'S DAY IS always the worst day of the year for me. Obviously all the holidays have their downsides and I loved my father, too, but Mother's Day was just extra lemon on the wound. Maybe it was spending hours taking down sweet messages from daughters to their mothers, but I never made it through the day without choking up at least a few times.

This year it was a six-year-old who walked in with a handmade card and a jarful of quarters for her mother's flowers. I filled the order and then excused myself to sit in the fridge. I felt the cold all the way down to my eyeballs, but it still didn't stop the tears from coming. After a few minutes, I managed to compose myself and return to work, but by closing time, I needed a drink.

I walked straight over to Lance's bar, pulled up a stool, and ordered a whiskey shot. Two shots later, Lance pulled up the stool next to mine.

"Want to tell me what's wrong?"

"Nope."

"You know management reserves the right to refuse service."

I slowly turned my head and met his eyes. They were concerned but also wary. "Today just sucks, okay?"

"Apparently it's not okay, so why don't you tell me more about it?"

"Why don't you leave me alone?"

"Because you look like you need someone to look after you."

I burst into tears. He ushered me into his office, sat me in his chair, and pressed a Kleenex into my hand. Maybe it was from working in bars and clubs his whole life, but he didn't even seem perturbed by me crying. He just waited patiently.

"Mother's Day," I managed to sob out. "The worst."

He nodded in agreement but didn't say anything else, just handed me another tissue. I blew my nose several times. He nodded at the wastebasket at my feet. After a few moments, the sobs turned into sniffles, and then I was quiet. The pot of clover on his desk had had grown an inch. He'd kept the clovers. My mother would have liked him.

I felt the waterworks sting my eyes. Not again, I thought.

"Queen bees never get to know their mothers," I told him.

His brows shot up.

"I raise bees," I explained. "For my candles. Hundreds of thousands of them in my backyard."

"What do you do for the bees?"

"Oh, you check on the health of the hive, feed them when their stores might be low, make sure the moisture levels are good."

"Sounds like you're the mother," he says.

"Huh?"

"Of the bees. You raise them. You're their mother."

I blinked, like that might help me understand what he'd said. He pulled a yellow tulip out of the bouquet of flowers on his desk and handed it to me. I took it, even though I didn't know why, and looked at him questioningly.

"Happy Mother's Day," he said.

I left the bar, thinking that I shouldn't have felt better, but for some reason, I did.

MY LIST OF reasons for not liking Lance keeps repeating over and over in my head as I look in on the reception where he's dancing with Harriet—without her stepping on his toes. Unfortunately, the list gets softer and softer until I'm left with other things in my head.

Easy things, like the fact that he's hot and successful. Other things, like how he's funny and nice and sweet. Uncomfortable things, like wondering how exactly I'd come to such horrid conclusions about him when I'm the only one I've ever seen drive off with him in his car. And then there are the harder things, like how he was all I thought about or how, whenever things were going bad, he seemed to make them better and...

Oh hell.

He always made me feel better until now.

Because I'm in love with him.

Being in love with Lance is the worst thing ever. It is one thing to be attracted to Lance. Or even to like him. But love? *Love*? Now that he's dancing in the arms of another girl and I just announced to half the town that I want nothing to do with him?

What am I supposed to do about that?

CHAPTER FIVE

QUEEN HONEYBEES DON'T have very long lifespans. At their best, it's seven years, and sometimes only two. Sometime she gets sick or doesn't lay enough eggs or gets hurt and loses a wing or the hive decides they don't like her. So they replace her.

They let the old queen go about her business while the hive starts to raise a new queen. At some point, the old queen dies. No one really knows for sure if the new queen kills her or if the worker bees kill her, but maybe she just dies from not being needed or wanted anymore.

I watch the dance floor from the foyer. Lance is swinging Taylor's aunt in a circle, and the woman is enjoying it. She holds her wide-brim hat to her head and lets out a whoop. Harriet bounces on her toes and kicks out her feet. How could I have thought she was frizzy and plain? It's easy to see that she's vibrant and beautiful and energetic. She doesn't need a queen bee telling her what to do. In fact, no one in Heartfield needs anyone telling them what to do.

The song ends, and the floor is cleared for the father-daughter dance. Taylor and her dad have prepared a special performance for the occasion, and I'm drawn back into the reception hall to watch. It's set to "Swinging on a Star." They even throw in a tap routine in the middle.

Dancers. They're so weird.

Taylor's dad taps over to West and reaches out his hand. We hold our breaths, but then West jumps up and joins the tapping. West probably had to practice every night for a month to get the choreography right. Then the rest of Taylor's family joins in.

I should be enthralled—they're a nationally ranked dance family whom people pay to see them and I love them like they're my second family—but for some reason, I keep scanning the room.

As the routine ends and we clap, I find Lance leaning against the wall across the room. He's looking right at me.

My breath catches. I wait for him to look away—he must be mad or annoyed— but he doesn't. The hard edge to his expression softens. He pushes off from the wall and walks the perimeter of the room toward me. I feel a zip of excitement and fear.

Because I love him, so now what?

I take a deep breath and walk in his direction. We meet in a relatively quiet alcove that overlooks the meadow, now dark except for the blinking white Christmas lights around the gazebo.

"I owe you an apology," I say. "I'm so sorry. I didn't mean to yell that out. I was feeling embarrassed."

"I know."

"I just felt so clumsy."

He nods. "I know."

"So...friends?"

He frowns, and my heart falls. He must still be mad at me. "Or not," I say. I clear my throat.

The idea of us not being even friends takes the wind from me and I stagger back a step. I hadn't realized, hadn't admitted to myself, how much I expected him to be in my life. I've only known him a year, but it hits me how much he's been there for me —not just for the big, important days, but the small, little ones, too.

We developed a routine over the past couple of months that had become comfortable. He stops by with coffee on his way into work since it's usually my afternoon busy period and I don't have time to grab one myself. On most days, I come by his bar when I close up. When I work late on major holidays, he drives me home. I hadn't realized how much I looked forward to those little moments, to our mundaneness.

There is a screech of the mic, and the singer comes on, saying it's time for the bouquet toss, and all eyes turn to me.

I walk away from Lance. My stomach is in shreds. I'm the only one in the group who is over twenty years old. I catch the bouquet of candy-colored flowers, the very one I made without realizing it would be my own again.

The wedding ends soon after that as the singer announces, "It's Christmas Eve, folks. Go home, be with your families, thank you for celebrating with us, and Merry Christmas!"

The band plays us out with a holiday medley. Everyone is kissing and hugging, but after a quick congratulations to Taylor and West and a thank you to Harriet for the dance lesson, I start the walk home.

The cold is good. Insulating. My breath comes out in short fogs of air. By the time I get home, shed my dress, and drop onto the couch with a blanket over my feet, I'm chilly, but I want more. More cold, more chill, as if it could still my beating heart, make it dormant until it's ready to thaw again.

I must have fallen asleep because my eyes pop open at the sound of heavy knocking on my door. It can't be Taylor. I open it, and Lance is standing there, still in his suit, though his jacket is gone and his top button is unbuttoned. I am in my sweatpants and a T-shirt that I think has a milk stain on it.

"I believe you owe me a favor," he says.

"I know. I'll live up to my end of the bet, I promise. But please don't be mad about earlier," I plead with him, but he's still staring at me with that intense look on his face. "What? Did I forget to return your jacket, too?"

"No, it's not the jacket. Why would you think..." He shakes his head. "I need you to do something for me."

He sounds so angry. All I can think is that I embarrassed him more than I realized on the dance floor. "Right now?"

He nods, so I step aside to let him in. He only takes a few steps before he closes the door behind him, his hands set at his waist.

"What's the favor?" I ask.

"I'm not your friend. Stop thinking of me that way."

I CLOSE WITH Love every Fourth of July. The entire block is shut down to cars for the Independence Day parade, and after the band and float come through, restaurants put up food carts and someone brings in a bouncy house for the kids.

This year, with my cup from Mansfield Perk in hand, I strolled up and down the street. Honeybees zipped around, enticed by the smell.

"You look nice."

I grinned over my shoulder at Lance. "You do, too."

"Bright red? Aren't you worried about bees?" He licked an ice cream cone. I had never wanted to be ice cream more in my life.

"Bees can't see red," I said, swiveling the skirt of my dress around.

"Too bad for the bees." He licked again. "I guess you've heard?"

"Yep!" West had proposed, and Taylor had said yes. "A Christmas wedding, I think."

"Crazy kids."

"Crazy-happy kids."

"Yep."

We wandered side by side, trying foods and even the bouncy house. I landed on him hard, laughing as he coughed to try and get back his breath.

"You smell like honey," he said as I rolled off him.

I touched my hair. "I use it in my conditioner sometimes."

"You have a real bee thing going on." Then he touched my hair. Lightly. The tips of his fingers rested just by my ear, but it was enough to send me down a dizzying road.

I stepped back and ran my hands over my scalp to stop the pleasant tingles buzzing about my head. It was too much. Too intimate. I needed something between us, something like tens of thousands of bees. "Want to meet them?"

It took a little more convincing, but I got him into my backyard. The beehive was inside a box next to a hawthorn sprig, a fair distance from my neighbors' fences. Fuzzy bodies came and went with busy abandon.

"I'm going to lift off the top."

"Maybe I need a red dress," he said.

"Just stay calm and still."

I lifted the top of the box, and the buzzing amplified. He took an initial step back but then leaned in over the box. I showed him the slats and how each one was part of the hive and how you could pull out the honeycomb. I walked him to my shed where I had some sheets laid out to drain the honey into plastic containers. There was already a healthy amount of honey dripping from them in a drizzling mound.

"May I?" he asked. "Do I need a spoon or something?"

"No, go ahead. It has natural antiseptic qualities." I dunked my finger in the honey and brought the sweep scoop to my mouth.

He dipped his own finger in and tasted it, staring at me. With an easy grin he took a step closer, swiped his thumb through the rich substance, and held it against my bottom lip.

Sanity fled. I licked it, hearing his intake of breath, hearing my heart over the buzzing of bees. He pulled back his thumb and ran it over his mouth, like he had the night we first kissed.

I wondered how many other times he'd done this. He was Lance. Bar owner. Overall flirt. If I didn't stop this, if I didn't reign it in, I'd drown in it.

My phone rang, and I let it break the spell. It was Taylor.

"Nope, not busy," I said when she asked. "Just with a friend." And I left it at that.

I SWALLOW HARD, taking in Lance's favor. *Stop thinking of me as your friend.* "I know what I said was catty and mean, but just because friends fight—"

"This isn't a fight." He cocks his head and takes a step closer. "Do you think this is a fight?"

"You're angry."

He laughs, which is confusing. "I'm not angry. I'm

frustrated. I'm desperate. Emma, I want you to stop thinking of me as your friend because I want to be more."

The words wind through my brain. "More?"

He steps closer. "More."

The thought is so tantalizing and perfect that I can't quite grasp it. "More."

"A lot more."

His palm wraps around my waist, pushing me back against the wall. There is heat and hardness and strength all around me. He dips his head and my lips part, but he tilts and draws his nose along my neck.

I gasp. "How much more?"

He drops a sizzling kiss on my collarbone. "All of it."

I curl my hands around his shoulders.

"Call me superficial," he says. "I want the queen bee, too."

"Drone bees die after mating with the queen, you know."

I feel his grin against my cheek. "Don't worry, love. I'll make it worth it."

Epilogue

LANCE AND I have our own Christmas. We stop by the church for service. He doesn't bat an eye as he slips his fingers through mine in front of half the town. Stranger even, no one else bats an eye, either.

We stop by his bar on the way to my house and raid the pantry for enough groceries to make a little Christmas ham with mashed potatoes and green beans.

After about a dozen insistent texts and one incredibly creative threat, I tell Taylor that, yes, fine, we'll stop by her and West's place for a cocktail. They own a Craftsman-style house a few blocks from my house so we walk. I manage to pack enough of the light dust of snow into a golf-sized snowball and throw it at Lance. He ducks and returns the favor, hitting me squarely on the forehead.

His face drops in horror. "I thought you were going to duck."

I wipe at my face, squinting. "I'm terrible at coordination."

With a laugh and a look of sympathy, he dries off my face and kisses me until I'm warm again. We arrive at Taylor's way later than we should.

Her house is filled with her family and friends. I'm a little nervous about seeing Harriet—was she interested in Lance?—and sip more eggnog than I should to calm my nerves. I finally find her in the kitchen—with her arm around another woman.

Her face lights up when she sees me. "Emma, come here. I want you to meet my girlfriend."

My face must be all screwed up because she laughs and says, "Surprise."

Taylor sweeps in a moment later and hugs me from behind. "Sorry, sweet pea, I'm just putting it all together. You thought Harriet was into Lance."

"She's not?"

They both shake their heads, and her girlfriend says, "Better not be. I would have told my job to shove it and fly in for the wedding if I had thought there was a chance of that."

"I knew you'd all be sitting together," Taylor says, "so I asked Harriet if she would talk Lance up, about how great he was, just to get you realize it. I didn't think you'd think she was into him."

"I felt so bad when I saw Elton kiss you," Harriet says. "I thought maybe you were together, and poor Lance didn't have a chance. But then Taylor explained what really happened."

"I feel so relieved! And so stupid," I admit.

Taylor winks at me. "I just figured, you know, you helped me see the light about West. It was time I returned the favor and played matchmaker for you."

For some reason, this, of all things—the idea that Taylor was looking out for me and so was Harriet—makes me feel weepy, but I don't want to cry in front of anyone because I'm not sad and happy tears are hard to explain. Lance will get it, though.

I find him leaning against the banister in the hall. He tucks me against his arm and points up at the mistletoe above our heads.

I think about that first night I met him. "We've kissed under the mistletoe before, you know."

His forehead crinkles. "We did?"

I nod. "I was there, at your bar, opening night."

His eyes close, and he groans, leaning back his head. "Oh, that night. I don't think I've ever been that wasted. I was just so excited about owning my own place. I heard I laid a kiss on everyone and a reindeer."

"Yep, me included."

His eyes pop open. "Wait. I do remember."

I punch his shoulder. "Don't lie to me. No, you don't."

"No, I do," he insists, getting serious. "I just thought it was a dream." He laughs and rests his head on the banister again. "That dream haunted me, Emma."

"What are you talking about?"

"I woke up the next day, hungover as hell, with a

headache that made everything hurt. Nothing made it better except these images I had of kissing you. I wasn't surprised because I'd been checking you out next door for a week or two. The dream felt so real I went over to see if maybe something had happened, but you acted like we were meeting at the first time. I figured it was a dream."

I snuggle against his shoulder, grinning. "I thought you'd forgotten it."

"I forgot everyone else," he says. "Never you."

ACKNOWLEDGEMENTS

Jessica: For being a (near-criminal) mastermind and bringing us all together.

The Oregon State Beekeeper Association: Thank you so much for all the info, and if I made any mistakes...my bad!

ABOUT THE AUTHOR

Cecilia Gray lives in the San Francisco Bay Area where she reads, writes, and breaks for food. She also pens her biographies in the third person. Like this. As if to trick you into thinking someone else wrote it because she is important. Alas, this is not the case. She reads a lot because books give her ideas of things to try—archery, lock picking, and swing dancing, among other adventures. To share your bookish inspirations or to check out what she's up to, e-mail her at cecilia@ceciliagray.com or check her out her website: www.ceciliagray.com.

It's a Wonderful Latte

Jessica Grey

For Marianne Rencher
my very own Victoria's Secret bag bearing angel
when I needed one the most.

EARLY AFTERNOON SUNLIGHT filtered into the small parlor, glinting off the fine china and silverware. Soft music piped in from somewhere unseen mingling with the soft clinking of glasses and the quiet conversation and laughter of the two sisters sitting together at the table enjoying a cup of tea.

"This really is my favorite time of day."

Jane nodded at her sister in agreement. "It is quite lovely that we can enjoy it whenever we wish. Quite possibly the best part of being here."

"Yes, that and the music. What are we listening to today?"

"I believe it is a gentleman named Barry Manilow. I heard about him from Emily. She has such unique taste in music."

Cassandra hid a small smile behind her teacup. "That is one thing that can be said about Miss Dickinson. Do you remember that awful screeching she was listening to sometime back? Something about…'punk' something or other?"

"At least this Manilow person does not scream, thank heaven for small favors. Mr. Clemens, whatever are you doing here?" Jane turned toward the corner of the parlor where a bright light had flickered into existence.

"How can you tell it is him before he is corporeal, Jane? I can never tell."

"His mustache causes a draft." Jane took a long sip of her tea. "And he never uses the door."

"Ah, my dear Miss Austen," said the flicker, which was now generally more or less in the shape of a lanky man clothed in a suit and sporting a mop of bushy hair along with said mustache. "It's lovely to see you as usual."

"Here to beat me over the head with my own shinbone, Mr. Clemens?" Jane took another long sip of tea before setting the cup neatly back in its matching saucer.

"My dear girl," said the flicker, who was now entirely Samuel Clemens, "you refuse to let that little jibe go. I wrote it, and all the others, so many years ago. For goodness' sake, I was still alive at the time; you shouldn't hold anything I said on earth against me."

Cassandra hid another smile behind her tea cup. "Truly Jane, Mr. Clemens has been quite the gentlemen ever since he died."

Jane raised an eyebrow. "Quite. Death does become you, my dear sir. 'Tis a pity it did not take you before you renamed yourself after a boating term."

Samuel ignored the barb as he sat down in one of

the empty chairs around the table. A steaming cup of tea appeared before him. He raised the small cup and drained it in one long gulp. Jane's eyebrow was now almost level with her hair line.

"I've an assignment for you," Samuel said as he clunked the cup back down.

Jane sighed. "I thought as much. Why does He always send you? Couldn't He send someone with a sharper wit to entertain Cassandra and me?"

"It was either me or a Brontë, my dear girl. I thought I'd spare you that."

Cassandra couldn't help herself and broke out in a fit of giggles. "Oh, Mr. Clemens, please do send one of the Brontës next time. Not Anne, she's too nice."

Finally Jane broke into a smile. "Cassandra, you are too wicked. You just want to have fun poking at one of those poor, depressed girls."

"It is not my fault they still manage to be depressed in heaven. That is a spectacular feat. It deserves to have a little fun poked at it," protested Cassandra.

"I thought you might have missed me, anyway," interrupted Samuel. "It's been fifty years since you've been on a mission."

"Fifty wonderfully peaceful years," agreed Jane. "Where does He want me to go?"

"Los Angeles."

"*California?!*"

"Yes."

"*In America?!*"

"That is where California is located the last time I checked."

"But why? Surely he should send you or that Chandler fellow...some American."

"Mr. Chandler is technically British, Jane," Cassandra chimed in.

"It's a special case; apparently you're quite popular in America now, Miss Austen, though He only knows why."

"But it's so far—Los Angeles —good gracious! And it is almost Christmas, what a horrible time to travel."

"'The distance is nothing when one has a motive,' and I do believe this case will interest you."

Jane's eyebrow shot back up. "Do not quote me to me, Mr. Clemens, or you might find I also can wield a shinbone effectively."

Samuel leaned back in his chair and laughed. "I do enjoy our little chats, Miss Austen. But He does insist."

"Does He? Well, then, one must do what one must..." Jane trailed off as she glanced down. Her pale muslin day dress had been replaced by a tee-shirt, a pair of ripped jean shorts, and fuzzy boots. "I see fashions have changed since I last went on a mission, but I really must protest. Why ever would I need boots with short pants?"

"I asked a similar question the last time I was on the west coast, I find it's better not to ask." Samuel laughed again. "Don't get all worked up, Miss Austen. Is that better?"

Jane looked down at the colorful flowing skirt and blouse she was now clothed in. "I suppose."

"I adore the hat, sister." Cassandra grinned as Jane

reached up to poke at the slouchy knit cap perched atop her now loose, long brown hair. "So exciting, Mr. Clemens, do tell us what Jane's assignment is."

Samuel rocked back so that the chair was balanced on two legs and grinned at the sisters. "A little place called Mansfield Perk."

"OF ALL THE books to name the stores after, why *Mansfield Park*?"

My cousin, Izzy, rolled her eyes at me from across the counter. Well, I wasn't looking at her, I was staring at the ornament I was placing on the shop's Christmas tree—it was a mansion with the store's famous MP logo scrolled across it—but I could feel her eyes tracing a circle on my back.

"I dunno, Evie…Because Mansfield Perk has a better ring to it than Pride and Perk? Or Sense and Espresso Shots?"

"But it's a horrible book," I replied. I pulled a face at the ornament portraying *Mansfield Park*. I've always hated it. Not just disliked it…hated it. With the kind of passionate hatred only a too-early reading at the age of thirteen (after consuming the dashing heroes of *Pride and Prejudice* and *Persuasion* in less than three days in a fit of teenage romanticism and angst) can produce.

Izzy snapped her gum as she stocked freshly baked muffins into the glass display case over the counter. "I wouldn't know; I've never read it. Or any of them."

"I know. Heathen. Don't let Grandma St. Laurent ever know that or you'll get nothing in the will."

"Grandma St. Laurent loves me and you know it."

I sighed. She was right. My cousins Izzy and Julian were favorites of my grandmother in spite of being completely clueless about anything Jane Austen related. At least she had the good sense to make me General Manager of the flagship Mansfield Perk in LA. She might be sentimental, but she was also a good business woman—who at the age of fifty-five had opened a Jane-Austen-centered coffee shop catering to the literary minded and had not only competed with the big S (saying that name out loud in a Mansfield Perk was considered sacrilege) in her local Los Angeles neighborhood but had ended up opening franchises across the country and two in England.

I hung up a *Pride and Prejudice* ornament on the miniature tree—a delicate painting of Darcy and Elizabeth on their wedding day. There was one ornament for each of the six novels plus a cameo-style one of Austen herself: the famous silhouette of Jane surrounded by a ridiculously gaudy Christmas wreath.

I put this tree up every year—five years now as GM and I loved almost every minute of it. I'd thought about going back to school to get my MBA...or maybe my Master's in Literature, my hatred of *Mansfield Park* notwithstanding; I had a pretty solid background in 19th century literature...but truth be told I was pretty content at the shop. I made an okay salary. I worked with family and people I generally liked. The location and the weather couldn't be beat. So I didn't have the most exciting life, or anything remotely resembling a steady boyfriend, I was still having fun. Isn't that what being twenty-seven in Los Angeles was all about? I sighed as I placed the Austen ornament on the tree and ordered myself to stop with the internal soliloquies and open the store.

"Well, the tree is up; it feels like Christmas now." I turned back to Izzy as I closed up the ornament boxes. "And we could officially kick off the season and open if you'd finished stocking the pastries instead of watching me hang ornaments."

Izzy snapped her gum. "It's supposed to be seventy-nine degrees today. It's not ever gonna 'feel' like Christmas."

"'Feel' is a relative term. If it snowed in LA we'd all freak the hell out anyway. We'll have to make do with these." I pointed at the sparkly snowflake garland decorating the counter. "And who wants to deal with snow anyway?"

Izzy flipped a strand of black and purple hair over her shoulder. "I could handle some cute snow boots in my life."

"Go to Big Bear."

"For two inches of snow," she whined.

"You've bought cute shoes for less."

"Fact. So can I leave early today? I'm meeting friends for lunch."

I raised an eyebrow. "You're running shift; are you

going to count down the drawers before lunch?"

"Nooooo. Frank!"

I glared at her. "Do not even try to make Frank do cash for you; it's part of your job, Izzy."

She heaved a dramatic sigh. "He'll do it for me, why not ask? It's not like he's got a hot date waiting for him like I do."

"I thought you were going to lunch with friends."

"'Friends is a relative term, Evie."

"Oh god."

"I don't mind doing the drawers, so you can leave early," Frank Nakatomi said as he came out from the back of the shop.

"See, now I can go. Frank, you're the best." Izzy kissed the air near Frank's perpetually shaggy black hair. "I'm gonna go open the front doors now!"

"You really need to stop letting her take advantage of you," I said severely.

Frank shrugged as he tied his apron around his slim waist. "It's not a big deal, and she takes forever. Morning shift would never get out of here."

"I'll help you with it if we aren't too busy," I promised.

"Clever, quite clever," a female voice said from directly behind me. I spun around to see a small, dark-haired woman dressed in a vintage looking hippie skirt and bright lavender knitted slouch hat.

"Oh, hello! I'm sorry, I didn't see you come in!" I glanced up to where Izzy was standing with the door half propped open talking to one of our regulars.

"I have recently developed a habit of popping into

places unexpectedly," the woman said as she stared at me through narrowed eyes. "You must be Evie St. Laurent?"

Her accent was odd. Definitely British, but unlike any English accent I'd ever heard. "Uh, yes, that's me. Do I know you?"

"I do not think we have ever met. I just heard your name from the person who recommended this delightful shop of yours. The titles of your beverages are entertaining."

"We get that a lot. Are you a fan of Austen, then?"

The lady looked back at me from the menu board with a small smile. "I am familiar with her work, I would not say I am a fan. The milk and tea is a Mr. Woodhouse…does it come with a side of gruel perhaps?"

I actually laughed at that. "You must be more than familiar with her books if you're making Emma jokes. What can I get you today?

"I think I'll try an 'All Astonishment!'"

"Thats basically just three shots of espresso and some cream; you up for it?" I raised an eyebrow.

"I believe so."

"Can I get a name for that?" I asked with my sharpie hovering over the light beige paper cup bearing the MP logo.

"Jane," she said as she rummaged around in the large hobo bag slung over her shoulder. "Now surely that rascal did not forget to give me local currency… oh here it is." She brandished a brightly colored wallet at me.

"So, you share a name with Miss Austen then. I always wanted to be named Elizabeth because of *Pride and Prejudice.*"

Jane nodded. "Yes, she certainly does seem to be everyone's favorite. Not very many people wish to be Fanny."

"Would you? Want to be Fanny, that is? *Mansfield Park* is my least favorite book…"

As I handed the cup to Frank to make Jane's drink I heard him mutter, "Here we go again."

"Shut it, nerd, I have to listen to your thesis on *The Godfather* movies on a biweekly basis."

Frank chuckled under his breath as he tamped down the first espresso shot.

"So, the thing is," I leaned over the counter to address Jane, "Fanny isn't all that bad, I mean she's wishy washy, but you know, consider women's roles in the time period *yadda yadda*, but it's Edmund Bertram I can't stand."

Jane looked up from fiddling with the wallet with an amused smile. "Is that so?"

"Oh yes, he's a horrible romantic hero."

"Maybe it's not a romantic book."

I stared at her blankly. "But—but—" I spluttered. "Huh, I've never thought of that."

"All of the romance does happen 'off screen' so to speak," Frank commented from mid-pulling of the second espresso shot. "We are just kind of told about Edmund and Fanny getting together, we never really see it."

I whirled around to stare at him. "You finally read it?"

"Yup, after listening to you bitch for years I decided it was time to see what all the fuss was about. I don't get why you hate it so much. Edmund is kind of an idiot and he friend-zoned the heck out of Fanny…"

"Friend-zoned? That's mild."

"But he's gotta have some redeemable qualities or Fanny wouldn't love him."

"I'm not gonna lie, Frank, I feel betrayed right now." I grabbed the coffee cup from his hand and handed it to Jane.

"First one is one the house, Jane."

"Oh! Why, thank you. I am sorry, could you tell me what is on this? It says 'Rivers of America;' what is that?" She held up the colorful wallet for me to look at.

"That's a part of Frontierland at Disneyland…it's an amusement park," I added at her blank expression. I was even more curious now. Who lived in or visited Southern California without having heard of Disneyland? "That white riverboat? That's called the Mark Twain."

Jane stared at me unblinkingly for a long moment. "Of course it is," she said. "Of course it is."

"Are you all right?" I asked in concern.

"Quite all right. Thank you for the coffee." She slipped the wallet back into her hobo bag with a thinly veiled sound of disgust. "I'm sure I'll be back…" she looked between me and Frank and shook her head. "Just remember, stories like the ones Jane Austen wrote, they're popular because they happen over and over; those stories always repeat in real life and in novels. Even *Mansfield Park*."

I nodded slowly. I was used to a high number of slightly crazy people coming through the store. We even had a group that came dressed as Austen characters for a book club once a month, so it wasn't unusual to have people speaking so sincerely about novels, but something about her tone—as if she knew something I didn't know—unnerved me. "Uhhhh, okay? Is there anything else I can get you?"

"No, thank you. Have a lovely day." She turned on her heel and swept out of the store, her long skirt flowing behind her.

"She was...odd." I commented to Frank.

"Seemed nice, a little eccentric maybe."

"Did she seem, I don't know, almost familiar to you?" I asked.

He shook his head, his shaggy bangs falling into his eyes. "Nope."

I brushed the dark hair out of his eyes absently. "Huh, I don't know, I have a weird feeling like I've seen her before, but I'm not sure where."

"Who?" Izzy appeared at my elbow, still snapping her gum.

"The lady who just bought an 'All Astonishment' from me and Frank."

"What lady? I didn't see a lady."

I rolled my eyes. "You are so unobservant sometimes, Izzy. She wasn't wearing Louboutin's so you probably wouldn't have noticed her."

"Whatever. Shoes are very important to me. Don't judge."

I shook my head and grabbed a cup. "Frank, make me an Evie special?"

"This much caffeine will kill you." He shook his head somberly but started my drink.

"But what a way to go." I grinned.

"**WHAT HAPPENED TO** the Austen ornament?" I demanded the next morning as I stared at the Christmas tree. "I had all of the ornaments on here yesterday, and now Jane is gone. Did someone break it?" I was suddenly sad, as if I'd lost a good friend. I'd been hanging that ornament for years. And sometimes when I was working the Christmas Eve shift, knowing I was going home to my cat—well first to the huge St. Laurent family Christmas Eve party and then home to Dr. Catson—I'd sometimes confide to Jane's silhouette that I was secretly lonely. Not enough to do anything about it, but enough to be a little bit sad during the holiday bustle.

"This is what happens when I let Izzy open by herself," I muttered under my breath.

"Hey, I heard that!" Izzy exclaimed from right behind me. "And I didn't lose your precious ornament, it was missing when I got here."

I turned around with a chagrined smile. "I didn't mean that the way it sounded. Well, actually I kinda did. Sorry."

Izzy glare at me for a moment before dramatically snapping her gum. "I forgive you."

"See, this is why I say things like that; lose the gum, sister."

"There's people here who want to see you..." she called back over her shoulder. Then she skidded to a stop and turned around. "The guy is hot. HOT. You might want to go..." she waved her hand in a circular motion in front of my face. "...do something with this. That something should possibly involve makeup."

"Fine. I deserve that. Who are these people, and more importantly, where are they?"

"Waiting in the reading room. But no seriously, I can go entertain them for a few if you need to freshen up."

"I'm cool, thanks," I said dryly as I handed Izzy my purse. "Can you go put this in the office for me? Where's Frank?"

"With the beautiful people."

"I'll go rescue him then." I headed toward the little library-like alcove in the corner of the store that we called the reading room.

"Oh, here she is," Frank said with what sounded like relief as I walked in. I almost smiled. Entertaining people wasn't Frank's cup of tea—actually, he was getting his masters in film production, so entertaining people was his cup of tea, as long as it was from behind the camera. Way, way behind the camera.

The two other people in the reading room stood up and turned toward me. Izzy hadn't been lying when she called them the beautiful people.

"Ms. St. Laurent?" The tall, sandy haired, Calvin Klein model in front of me asked.

"Uhhh…yes, that's me."

"Jake Piper. This is my sister Maggie."

Maggie Piper extended her manicured hand in my direction and I tore my eyes off her brother's dimples long enough to shake it. She had the kind of red hair you swear could only come from a bottle but know because of her pale skin, green eyes, and too adorable freckles is actually natural. Because the hair gods are sick, twisted bastards who just do not give a damn. I resisted the urge to pat down my slightly wild brown curls.

"What can I do for you?" I asked.

"Jake and I are the interim marketing directors for The Highlands," Maggie said. The Highlands was the upscale shopping center that Mansfield Perk was located in. In fact, it had been built around the original MP about ten years after the shop had opened. It was very trendy. I often wondered how they tolerated us cause we were a bit on the lit-geek side here at MP, but then I would remember just how much money we brought in every year. Plus, hipsters loved us and The Highlands loved Hipster money.

"What happened to Nora Harris?" I managed as I switched from Maggie's hand to shaking the Calvin Klein model's…er, Jake Piper's…hand. His warm, strong, also well manicured hand. I tried not to notice. I had a thing about guys who got manicures, but in this case I assured myself I could overlook it.

The siblings shared a look. "She's gone," Maggie

replied. "And unfortunately without any real holiday celebration plans. But we're here now!"

"There's Christmas lights on the palm trees," Frank pointed out. "That's about as festive as The Highlands has gotten the last few years."

Maggie smiled. Her teeth were very even and very white. I wondered if she'd temporarily blinded Frank. "Holiday lights," she corrected. "And even though it's *super* close to the holiday already, we are hoping to rectify the lack of community involvement and wanted to talk with you about our plans."

"Oh?" I realized suddenly I was still awkwardly holding Jake's hand and dropped it like a hot potato. Which was also awkward. "Why me?"

Jake grinned. His teeth were equally even and white. These people were "oh so very L.A." as Frank often said about his fellow film students. Usually that turned me off. Most "oh so very L.A." people weren't even from L.A. We St. Laurents (and Frank) liked to consider ourselves superior Angelinos and to prove it by doing things like shunning high end restaurants for guaranteed food poisoning at local taco trucks. But for some reason it wasn't turning me off of the Pipers yet. Maybe because Jake was so ridiculously hot (and I am apparently so ridiculously shallow).

"You are the general manager of the store that the Highlands was built around, the oldest and most respected store in the shopping center."

"True. I mean, yes, I am the GM. And yes we are the oldest store." My tongue wasn't quite working correctly. I'd just noticed his eyes were green too. I didn't necessarily believe in love at first sight, but those eyes were leading me into a strong case of lust at first sight. "What are you planning to do for the holidays. Oh, I'm sorry, where are my manners. Sit." I gestured to the chairs and then plopped down in one myself. Frank gave me an odd look, but I ignored him.

Maggie sank gracefully onto the seat across from me and Jake took the chair next to hers. He leaned forward, bracing his forearms on his thighs. I tried not to notice that his shirt sleeves were rolled up. Or his thighs. I failed on both counts.

"We are planning a fundraising campaign, hosted by all of the retailers here at The Highlands. We want there to be a community involvement component—displays in stores, chances to give, that sort of thing, as well as a holiday extravaganza fundraising event right before the holiday."

I blinked. "Right before Christmas?"

"Yes, before the *holiday*…the Friday night before, to be precise."

I blinked again. Her use of the term holiday over and over was starting to irritate me, but I tamped it down. "That's like less than six weeks away, isn't that cutting it a bit close for planning a large event, not to mention getting all the, what, twenty-six other retailers involved?"

"I believe there are twenty-five other retailers, but we think we can get everyone on board as long as Mansfield Perk is on board," said Jake.

"No, twenty-six, everyone always forgets the Piano

Girl, but she's still there," Frank interjected. I glanced up. He was leaning his hip against my chair, his arms crossed casually across his chest. He looked totally chill but I could read the Frank body language for "I don't like you people" a mile away.

"It's true, people do tend to forget the Piano Girl," I turned back to Jake with a smile. "But Mary is a lovely woman and actually would probably be really excited about this. So what charity are you thinking of supporting?"

"There's a lovely independent theater group here on the Westside called The Actor's Stage."

I blinked yet again. Maybe I was developing an eye issue. "A...theater group?"

"Oh, yes, they are a *very* talented group," Maggie assured me.

I looked between Jake and Maggie. They were sporting almost identical expressions of completely non-ironic sincerity. "But, I mean...and don't get me wrong, I love the theater, but wouldn't it be easier to get people behind supporting like a women's shelter, my grandmother has one that she's donated to for years. Or um, something with the ASPCA? People are really into their pets around here."

"The Actor's Stage does amazing work with inner city children." Jake leaned even more forward and rested his hand on my arm. I felt the inside of my mouth go dry.

"Oh?"

"Amazing. Work." Maggie nodded.

"Oh..." I swallowed. Kids were good. Almost as

good as pets. Kids brought in donations and looked cute on posters and totally needed whatever services The Actor's Stage was offering them. This was L.A., after all; acting skills were almost as good—or maybe even better than—reading, writing, and arithmetic. These kids needed The Actor's Stage! The Actor's Stage needed our money!

Jake's hand was really warm.

"I guess that's okay, then. I mean, inner city kids. Right, Frank?" I tore my gaze off of Jake's hand still on my forearm to look up at Frank.

He was still standing with his arms crossed and looking more irritated by the second. Frank let out what sounded like a long-suffering sigh. The movement caused his t-shirt sleeve to ride up and expose the tattoo around his bicep. "I honestly don't know how you're going to get that past your grandmother." He looked over at Maggie. "Maybe if there was some assurance that all funds raised would go only to the children's program?"

I swiveled my head to look at her as well, momentarily surprised by the predatory look on her face. Then I followed her line of sight to his bicep and almost laughed. Girls always underestimated Frank until they got a closer look. I could tell Maggie was definitely an arm woman.

"I'm sure we could make any assurances that Mrs. St. Laurent would need," Maggie almost purred. "Speaking of your grandmother, Evie, we would love for her to be involved."

Jake finally removed his hand from my arm as his

sister was talking. I was torn between relief—at some point it would become socially awkward to have him attached to my arm—and sadness. "I don't know, she's making more of an attempt to take time for herself," I said.

"She's still involved in a lot of charity work though, isn't she?" Jake asked.

"Well, yes. I'll talk to her about it. I'll have to run the whole idea past her anyway." I bit my lip, Frank was right. It would be easier to sell if it was a different charity, one that Grandma St. Laurent was already supporting, but I had faith in my persuasive abilities. Mostly.

"We are so excited to have Mansfield Perk on board," Maggie smiled at Frank and I as she stood up and smoothed down her skirt. "Jake and I have some quick visits to make to the other retailers, but it was lovely to meet you."

Jake and I both stood up. "It was nice to meet you both as well," I replied as I shook hands with both siblings. "Frank?"

Frank glanced at me sideways but shook hands with Maggie and Jake as well.

"It was so nice to meet you as well, Frank." Maggie was back to purring. Really, the ASPCA might have been the better choice as she was obviously part cat. I grinned at Frank. He ignored me.

"You as well, Ms. Piper."

"Oh, please call me Maggie."

"Maggie," he nodded gravely. I choked on a giggle as Maggie reluctantly let go of his hand and followed her brother to the shop's front door. "Really?" he demanded once we heard the tinkle of the bell as the door closed.

"Oh, *pleeeeease* call me Maggie." I batted my eyelashes furiously at Frank.

"You're one to talk. The only reason you're going along with this ridiculous theater group charity idea is because you think Jake Piper is hot."

I snorted. "Dude, he *is* hot. More importantly, Maggie has it bad for you. Did you see her start drooling when she saw your tattoo?"

Frank glared at me. "I am not at all interested in Maggie Piper."

"Why? She's pretty! Like if you like that sort of cool, perfect, barely touchable sort of pretty."

"You've got issues."

"I know! But you love me anyway."

Frank huffed out a frustrated breath. "Good luck convincing your grandmother, by the way."

"I don't suppose you want to talk to her for me?"

"Nope."

"Frank, why not? She likes you better than me," I protested.

"Evie, if you want to get in bed with Jake Piper, it's on you. I'm not gonna go butter up Grandma St. Laurent so you can look good to a guy."

I gaped at Frank. "Wh-what? That's crass. And harsh."

"But let's be honest, that's the only reason you're on board with this idea."

"No, it's not! It's a good idea! Why are you being

so judgey? Have you not had enough caffeine yet? Go get an espresso before you talk to me again."

Frank shook his head at me. "I'm not planning to talk to you about it again. It's your project, not mine. I'm gonna go help Izzy on counter." He turned and walked out of the reading room and into the main shop, leaving me sputtering in rage behind him.

"Not helpful, Frank!" I yelled after him. He didn't respond.

"YOU'RE SITTING ON a rooftop? This seems so very... unJane of you."

"Good evening, Mr. Clemens." Jane responded without glancing up as the author appeared next to her on the roof.

"It is a lovely evening. All of these lights are impressive." Samuel waved a hand at the expanse of twinkling lights that could be seen from the rooftop of the shop across from Mansfield Perk where Jane was perched.

Jane sighed. "Yes, a lot of busyness and electricity. It iss all very...modern."

"Indeed. How are you finding your assignment."

"She's an interesting one, Evie St. Laurent." Jane glanced up at Samuel before nodding her head back down in the direction of Mansfield Perk. Through the lit window they could see Evie wiping down the front counter. She occasionally would pause and fiddle with her curly brown hair as she glanced over at Frank Nakatomi, who was stocking a shelf in the corner and completely ignoring her. "I do not think I have ever met a more obtuse woman."

Samuel laughed. "Oh please, Miss Austen. Your very own Lizzy Bennet—not to mention your Emma —were both completely clueless about the men that were in love with them."

"They were also completely fictional, a fact which seems to elude most of these modern readers," Jane said dryly.

"Pfft. So you're telling me that non-fictional women are always aware when a man is desperately in love with them?"

Jane shrugged her slims shoulders. The evening breeze was blowing the peasant blouse around her frame, but it was warm at least. That was the best thing about being on assignment here, she reflected, the warmth. "No, it is not so much that she does not realize he's in love with her…" she propped her hand on her chin, watching in interest as Frank headed out to the outdoor patio. "It is that she does not realize she's in love with him."

I FOLLOWED FRANK out onto the patio. I hate it when Frank isn't talking to me. Not that it happens often 'cause we are usually just so chill together, but every once in a while he gets a bee in his bonnet over something and cuts off the lines of communication. Usually that lasts for about a day before I pester him out of it. We were at eight hours since our fight about the Pipers and it was driving me not so slowly insane.

"So, how long are you planning to not talk to me?" Great opener, Evie.

Frank ignored me as he started putting chairs upside down on tables so he could sweep the patio for the night.

"I don't really know why you're so upset. Is it just because I thought Jake Piper was hot?"

A few more chairs clunked up onto tables.

"Come on, Frank, I'm not gonna stop bothering you until you talk to me."

He finally turned to look at me, his face was in a shadow so I couldn't really see his expression. But Frank was an expert at masking his emotions so I doubt being able to really look at him would have helped. "No, it's not that. It's that I think you're agreeing to kind of a stupid idea just because he's hot."

"No, not just because he's hot, though that helps. Don't you think it would be good for The Highlands to have more community interaction and involvement."

"Well, yeah, if the Pipers were actually concerned about what The Highlands as a community were interested in, but they're not. They just want to push their theater thing."

"It's not a totally bad idea, especially because of

the inner city kids thing," I said defensively. "The thing is, I think it will be good for the shopping complex, and for MP to look more involved. We can be kind of isolated."

"All true, but I just think you jumped into it for the wrong reasons. And there's no saying how much time it's going to take up right at Christmas, and the store gets insane busy, you know that."

"I won't let it take time away from running the store properly!" I insisted. "You know I'm a good manager."

Frank pinched his forehead with his thumb and forefinger. A sure sign that he was upset.

"Yeah, you are. It's cool. You're the GM and you'll make the decision. I'll just do whatever you want me to do."

I crossed my arms over my chest. "That's not fair. I can tell you're just trying to end the fight."

"I'm not even sure what we're fighting about," he admitted.

"Me either! And you know I hate it when we fight!"

Frank shrugged. "Well, then let's not fight. Back to the status quo we go."

I squeezed my arms together tighter as the wind picked up. "What's that supposed to mean?"

I could swear I heard a laugh on the breeze. I glanced around but didn't see anyone.

"It doesn't mean anything, Evie. Let's just go back to not fighting. That's all it means."

I stared at him. There was something wrong. More

wrong than just a disagreement over...whatever we were disagreeing over. "Is it because the charity is a theater group? You always say we should support the arts."

Frank laughed. "Yes, Evie, I am morally opposed to giving money to a theater group. That's why I'm a film major."

"You're a film major?" Maggie Piper's voice cut off my response. I nearly jumped out of my skin. I'm not sure how I'd missed the clicking of those high heels on the cement, but suddenly there she was...like a creepy jack-in-the-box popping up out of nowhere. I shook my head. Why was I thinking negative things about Maggie Piper? I liked her. I wanted her to be my potential-future-sister-in-law. My fight with Frank was throwing me off.

"Hi, Maggie. Do you usually stay this late?" I asked after a long, awkward pause. Frank was back to pinching his forehead über dramatically, so someone had to make conversation.

"Much to do. New job, new people." She smiled in my general direction but her green eyes were glued on Frank. "So what is it you do? Do you have a camera?"

"Yes, he does. He writes and directs. He's very good," I responded. Frank shot me a look and I shrugged back as if to say, "If you'd talk I wouldn't have to."

"That's brilliant." Maggie leaned over the iron railing to be closer to Frank. "Would you be willing to help us with some promos and things for the fundraiser? I would so very much appreciate it." She drew out each word as if she'd suddenly developed a southern drawl. I narrowed my eyes at her. It was fine and all if she wanted Frank to do film stuff for her, it was even fine if she *wanted* wanted him…but something about how strong she was coming on made me…edgy.

I could swear I heard another laugh. I whipped my head up and down and around, but still didn't see anyone else materializing out of the dark.

Frank looked at me for a long moment, probably wondering why in the world I was spazzing out, before replying, "Yeah, sure. I could help."

"Wonderful!" Maggie almost fell over the railing in her excitement. "Here, give me your number; we need to set something up immediately so we can discuss."

Frank reached out and took the iPhone she was offering him and added his name to her contacts. "I put Evie's number in there too."

"Great! Oh, and Evie, I wanted to ask if you'd gotten a chance to talk to your grandmother yet?"

"No. But I don't think it will be much of an issue."

Maggie smiled at me, now leaning in my direction over the railing. "Just let her know how happy we are to be working with Mansfield Perk and how much we'd love for her to be involved."

I nodded. "Okay, will do. All right, then, I'm gonna go lock up the store."

Frank started forward. "I'll come with you."

And maybe it was because I was still slightly miffed at him for not talking to me all day, or maybe because I was upset with myself over how much it had bothered me, or maybe because I'm just generally evil, but I held up a hand and said, "Oh no, go ahead and finish putting up the chairs; I'm sure Maggie will keep you company."

"OH HELLO AGAIN, Jane."

I'd seen the woman named Jane a few times since that first day she'd ordered an All Astonishment. She always came in first thing when we opened and she always seemed to be wearing the exact same outfit. It was a little strange, but then we were a city full of eccentrics. She also seemed to be working her way through the entire MP menu.

"What will it be today?" I asked.

"I believe I will have a medium Emma Woodhouse."

"Ah, strong but sweet, that's how we make it, just like Emma Woodhouse." I stifled a yawn as I grabbed a cup and marked off the appropriate boxes with my sharpie. "Anything else?"

"Strong and sweet is a complete misread of the character, in my humble opinion."

"Uhhh, okay." I yawned again. Frank hadn't worked mornings with me all week, he'd been working only night shifts so he could help Maggie and Jake with their video promos for the holiday fundraiser—glossy posters for which were papering every corner of The Highlands. The last night shift we'd worked together had been two weeks ago and I missed our morning banter. It had apparently been the only thing keeping me awake at 5 a.m.

Of course I hadn't scheduled myself for any night shifts because I didn't want to schedule them over my dates with Jake. There had been five…five actual "get dressed and go out and kiss (and stuff) at the end" dates in two weeks. Basically we were a weekend on Catalina away from 2.5 kids and a white picket fence.

"Gum, Izzy," I reminded as I flashed Jane's cup at her so she could ring up the order. "Who even chews gum this early, it's inhuman."

Izzy rolled her eyes at me and gave Jane her total. Jane dug out her brightly colored Disneyland wallet and handed over a five dollar bill.

"She's just not a morning person," Izzy said as she made change. "Obviously you and I are 'cause we manage to be sweet even with no caffeine yet."

"I heard that," I muttered as I squirted flavor pumps into the cup. "I'm just…tired. I was out late last night."

"Oh yes? And how is Jake the Perfect?"

"Still perfect."

"Gag. I'm suspicious of that much perfect."

I dumped a shot of espresso in with the flavor pumps. "I don't know. It's not that I'm uncomfortable with how perfect he is—which is a lot of perfect, by the way; it's just there's no…" I shrugged.

"Spark? Does he suck in bed?"

"Izzy!" I snapped at her. "That's not appropriate." I glanced at Jane but she didn't seem to be paying attention to us. "I just...I don't think I'm in love with him, and I don't know that I could see myself falling in love with him."

"Perhaps the problem is you do not know love when you see it. You have imagined it one way and the real thing never looks like that," piped up Jane from across the counter.

I stared at her, mouth agape, trying to decide if I should be offended or just laugh.

I finally settled on laughing. "This is feeling like a very *Anne of the Island* moment. Are you trying to tell me that Jake Piper is my Gilbert and I somehow missed breaking my slate over his head?"

"Lucy Maude...lovely, lovely woman. Enjoys a good cup of tea." Jane said.

I raised an eyebrow. "I'm sorry, what?"

"Perhaps you have a Gilbert," she shrugged. "Or a Mr. Knightley, or maybe even a Fanny."

"Well, I don't really...swing in the Fanny direction, if you get what I mean," I said carefully.

Jane glared at me. "No, but you are a bit like Edmund...or Emma. Emma was basically Edmund in a dress. Can I ask, do you always speak of fictional characters as if they are real? I never did before I spent time here at Mansfield Perk."

"Really? I mean, yeah, I guess I do. And mind blown about Emma. That's like, a really astute observation. Are you sure you're not an Austen scholar or something?"

Jane shrugged. "I could be considered a foremost expert on Austen's life and times, I suppose."

"Seriously?!" I raised both eyebrows this time. "How cool. Do you have a book or anything? You could do a signing here."

"I have several books, actually, but somehow I do not think a signing is a good idea. I do not do well with large groups of people. It is really more of a one-on-one thing."

"Several books? Have I heard of any of them? What did you say your last name was?"

Jane grinned. The first full-fledged smile I'd seen from her. "I did not give it, and it is possible that you have read a few of them. One never knows. But, really, I must be going. Remember what I said."

I was shocked by the abruptness. "Wait, your Emma Woodhouse is ready!" I held out the cup to her. Jane took it and sailed out of the store. I stared after her. "She's weird, right?" I asked Izzy.

"I guess. You all lost me there when you were talking about Emma being a dude in a skirt; it was all very confusing."

"She still seems really familiar, though, like I've— Oh my god."

"Are you okay, Evie?" Izzy asked in concern. "Evie? You look weird." I felt her cool hand against my forehead. "Hello?! Okay, I'm getting concerned."

I turned to her and grabbed her shoulders. "Izzy!"

"Holy crap, girl, what's your problem?" Her light blue eyes were so wide they seemed to take up half her face.

"I am not insane, right? Tell me I'm not insane!" I almost shouted at her.

"Well, up until a minute ago I would have said 'no, you're not,' but I'm a little afraid of you right now!" she shouted back.

"Isabella Francesca St. Laurent!" I shook her shoulders hard enough that her black and purple hair flew around them. "I think Jane Austen was just in our store!"

Izzy gaped at me. Then she gently placed her hands over mine on her shoulders and pried my fingers out of her shirt. "So…" she said in a cautious tone of voice, the kind of voice you use with rabid dogs and tantrum-throwing children. "I'm just gonna go call your mom real quick and see if we can get you the help you so obviously need."

"I'm not crazy! Okay, well, maybe I am crazy… wait!" I ran around the counter, through the store, and to the reading room, ignoring the startled looks from customers trying to enjoy their beverages in peace. "One of these books has to have it," I hollered over my shoulder as I stumbled into the reading room. I grabbed a handful of Austen novels off one of the side tables and ran back to the counter, plunking them down on the wooden bar. "Let's see…aha!" I nearly shrieked in excitement as I located the famous watercolor of Jane by her sister Cassandra in the back of a copy of *Pride and Prejudice*.

Izzy peered down at the picture, then up at me, then down at the picture again. "Either we are both insane or Jane Austen was just in our store."

I bit on my knuckle to keep from screaming. "Right?! So is she a ghost? Is she a..what? WHAT IS SHE, IZZY?"

"There is the third possibility: we're both on some weird trip. Maybe the coffee beans are spiked?" Izzy held the book up, turning it this way and that, squinting at the picture. "Yeah, that's definitely her, except with a slouch hat. Where did Jane Austen get a slouch hat, that's what I want to know."

"That's what you want to know? She's been dead for two hundred years but somehow she's been drinking her way through our entire beverage menu over the last few weeks, and you want to know where she got the hat?!"

Izzy squinted at the picture some more. "It was actually a super cute hat, way cuter than this bonnet thing she's got going on here."

"She's a ghost, Izzy. Maybe you get cool hats at ghost school."

"Or an angel."

"An angel?" I squeaked. "Like she's on a mission from God?"

"No, that's *The Blues Brothers*. But she could be an angel. A JANE-GEL." Izzy doubled over in laughter, leaning on the counter for support. "Oh my god, a Jane-gel!"

"You cannot be serious right now."

"I am, actually I am," she sputtered through the laughter.

"Okay, so ghost or angel, what do we do about it?"

Izzy stopped laughing and stared at me. "What do

you mean, 'do about it?' Is it something that needs doing about? I mean, if she's a ghost, why not hang out at a Mansfield Perk? Where else would she hang out?"

"I don't know! Chawton Cottage?"

"I have no idea what that is," Izzy admitted.

"Yeah, I know you wouldn't. It's like her house. Why haunt a Mansfield Perk and why this Mansfield Perk? Why L.A.? Also, and this is an important question, I think...*can ghosts drink espresso?*"

"I really don't think that's actually an important question." Izzy shook her head at me. "The really important question is, if she's a Jane-gel who is she here for?"

I widened my eyes. "What do you mean by 'here for,' like Andrew in *Touched by an Angel* 'here for?'"

"Yes, Evie, you're going to be escorted to the afterlife by Jane Austen." Izzy rubbed her forehead in mock exasperation. Or maybe it was real exasperation. It was hard to tell. "But if she is here for you, the question is why? She's not here for me; I'm not an Austen person like you are."

"*Janeite.* How have you worked here for five years and not picked up on that?" I asked.

Izzy grinned. "You'd be amazed what I have managed to not learn while working here. So back to my point; God sent you Jane Austen...why? You need to examine your life, Evie. I'm gonna start playing some slow music now and extend an altar call."

"And I'm going to end this conversation now," I tossed over my shoulder as I walked the books back to the reading room.

"But ask why, Evie, ask...Oh!"

I stopped and turned back around. "Oh, what?"

Izzy's eyes were wide and her mouth was open in a perfect circle. "Oh. Oh. Oh."

"Do you know something I don't?"

"Maybe, maybe not, I dunno. Is one of those books *Mansfield Park*?"

I glanced down at the books in my arms. "Yeah."

"I'm going to read it," she announced.

"You are? Mansfield Park?" I asked doubtfully. "Don't you want to start with *Pride and Prejudice* or *Persuasion* or something?"

"Nope, that's the one I want." She held out her hand.

"Okay." I handed her the book. "But I don't want you to judge based just on this story."

"I thought this conversation was over, Evie."

"Fine," I huffed as I spun on my heel and stomped back to the reading room. I tried to ignore Izzy's cackling laughter behind me.

"LONG TIME, NO see." I pretended not to stare at Frank as I tried unsuccessfully to unlock the MP door to let us both in.

"Morning, Evie," he responded.

"How's things?" I asked. I had the wrong key. I tried not to blush. It's not like I hadn't been unlocking this door for half a decade, and here I was trying random keys.

"Things are good. Busy." Frank shrugged.

"Hmm. What the?" I muttered a string of curse words under my breath as I tried yet another wrong key.

"You need some help there?"

"No. Nope. Got it." The correct key slid home and I breathed a sigh of relief as I turned it and let us in.

We walked into the empty store. It seemed really quiet and large. Usually when we opened Frank and I were laughing and joking...and comfortable with each other. That comfort factor was definitely missing now.

"I saw the commercial thing you filmed for The Highlands." I broke the silence. "It looked really nice."

"Thanks," Frank responded.

Silence descended between us again.

I swear I heard crickets from the corner of the store.

"I'll go turn the machines on..." Frank started.

"So are you dating Maggie Piper or what?" I interrupted him, then almost smacked my forehead. That had come out of nowhere. Well, not nowhere, I'd been thinking it for weeks but I hadn't gotten up the courage to ask.

Frank shrugged.

"What's with the shrugging?" I asked irritably. "You never used to shrug this much. Like, answer or don't, but enough with the shrugging."

"Are you feeling all right?"

"Yes, I'm fine," I snapped. I was far from all right. I wanted to know if he was dating Maggie and I wanted to know why I wanted to know. It had never bothered me before when Frank dated girls. Not that he'd ever dated any as generally irritating as Maggie Piper.

I walked over to the counter and slammed my purse down onto it. Irritating was the wrong word. I didn't find her all that annoying when I'd hung out with her and Jake. It was more the thought of her running her red nails all over Frank's tattoo that I found…maybe irritating was the right word after all.

"You're dating Jake Piper." It wasn't a question.

"I'm…not *not* dating him," I sputtered.

Frank sighed. "Either you're dating him or not."

"Well, I guess I am. Casually. Like we've gone on dates."

Frank's dark eyes seemed to study my face. Why had I never noticed how unreadable his expressions were before? Maybe because I'd never had trouble reading them. "What does it matter to you if I'm dating Maggie?"

I opened my mouth, then shut it again. Then opened it to say something really pithy, but I forgot what, so I closed it again. "She's not your type," I finally said.

"Maybe I'm changing my type." He shrugged again. It was the shrug that broke the camel's back.

"Fine. Okay. Good. I hope you're both very happy together. Though I think she will make you miserable." I turned away from him, slinging my purse back over my shoulder as I made my way to the office. "I'll do the paperwork, you can open front."

"Fine," he responded.

"Fine," I shot over my shoulder before locking myself in the office. I took a deep breath. I felt like crying. I actually was crying if the wetness on my face was anything to go by, but I was ignoring it.

The question was: why was I so upset? Why was Frank dating Maggie making me angry and edgy?

Maybe it was because I felt like I was losing my best friend. I'd barely seen him in weeks and I missed him. Maybe it was because I so desperately wanted to tell him about everything: about Jake and how I liked him but didn't think it would work out, about how I was convinced the ghost of Jane Austen was haunting Mansfield Perk.

Would Frank think I was crazy or would he believe me? He'd seen Jane, right? I was pretty sure the first time I'd met her he'd been there. Maybe he'd even seen her when I wasn't there. Izzy said she'd sold her an Iced Pemberley Whip the other day, so if she was working her way through the menu alphabetically she was nearing the end. Maybe the Jane sightings when I wasn't there meant she wasn't really here for me. I'd seen her twice this week, skulking around the store; I caught her staring hard at me once or twice but she hadn't talked to me. I choked back a laugh at the thought of Jane Austen skulking around, but it's true. More proof that I wasn't the intended target of her haunting/angelic mission. Maybe Frank was her target. Or Izzy.

Maybe I needed to stop coming up with more maybes and go apologize to my best friend for being a crazy female.

Or maybe I could pretend this morning never happened, that I didn't desperately miss him, and that I had wanted to ask him to go with me to this charity gala thing that the Pipers were putting on. Jake had asked me to go with him, but the thought of hanging on his arm while he schmoozed everyone, including Grandma St. Laurent who I'd talked into putting in an appearance, was unappealing.

I pulled a mirror out of my purse to check the not-crying's damage to my mascara. I looked like a sad, lost little girl. I pulled a face at myself.

"And maybe, Evie St. Laurent, you should just put your big girl panties on and take yourself to the ball."

FRANK DIDN'T GO to the gala. He volunteered to be the closing manager for MP that night instead so the rest of us could attend. I was torn between feeling grateful that he wouldn't be there so we could enjoy some more awkward silences and disappointed that he wasn't going to see me in my knock out, sparkly silver dress.

"Evelyn, darling, you look positively radiant." Grandma St. Laurent, my date for the evening, air kissed near my cheek as I helped her out of the back of the limo we'd driven over in.

"Thank you, Grandma."

"It's too bad young Frank can't see you in that dress."

"I don't think he'd care, Grandma." I fiddled with my purse as we walked up the red carpet leading into the gala. Grandma St. Laurent paused the requisite few moments in front of the photographers, nodding and smiling in their general direction. This always made me uncomfortable. Not that I had to deal with it often, but occasionally being a St. Laurent meant you had to show up to some event with Grandma and then live through bad pictures of you being captioned "Diane St. Laurent and unidentified companion" in the media the next day. Grandma always looked impeccable: silver hair sleeked into a bob, ridiculously gorgeous dress, fabulous shoes. Invariably I was pulling a weird face or my curls were standing up like I'd stuck a fork in a light socket.

I took a deep breath and smoothed my hands down my sparkly, one-shouldered dress. I think I had a fighting chance of not looking like a moron tonight. The dress had been a last minute gift from Izzy who had found it online at a shop called Cate's Creations. I didn't know who Cate was, but tonight she'd made me feel like a million bucks. Izzy had lent me shoes, high heeled and strappy and better than anything Cinderella ever dreamed up.

"Oh I don't know about that," Grandma said once we were past the photographers. "Frank's always cared, hasn't he?"

"What?"

"Cared. He cares quite a bit about a lot of things, especially you." Grandma winked at me.

"What do you mean esp-"

"Evie! Sweetie, there you are!" Jake's voice cut me off as we entered the ball room of the hotel where the event was being held.

Sweetie? I stared at him. Since when was I "sweetie?"

"This must be your Grandmother; we are so thrilled to finally meet you." Jake's voice dripped with sincerity. "This is my sister Maggie," he said as his sister appeared at his side. I was pleased to notice that my dress was way more kick-ass than hers.

"Mrs. St. Laurent," Maggie cooed. "So excited you've blessed our little event with your presence."

I felt vaguely sick. Possibly from the amount of syrupy sweet buttering up I was witnessing. It suddenly occurred to me that the only reason Jake had been so interested in me was my family name, and my family's money. It was weird how not disappointed I was.

"It's nice to meet you both," Grandma said. "Evie has told me a lot about you."

I glanced sideways at her. I had?

Grandma smiled at both of the Pipers. It was a cool, aloof smile, one I'd seen before. Grandma St. Laurent could take care of herself.

"Evie!" Izzy appeared at my side wearing a low cut ice blue number that almost exactly matched her eyes. "Can I see you for a moment?"

"Run along, dear," said Grandma. "Isabella, you look lovely tonight as well."

"Obviously, but thanks." Izzy blew a kiss in Grandma's general direction before pulling me away into the throng of party goers. It was very crowded and dimly lit. Large, sparkling snowflakes dangled from the ceiling and a band was playing Christmas classics in a big band style. Loudly.

"What's going on?" I shouted at Izzy.

She turned to me, her light blue eyes glittering in excitement. "I read Mansfield Park!"

"Um, okay? Congratulations?"

"*Aaaaand...*" she drew out the word dramatically, "I think I know why Jane-gel Austen is here!"

"Really" I asked. "Because you read her worst book?"

"Yes! But, I'd hate to spoil the surprise, so I'll let you ask her yourself." Izzy pointed to the corner of the ball room. I peered through the darkness.

"Jane is here?!"

"Yup! You should go say hi!" Izzy grinned at me.

I was suddenly nervous. "And you're sure she's here for me? It's not, like, presumptuous of me to assume that ghostly Jane Austen is visiting just for me?"

"Pretty sure! I'm gonna go back and rescue Grandma from the Pipers now, bye!" Izzy kissed me on the cheek, not an air kiss like she'd given Grandma, but a real leave-your-bright-pink-lipstick-behind smooch.

"Okay, if you're really sure..." I said somewhat doubtfully as I rubbed at my cheek, but Izzy was already gone so I started in Jane's direction.

She was standing almost in the corner of the room nursing what looked like straight whiskey. It both entertained me and kind of freaked me out to think about Jane Austen drinking whiskey. She was still wearing that same hippie skirt, peasant blouse, and purple slouch hat. Izzy was right, it was a cute hat.

"Uh, hello, Miss Austen?" I wasn't sure how to address her. Before I'd called her Jane, but that was before I knew she was...well, dead. How does one address the dead?

Jane smiled. "Finally figured it out, Evie?"

"I...think so? You are *her*, right?"

"Yes, I am Jane Austen."

This was so surreal. I glanced around, half-expecting a camera crew to jump out from behind one of the oversized, pastel Christmas trees.

"Are you an angel?" I asked.

Jane took a long sip of her whiskey. "No. Angels are not to be trifled with. They are not good people given wings, you know. They are very powerful spirits. It would frighten the wits out of you to see one."

"Oh." I didn't really know how to respond to that. "Have you seen one?"

"Indeed. There is one over by the door right now." Jane nodded to an empty space by the large double door entrance. I stared at it with wide eyes.

"I think maybe I don't want to know," I replied carefully.

"No, you really do not."

"So, if you're not an angel are you a..., a..."

"Ghost?" she supplied helpfully. "No, not one of

those either. There is not really a title for what I do. I get called upon for special assignments—visitations, I suppose you would call them. It does not happen frequently and there is usually some connection to my life's work."

"So am I your assignment?"

Jane took another sip of her drink, looking at me thoughtfully over the rim of her glass. "You seem surprised you would be worth making the trip for."

I laughed, but it came out as a nervous giggle. "From heaven? Yeah, making a trip like that surprises me. I mean how screwed up does my life have to be to rate coming from the afterlife?"

"Oh, it is not 'screwed up' at all. You are just missing a piece. And I suppose He wanted to you have it for Christmas this year."

"He being?" I pointed toward the sky.

"The very One."

"Wow." There didn't seem to be much else to say to that. Jane seemed to be expecting me to ask more questions, even though I was now officially scared to ask them. "So, um, it's the Mansfield Perk thing, that's why you got assigned to me?"

"Partly. That and because of the story."

"The story?" I asked.

"Do you remember how I told you that the stories are popular because they always repeat? They always repeat—in novels and in real life? Even stories like *Mansfield Park*, which, by the bye, I think you are not only missing the point of, but much too critical of?"

I stared at her for a long moment. What was she talking about? Was she saying *Mansfield Park* was repeating? And in my—*Oh, holy crap.* I whirled around and looked back toward the front of the ballroom where the Piper siblings were still sugaring up my grandmother, though now Izzy was there running interference. Then I turned back to Jane with wide eyes.

She laughed. "Quite a revelation, then, Evie?"

"I...I..." I stuttered. "Edmund in a dress!"

"You are." She nodded.

"I'm crazy in love with him aren't I?" I asked in a whisper.

"You are," she repeated.

"But he's dating Maggie Piper?"

"Is he?"

I stared at her.

She laughed again. My moment of absolute, utter know-thyself devastation and I was being laughed at by a long dead author. Someone, somewhere had a sick sense of humor. "Perhaps you should go find out?"

I nodded mutely then turned to run out of the ballroom. I only got a few steps before I stopped and ran back.

"Um, thank you! Thank you very much, Miss Austen."

"Jane," she said firmly. "You're welcome. Merry Christmas, Evie."

"Merry Christmas!" I called back over my shoulder. I was already on my way to Frank.

MY HIGH HEELS made a strange thudding sound as they hit the sidewalk, competing with the wild beating of my heart. I was running...running in heels and a fancy dress like some kind of errant Cinderella through the streets of Los Angeles.

I had to get to the store and talk to Frank. To see him, to make sure he was still there...still the same Frank. The same Frank I'd been overlooking for years. How had I been overlooking him? He was just always there, solid and dependable and so very...FRANK. And he was just what I needed, what I wanted, what I didn't even know I had until he was almost gone.

Or maybe he was already gone.

I stopped at a corner, bending down to put my hands on my knees, trying to catch my breath while I waited for the light to change. Everything in me wanted to keep running, but that damn red hand on the crosswalk refused to change.

I searched in my bag for my phone. I'd texted Frank that I needed to talk to him as I'd run out of the ballroom. He still hadn't texted me back. I heaved a sob, or tried to...I couldn't get enough breath into my restricted lungs for an actual sob, it came out as a strangled, sad sound.

Finally the red hand blinked off and the little silver walking man blinked on. I ripped off my heels and ran across the street in bare feet. I was finally into The Highlands. Ode to Joy was blaring through the loud speaker. I was running so fast that the little white Christmas lights decorating the palm trees were blurring together. I was probably going to break an ankle and cut my bare feet on something, but the calm, reasonable voice inside my head that usually argued against dramatic action had apparently gone as insane as I had. It should have been telling me to walk, to put my shoes on, to text Frank again or maybe call.

But instead the voice was screaming at me, "Run! Run faster and find your man."

But Frank wasn't my man. He might even be someone else's. And I'd wasted years of opportunity.

I was almost to the store; I rounded the corner and I could see it now. I didn't break out of my run, just reached forward to push the door in…

I bounced off the locked door with a thud and fell in a heap to the pavement.

"Oof! Ow! Damn! Ow!"

I propped myself and searched for major injury. Everything seemed to be intact other than some minor bruising to both my ass and my ego.

I heard the key turn in the door, unlocking the store from the inside. "Evie?"

I stared up at Frank silhouetted in the light of the door. He was there. Just like always. Solid and dependable with too shaggy hair. Just like always but altogether different.

"Hi," I said.

"Hi. Did you just run into the door?"

I felt myself start turning red. What was wrong with me? I was sitting on the pavement staring up at him like an idiot. "Uh, yeah."

Frank extended his hand and I took it. Warm and reassuring…and yet suddenly I was nervous.

"Jane Austen was in our store," I blurted as he pulled me up to standing.

"What?"

"She was. And at the gala. Izzy called her a Jane-gel…and she took exception to my saying *Mansfield Park* was her worst book. I'm pretty sure the whole point of the novel is that sometimes you miss what's right in front of you. And it's happened to me!"

Frank raised an eyebrow. "Have you been drinking?"

"No. Well, yes, I had a glass of wine before I went with Grandma cause you know how I hate the press photographers."

"Yeah, I do."

"But I was feeling okay, I looked good…"

"You do. You look amazing."

"Thanks—wait, I do?" I glanced at him from under lowered lashes. This was weird. Usually I'd just accept a nice compliment from Frank and move on, but now I was over analyzing and wanting it to mean more than it probably did.

He nodded. "Of course you do, you always look amazing."

"Oh." I abandoned my covert peeking tack and stared at him. "Are you dating Maggie Piper? Serious answer this time."

Frank sighed. "Are we really going to do this here?"

I belatedly realized we were still standing in the half-open door of Mansfield Perk. "No. I mean, I guess we could go inside the store."

Frank held the door open and I walked past him into the lobby of the store. The floor was cool against my feet. I felt sick to my stomach. If Frank felt about me how I felt about him, wouldn't he have recognized my flying into the locked door as the desperate act of love that it was? Or maybe, Evie, I told myself severely, he thinks you've gone around the bend.

I glanced at the tree in the corner and noticed that the Jane Austen ornament was back hanging with the others. It gave me courage.

"Here's the thing," I said, whirling around as he closed the door. "It doesn't really matter if you're dating Maggie Piper."

"It doesn't?" He looked surprised, and maybe a little bit…angry? I hoped that was a good sign.

"No, it doesn't. It doesn't change how I feel. I love you. Which is what I ran all this way to tell you. I've been blind and stupid for years, totally missing what was right in front—" and suddenly I wasn't talking anymore because I was kissing Frank. Or really, he was kissing me. He'd cut off my rambling explanation with the most world-spinning, mind-altering kiss I'd ever experienced.

I'd always hated books or movies where the hero cuts off the heroine mid-sentence with a kiss. Like, dude, let the girl finish her thought then kiss her…but as I reached up and ran my fingers through the hair at Frank's nape, pulling him in closer to me as I kissed him back with every ounce of my being, I reconsidered my opinion. Mansfield Park, for example, could have been vastly improved with this kind of a kiss.

After what seemed like forever, but at the same time way too soon, Frank ended the kiss and looked down into my eyes. "I'm not dating Maggie Piper," he said seriously.

"No, you're not," I agreed. "You're dating me." And then I pulled him back for another kiss.

"ANOTHER SUCCESSFUL MISSION then, Miss Austen?" Samuel tilted the chair back to balance it on two legs as he stirred sugar into his tea.

"Yes. I actually enjoyed this one. The coffee was a nice addition, so many interesting flavorings." Jane took a sip from her tea cup. As much as she had enjoyed the coffee, being at home in her own parlor was a blessing.

"It is a pity you could not have brought any home," Cassandra said sadly. "I do wish I could have seen the cups with the store name one them. How sweet that they named it after one of your books, sister."

Jane smiled. "Yes, although Evie St. Laurent made it quite clear that she despised *Mansfield Park* with a passion."

"Well, I do admit it was never my favorite." Cassandra giggled. "I much preferred Captain Wentworth to Edmund Bertram."

"There is something to be said for a man in uniform," agreed Jane.

"Indeed." Cassandra giggled again.

Samuel grunted. "If this is going to turn into a silly female discussion about what types of men are more attractive, I must excuse myself."

Jane winked at Cassandra. "The quickest way to get rid of Mr. Clemens."

"I know when I'm not wanted," Samuel teased. "However, He's sent you a small Christmas gift; I must deliver it before I go."

"Oh? Lovely," Jane said. "What could it be?"

Samuel opened up his suit coat and from a large pocket inside pulled out two tan coffee mugs with the Mansfield Perk logo emblazoned in lavender on the side. "It will always refill with your favorite beverage from the store, of course."

"How pretty!" Cassandra exclaimed. "What a lovely gift. Do express our gratitude, Mr. Clemens."

"I will do that." Samuel let the chair fall forward with a thunk.

Jane winced. "But please spare the chair."

"Always a pleasure, Miss Austen. You ladies have a Merry Christmas now."

"Merry Christmas, Mr. Clemens, wish Him a Happy Birthday for us," Jane said to the smudgy colored blur that had a second before been Samuel. "Now, Cassandra," she leaned forward with a mischievous grin. "You really must try an 'All Astonishment!'"

ACKNOWLEDGEMENTS

A huge thank you to Jane Austen for creating such an amazing sandbox for us to play in and for consenting to be a character in my story, you've done Clarence proud.

To Kim, Cecilia, Jennifer, Melissa, and Rebecca: thank you all so very much for agreeing to tell stories with me and for putting up with all of the birth pains that accompany a new project.

Rebecca Fleming and Mark House, thanks for fixing my errors and pointing me in the right direction.

As always, thank you so much, Maddie and James, for sharing Mommy with the people that live inside her head.

ABOUT THE AUTHOR

Jessica Grey is an author, fairytale believer, baseball lover, and recovering Star Wars fangirl. A life-long Californian, she now lives with her two children in the Rocky Mountains where she spends her time writing, complaining about snow in April, and drinking way too much caffeine.

You can connect with Jessica on her website: www.authorjessicagrey.com or on Twitter @_JessicaGrey.

PRIDE AND
Presents

KIMBERLY TRUESDALE

'TWAS THE NIGHT BEFORE CHRISTMAS, WHEN ALL THROUGH THE HOUSE

LIZ BENNET SHIVERED as the snow hit the back of her exposed neck. She'd committed the cardinal winter sin of not checking the weather this morning and now she was stuck hobbling down the icy sidewalk in her high heels. She would have been fine on any other day, wearing her usual uniform of jeans and t-shirts and sensible shoes. But today she'd gotten dressed up and put on her power heels to make the annual round of "wouldn't you like to give us money or services for our Christmas party, please, it's for the children" meetings. Liz wasn't shy on a normal day and it wasn't as if she'd never done these meetings before, but this year she had asked to do them alone and the heels gave her an extra boost of confidence.

Good thing it had worked. Her whole day of meetings had resulted in some of the most generous donations they'd had in twenty years of running Longbourn Community Center. It was going to be a very good Christmas.

Nearly frozen, Liz finally made it up the steps and opened the door to her beloved Longbourn. She could barely remember her life before they'd had this place. And though sometimes Liz and her sisters and their effusive mother complained about it, none of them could really imagine life without the hum of activity. It was like the blood that ran through their veins. Or, since it was only a month before Christmas, more like the tinsel and candy canes that decked their tree.

As she stepped inside, the rush of noise and activity warmed her. She stomped her feet on the large mat just inside the door, trying to dislodge all the snow she'd accumulated. Then she looked up into the mirror that lined the front entrance and used her sleeve to wipe away the snow that had already started to melt down her dark skin. She wanted to look her best when she told her father the good news.

Around the corner in the main room, Liz could see the usual holiday festivities. In one corner, her older sister Jane was making hand-loom potholders with a group of kids. They seemed to be throwing the loom bands at each other more than putting them on the loom. And Jane was joining right in. In another corner, Mary was teaching some of the children how to play Christmas songs on a few old guitars that had been donated many years ago. She looked very serious and patient as she showed the small group how to play a new chord.

Liz's mother, Mrs. Bennet, was in another corner happily crafting all manner of Christmas decorations out of construction paper. They would have a lot to hang on the walls and on the tree at Friday night's decorating party. "The more the merrier" was kind of the Bennet family motto.

But by far the loudest and giggliest corner held Liz's two youngest sisters and a large group of boys and girls. Kitty and Lydia were teaching the kids a dance routine they would perform on the night of their Christmas party in a few weeks' time. Right now it didn't look very coordinated to Liz, but that was hardly the point of it. They were all having a grand time.

Smiling broadly at the utter joy of it all, she threaded her way through all of the hullabaloo and toward the office just behind the main room. There she found her beloved father bent anxiously over some paperwork.

"Hi, Dad," she said as she set her bag down on her desk.

"Hi, sweetheart," he said and smiled up at her. "How did everything go?"

Liz unbuttoned her coat and tried to play coy. "Well..."

Immediately her father began to worry. "Do you need me to make some calls? See what I can rustle up?"

"Well, maybe...if you think that we'll need it. But Lucas Catering said they'd be happy to provide finger foods for the party again this year. And Lady

Catherine's Tea Shop is going to provide hot coffee and tea, as usual. And Philips Drugstore is already running their annual toy drive."

"That's wonderful!" Mr. Bennet exclaimed. He jumped up from his chair and came around Liz's desk to give her a hug and a kiss.

"But..." Liz hadn't yet revealed her big surprise.

"But what?" Mr. Bennet drew back in concern.

"Meryton Market..."

"Oh no. Have they said no? I'll call them." He moved toward the phone.

"Dad, wait." Liz couldn't help but grin. "Meryton is in. They said they would be honored to provide all the cakes and cookies we could need."

Mr. Bennet laughed in relief. "You had my heart going there for a minute, Lizzy."

"There's more."

"More?" Now her father was grinning too.

"Yes, and they agreed to donate a full Christmas dinner to all of the families who come to the party. Turkey and stuffing and vegetables and pie. All of it."

Mr. Bennet whooped and swept Liz up into another big hug. "Oh my dearest Lizzy! This is wonderful. I knew you could do it. This is going to be the best Christmas we've ever had here at Longbourn."

When he finally let her go, Liz saw see tears in her father's eyes. This community center was everything to him. Making a difference to the people in this town was everything to him. And she'd just made Christmas better. It was a wonderful feeling.

"Now that you've seen what I can do, will you consider retiring?" Liz teased.

Mr. Bennet laughed. "I just might have to. Your mother has been begging me to take her on a vacation. But you know I always put her off because of something here."

Liz had been trying to show her father for years now that she was ready and willing to take over running the community center. He'd reluctantly let her take over some of the responsibilities, like going to all these meetings today. And while Liz had known the donations were pretty much a sure thing—these places had been donating to the center for years now —she was still anxious to do a good job of it and to show her father what she could do.

And now everything was coming together so nicely. Maybe she could venture it.

"Dad?"

"Hmm?" He had returned to his desk and was once again absorbed in his papers. Liz walked over to him and grabbed them away.

He protested while she spoke. "I have a proposition for you."

"Uh oh. That's what your mother said to me many years ago..."

"Hush and listen." Liz laughed. "You know we've all been trying to get you to retire or at least step back and let us take over here."

"Yes?" He looked dubious.

"Well, now that you've seen what I can do, maybe you could actually retire now."

"But we have all of the paperwork to get done before the new year. The lease is up this time around and —"

Liz interrupted. "But how many years have I hovered over your shoulder while you did all of that? I can do it, Dad. I know I can."

"I know you can, too, Liz, but —"

"But nothing. Why don't you let me do all of this? I'll take over most of your responsibilities and you and Mom can finally enjoy the Christmas season together. You never get to do that."

"Did your mother put you up to this?" Mr. Bennet asked suspiciously.

"When have I ever done what Mom told me to do?" Liz retorted.

"True." Her father chuckled.

"So if I can do this, I want you to promise me that you'll retire and let me and the girls take over."

"How about I let you do all of this and I'll *consider* retiring?"

"That's the best I'm gonna get from you, isn't it?" Liz sighed.

"Yes, take it or leave it," Mr. Bennet declared.

"All right."

"All right."

As they shook hands over their bargain, there was an unusual commotion from the main room.

WHEN OUT ON THE LAWN
THERE AROSE SUCH A CLATTER

LIZ AND HER father moved quickly to see what all the noise was about. They found that the different corners and activities had been abandoned and all the children—and her mother and sisters—were crowded in a clump at the center of the room, clearly excited about whatever or whoever was there.

Liz quickly assessed the situation, making sure that no one was hurt. Her eyes stopped on her older sister Jane, who was ushering someone, two someones, forward through the swarm of children. Liz only had time to shut her mouth and thank god she was dressed up today before the visitor was standing right in front of her.

Jane spoke with barely restrained excitement. "Dad, Liz, this is Charles Bingley."

Liz couldn't even smile, she just stared. She'd never

been starstruck before, but there was a first time for everything.

Mr. Bennet had no such problem, however. "Mr. Bingley!" he effused and reached out to shake his hand. "Of course we know who you are. It's hard to miss the newest star player on our basketball team."

"Thank you, sir." Charles Bingley reached forward to shake their hands. "I'm excited to be here in the city and especially here at Longbourn."

While they went through the motions of small talk, Liz stared some more. Charles Bingley had joined their city's basketball team this year and he was already making waves. He was the best player they'd had for some time and, on top of that, he was gorgeous. (She and her sisters had already agreed that "gorgeous" was the only appropriate adjective for him.) Tall and muscled with beautiful brown skin and a brilliant smile that lit up the room. Right now he was wearing a coat, but she could imagine (and was enjoying imagining) the broad shoulders underneath the heavy material.

After some more talk between Mr. Bennet and Charles Bingley—talk that managed to pass Liz right by—Charles gestured to a man standing next to him. Liz hadn't even noticed him.

"This is my friend and my lawyer Will Darcy."

Mr. Darcy's greeting was downright cold compared to the warm smile Mr. Bingley had bestowed on them. Liz didn't linger long over him. Mr. Darcy was as tall as his friend, with deep black skin and close-cut hair. Under his coat he might be just as broad as Bingley, but his face seemed set into a permanent scowl. He did not look happy to be here. And Liz was certainly not happy to have him.

The children were starting to inch toward Charles Bingley, their patience with the adults running thin. Liz made eye contact with Jane, who had noticed this too.

"Mr. Bingley —" Jane said.

"Charles, please," he smiled. Jane blushed.

"Charles, if you wouldn't mind, I think the children would like to take some pictures, if that would be okay..."

He smiled and Jane blushed even deeper under his attention. "I'd be happy to, Ms. Bennet."

"Jane, please." They waded into the crowd of kids, leaving Liz and her father with the sullen and silent Will Darcy.

Charles looked back over his shoulder. "You'll take care of things, Will?"

His friend nodded curtly and turned to Liz and Mr. Bennet. The mood changed immediately. Liz didn't like it at all. It felt as cold as the snow that had spilled down her neck half an hour ago.

Mr. Darcy spoke. "Charles would like for us to volunteer here on a regular basis."

Mr. Bennet didn't seem to feel the same chill that Liz did. He was thrilled at the suggestion. "That would be wonderful, Mr. Darcy —"

"You can call me Will."

"Excellent. We would love to have Charles and yourself. We always need help during the Christmas season."

"Charles wants us to give back," Mr. Darcy declared.

Charles this and Charles that. Did Will Darcy do anything because he wanted to? He didn't seem too thrilled with the idea of volunteering here at Longbourn.

Liz felt the desire to needle him about it. "And what made you choose to grace us with your presence, Mr. Darcy?" She deliberately used his formal name. If he didn't really want to be here, she wouldn't make him feel welcome.

"Charles and I both grew up involved in our local community center. That's where we first met each other."

"And now you're a hoity-toity lawyer." Liz couldn't help her confrontational tone.

"Liz," Mr. Bennet warned. He clearly knew what she was thinking. He went on the offense with their guest. "We're happy to have you both, Will. It is always good to see celebrities giving back."

Mr. Darcy made a noise in his throat that her father took as agreement and then all three of them descended into silence. Liz watched as Jane introduced their visitor to each of the children. He kindly took pictures with them and gave them all high-fives or hugs. And every once in awhile Liz saw his radiant smile turn on her sister.

Eventually Mr. Bennet wandered back into the office and left Liz to babysit Will Darcy. It was no easy task. In the spirit of goodwill (and remembering her father's warning), Liz tried her best to start a conversation. Each time his curt answers shut her down. When Charles was about halfway through the crowd of kids, Liz clutched at the last straw she could find and offered to show Mr. Darcy around the center. He accepted, but didn't seem the least bit interested in what she was showing him. He managed to rub some of the shine off of her good day. And she was beginning to resent him heartily for it.

So it came as a great relief when Charles was finally finished with the kids and Jane announced that he had to go. The kids moaned and whined and tried to coax him into staying. Charles mollified them by promising to come back.

"All right, Darcy?" Charles enthused as they got ready to leave. "Nice place here, isn't it?"

Mr. Darcy gave his friend a grunt and a nod. The lackluster gesture infuriated Liz, but she held her tongue.

"So when do you want us back?" Charles asked.

"Well..." Without the kids between them, Jane grew shy of their famous visitor, so Liz stepped in.

"We're having a decorating party this Friday evening about six, if you'd like to come. We usually have some pizzas and the kids come and decorate the center for the holidays."

"Sounds like a plan! We'll be here." Charles' evident enthusiasm spilled over to Liz. After a chilly half hour with his friend, it was good to see that at least someone was as excited about Longbourn and Christmas as she was. Mr. Darcy didn't say anything, he stayed as cold and wet as the weather outside.

The two men said their goodbyes and, without any further pomp, left the center.

What they left behind them, though, was a room full of children talking at high volume and comparing the pictures on their phones. They were excited beyond belief. But not any more excited than Liz's squealing younger sisters and their mother who rushed over to Liz and Jane immediately after Charles and Mr. Darcy left.

"I cannot *believe* that Charles Bingley was here!" Kitty's voice was almost too high-pitched to hear.

Lydia flipped through the pictures on her phone. "Wait until everyone at school hears about this."

Even Mary, normally somewhat reserved, was starstruck. "He's so handsome."

Mrs. Bennet wondered aloud, "Do you think he's single? I think he was flirting with you, Jane. You should get his phone number next time. Have him take you out to dinner or something...And that Mr. Darcy was a lawyer, wasn't he, Liz? He was quite good-looking, even if he never smiled the whole time he was here...I wonder what you father thinks of all this. Where is your father, anyway? Don't tell me he's hiding away when we have such guests visiting us!"

While they all tittered, Liz and Jane looked at each other and smiled. Yes, in spite of Mr. Darcy's coldness, this was going to be the best Christmas they'd ever had.

When what to my wondering eyes should appear

BY THE TIME the decorating party came around on Friday night, they'd nearly elevated Charles Bingley to sainthood. Excitement had built to a fever pitch by the time he finally arrived.

Luckily, Mr. Bennet had prepared for this. He had all the kids and their parents sit down in the rows of chairs he had set out. He stood in front of them and spoke.

"Thank you all for coming down to the center tonight. We're going to make this place sparkle with holiday cheer!" Everyone clapped and hooted. "You may have noticed," there was a twinkle in his eye, "that we have a special guest tonight. Basketball superstar Charles Bingley has come to help us." More hooting and clapping. "I know you will all say a big thank you to Charles for spending his time helping us and you won't bother him too much. Remember that we are all here to have fun and to get the holiday season started right! In about an hour we'll have some pizzas, so let's see what damage we can do before then." There was a flurry of movement as Mr. Bennet shouted out some final instructions. "Remember that it is only adults who should go up the ladder. Everyone else needs to keep their two feet on the ground."

Soon, the center was filled with decorations, all of them made by the children. The only thing they hadn't made was the big tree in the corner. About ten years ago, Mrs. Bennet had somehow wrangled a local hardware store into donating the most enormous fake Christmas tree they had ever seen. Mrs. Bennet treated it like her sixth child. When they took it out of the basement each year, she carefully cleaned it and fluffed out all the branches. She had been especially careful with it this year, as she knew that Charles Bingley was coming and she wanted to show it off.

In fact, Mrs. Bennet claimed his attention before anyone else and asked him to help her decorate the tree. Liz knew exactly what her mother was up to once she heard her calling out across the room, "Oh Jane! Come help me and Charles with the decorations over here by the tree." Liz hoped her mother wouldn't be too obvious about it. Jane was so easily embarrassed.

Before long Liz found herself enlisted to hang garland. The kids needed an adult to climb up on the ladder for them and she was it. They'd made it to the corner of the room before Liz noticed Mr. Darcy sitting there. She had been made too cheerful by the atmosphere of the room and the fact that she loved Christmas to respond negatively to his scowl. As she moved the ladder toward where he was sitting, she spoke cheerily to him.

"Mr. Darcy, would you help me and the kids hang up this garland? You can probably reach higher than I can." One of the children held out the next bit of garland to him.

"No, thank you." His refusal was firm.

Liz got angry. How could he be so surly at such a happy party? Didn't he see the kids here who just wanted his help? And she had asked so nicely, even after he'd been so rude the other day. Liz spoke more bluntly than she should have.

"Well, Mr. Scrooge, if you're not going to help, you could at least move out of the way so we can get this beautiful garland hung." She planted the ladder firmly in front of him as the kids laughed.

Without answering or showing much emotion of any kind, Mr. Darcy got up and moved away. Liz had a momentary pang of dismay. She knew he was a guest here and she shouldn't have treated him like that. But still, what business did he have sitting in the corner and refusing to help? Get some Christmas spirit already!

Liz tried to put him out of her mind, but every once in awhile as she and the kids hung the garland, she felt eyes on her. She was sure it was Mr. Darcy, but she didn't want to give him the satisfaction of paying any further attention to him. She didn't know what his game was, but she wasn't about to play.

By the time the pizzas arrived, most of the decorations had gone up. People were sitting everywhere eating and laughing. Christmas songs played from the dock in the corner. Longbourn was decked out in all of her holiday resplendence.

Liz couldn't help but smile. She loved this place. And she loved these people. They were all a part of her family and she would do anything for them. Her heart swelled even more when she saw her father carefully holding a plate for her mother. She never understood how they had married each other in the first place, but their love was evident even after all these years. Liz wanted them to be happy. And she wanted them to be able to enjoy all of the hard work they'd put into this place. She had to step up and take over. It was time to prove to her father that she could do this.

With that thought, Liz ducked into the office, deciding that she would just get some work done. This was the year their lease was up, as well as the year they had to renew their non-profit status. There was a lot of nearly incomprehensible paperwork and accounting that had to be done. And she wanted to make sure everything was correct.

While the party continued to buzz in the main room, Liz lost herself in her work. She was reading one of the more confusing questions out loud when someone interrupted her.

"I wanted to say goodnight."

Liz was startled to see Mr. Darcy standing in the doorway with his coat on. He was looking intently at her.

"Goodnight." Liz was too astonished to be upset. He hadn't said two words to her tonight.

Mr. Darcy continued to stand there. Liz was just about to say something when he spoke all in a rush. "I'm sorry I didn't help with the garland. I'm a little afraid of heights and didn't want to make a fool out of myself. I'm sorry."

Before Liz could reply, he'd left the office. It took her a moment to register that if Mr. Darcy was leaving, so was Charles Bingley and she should probably go say goodbye to their guests. Half in a daze at Mr. Darcy's strange apology, Liz left the office. She shook Charles' hand and made the appropriate farewells.

While Charles said goodbye to each of the kids, Mr. Darcy was standing by the front door, refusing to look at anyone. Still astonished by his apology, Liz stared at him. Where his expression had seemed rude and uninviting before, now she thought she actually saw a bit of shyness behind it. Not enough to excuse his previous behavior, but enough to make her think that maybe Charles Bingley saw something in him that no one else saw.

I KNEW IN A MOMENT IT MUST BE ST. NICK

LIZ KEPT HER thoughts about Mr. Darcy to herself. All anyone could talk about anyway was Charles Bingley. The day after the party, Jane confessed to her sisters that Charles had asked for her phone number. They were sworn to secrecy, though, as Jane didn't want their mother to start making wedding plans.

In her usual reserved way, Jane stayed pretty quiet about it, but every time her phone beeped with a new message, Liz saw a little smile cross her face. Charles even stopped by a few times during the next week, ostensibly to say hello to the kids, but he wasn't fooling anyone.

The kids treated Charles just like anyone else now. They were thrilled to have someone new to show off for. Each time he came, Liz held her breath a little until she could verify that Mr. Darcy wasn't with him. She didn't want another strange encounter like the one the other night. He put her dander up for no reason except his refusal to have fun. And then there had been that strange apology that put her on the wrong side of things. No, she didn't want to meet Mr. Darcy again and was glad when he didn't show up.

About halfway through the week, Charles showed up and asked Jane to have some coffee with him at Mansfield Perk, the coffee chain just down on the corner from the center. It was hardly a date, but Jane was beaming when she came back. Liz was happy that her sister was happy, but she was also a little bit jealous. Christmas was a time that made Liz feel like it would be nice to have someone. But there was only one Charles Bingley in the world and Liz didn't have time or energy to search for anyone else.

She spent most of her days working hard on the paperwork and getting more things settled for their Christmas party. They'd been running a toy drive since Thanksgiving and had collected a truckload of gifts to give the children. Charles had donated another truckload, all of which needed to be wrapped. So Liz had organized a wrapping party for Friday evening after the kids went home. She didn't want them peeking at any gifts. It would just be adults and toys and wrapping paper. And wine. Definitely some wine.

Jane invited Charles and Mr. Darcy. And Lydia hinted around all week about a new friend she was going to bring. She wouldn't say who it was, only that it was a he and he was very kind and very good-looking and she had met him at the store or something. Liz and her sisters just rolled their eyes. As a teenager, Lydia found nearly everyone good-looking and she had the uncanny ability to pick up adoring men anywhere she went. At least whoever he was, he'd be another pair of hands to help them. He couldn't be worse than that kid Dennys she'd brought home a month ago. Mr. Bennet had been having none of that nonsense. Hopefully, this new guy was somewhat better than that loser.

And so the days rolled on. The women were busy getting everything in order for Christmas and keeping the children relatively calm after school. Mary's guitar players were actually starting to sound musical. And Kitty and Lydia's dancers were getting most of their steps together. Jane's group had made more potholders than anyone knew what to do with. And Mrs. Bennet's crew was crafting decorations for everyone to take home. There was a lot of happy buzz going on.

With her sisters joyful and the Christmas stuff going smoothly, Liz was feeling pretty confident about all of her new responsibilities. She'd only had to shoo her father away a few times a day. He was now to the stage where he was teasing her more than he was worrying about her actually getting the work done. And Liz was glad to see that he was spending more time with the kids. He was so good at it. She grew more determined than ever that she would take over the business side of things and let him enjoy his semi-retirement.

When Friday came around again, Liz was

definitely ready to put aside the soul-crushing paperwork and have a good time with her family and friends. After the kids went home, they unloaded both trucks and made a huge pile of toys in the middle of the main room. Liz hadn't thought it possible, but the pile actually dwarfed the Christmas tree in the corner. The kids would be delighted come Monday. She hoped they didn't break anything in their eagerness to shake every box and guess what was inside.

Once they had unloaded everything, Mr. and Mrs. Bennet headed off to the store to grab more wrapping paper and bows and to bring back some Chinese take out for dinner. The girls and their friends grabbed some presents and started wrapping and chattering. At some point someone put on a playlist of Christmas carols and they all started singing.

Liz was having such a grand time, that she didn't notice Mr. Darcy had arrived until he sat down in the empty seat next to her. He didn't say hello. He just sat down by her and started wrapping. Liz was embarrassed and didn't know what to say. Should she mention the apology? Should she act like nothing had happened? She hated always being in an awkward position with him.

A moment later Charles came in and some of the tension was broken. He gave effusive greetings all around, making small talk with everyone and smiling that brilliant smile of his. Liz made eye contact with Jane, who was performing the odd feat of shining like a sunbeam and trying to stifle it behind a fierce blush.

Liz grinned. Jane had fallen harder than she'd thought.

When Charles had retrieved some toys from the pile and settled down next to Jane to wrap, Mr. Darcy finally spoke to Liz.

"I see that you got the truckload of toys." It was a matter-of-fact statement.

Liz answered him in the same flat tone. "Yes, we did. Charles has been entirely too generous."

"You object to the toys?" Mr. Darcy inquired.

Liz backtracked. Clearly Mr. Darcy was socially inept as well as surly and abrupt. "Not at all. I meant that we seldom see such generosity here at Longbourn."

"I can't believe that. I'm sure you do your job very well and the community is happy to give back." It was the longest statement she'd ever heard him make, and it startled her. How did he know what kind of a job she did? Mr. Darcy stopped wrapping his gift and turned his full attention on her. It made her feel strange and she stumbled over her next words.

"Of course...I mean...the community is great...and they are...happy to give what they can. But it's never enough, is it?"

He didn't respond right away. He just kept looking at her. Liz finally met his eyes. There was no reason not to, after all. He seemed to be studying her intently in a way that made her feel squirmy. She didn't know what to say.

Finally, he spoke again. His words came out in a rush, as if he didn't know whether he wanted to say them and better get them out before he changed his mind. "If you could have whatever you wanted for Longbourn and these kids, what would you wish for?"

"Uhhh..." Liz stuttered. The question threw her off balance and she tripped over her answer. "Anything? Uhhh...where to start?"

Liz was rescued from her answer by the door swinging open with a bang.

"You came!" Lydia squealed and ran toward their new guest. Liz felt Mr. Darcy go rigid. Whatever had just been passing between them was completely gone, replaced by something even colder than the first time they'd met. He was staring at their new guest. Liz barely had time to think to herself that the two men must know each other before Lydia brought the visitor over to the table and introduced him around.

"Everyone, I want you to meet George Wickham." Lydia had twined her arm through his and was smiling so big that even her back teeth showed.

"Delighted to meet you all." George Wickham smiled. Liz couldn't help but smile back. He was a handsome man. Tall and blonde. Well-dressed and, from what she had seen so far, well-mannered. At least he was smiling. She liked him already. Maybe Lydia had picked a good one this time.

"Wickham is the guy I've been telling you about," Lydia gushed.

"Good things, I hope!" He chuckled.

"Oh, *very* good things," Kitty giggled.

"Kitty!" Lydia's eyes went wide with mock

embarrassment. Liz and Jane just rolled their eyes and tried to stifle their smiles. They knew this was exactly what their sister wanted. She was the center of attention and had a handsome guy on her arm. There was nothing better in Lydia's world.

Lydia took great delight in introducing George Wickham to each of her sisters and their friends in turn. But when she got to Mr. Darcy, Wickham's smile cooled quickly. He nodded curtly.

"Darcy."

"Wickham." Darcy didn't move. If it were possible, Liz thought, his back went even straighter. They must know each other and whatever they know is not good. For a moment, Liz wondered what had happened between them, but her curiosity was quickly muffled under the lantern of good cheer that George Wickham shone around the table.

For an hour they all wrapped gifts while Wickham kept them entertained with stories and had them all singing songs. He had a beautiful voice that he wasn't shy of showing off. Liz liked him more and more. But always there was that cold silence from beside her. Darcy hadn't left, but he hadn't spoken again either. Their earlier conversation was forgotten.

Just as she was getting up to retrieve more toys from the pile, her phone rang and she excused herself to the office.

"Hello?"

"Liz?"

"This is Liz."

"Hey, Liz, it's Carl. I'm sorry to do this to you, but

something's come up with the family and I have to go out of town, so...I can't be your Santa this year."

"Oh no." Liz vaulted into panic mode. No Santa for the kids' party? What was she going to do? She remembered herself before she spiraled too far. "Is everything okay, Carl?"

"Oh, nothing serious. Just have to be away. I hope this doesn't put you in a bind for the party."

"Not at all," Liz lied. Carl had been their Santa for years now. It was just a given that he would do it. She didn't have any other Santas. One of the threads of her perfect Christmas was unraveling.

"I'm sorry again," Carl said. "Please let me know if there's anything at all I can do."

"Thanks for letting me know. We'll miss you. And I hope everything's okay with your family."

"Thanks. Bye."

"Bye." Liz hung up the phone and stood in the office. She needed a moment to herself. What was she going to do?

Her moment didn't last long. She had barely hung up the phone when Lydia and Wickham came in.

"Wickham asked for a tour of the place," Lydia announced to her sister. "This is the boring old office where Liz and Dad do all the work."

Wickham looked around with some interest. "Nice place. Very well-organized."

"Thanks," Liz was still thinking about her phone call.

"Is everything all right?" Wickham asked, concern in his voice.

"Oh fine," Liz sighed. "Just got a call that our Santa can't make it to the Christmas party this year."

"Oh no," Wickham seemed genuinely concerned. Lydia was almost tugging on his arm to get him to move on. She couldn't be concerned about her sister's problems. "Could I help?"

"Only if you want to be Santa this year." Liz said it jokingly.

Wickham's face lit up. "I'd love to."

Liz couldn't believe it. Did life really work like this? "Are you serious? If you are, I'm sure we would love it."

Lydia beamed up at her date. "That would be amazing, Wickham! Would you be our Santa? Isn't he so great?" The last question was directed toward her sister.

"I can hardly leave such lovely damsels in distress, can I? I would be happy to be your Santa." Wickham boomed out a "ho-ho-ho."

"It's settled then!" Liz was overjoyed. Problem made and solved within two minutes. Whew.

As they left the office, Wickham continued ho-ho-ho-ing, happy to announce to all that he was going to step into Santa's boots and make all the little children happy. As she looked out over the main room, decorated to the hilt and piled high with presents, she counted her blessings. The perfect Christmas was back on track.

AS LEAVES THAT BEFORE THE WILD
HURRICANE FLY

BUT THE SHINE of holiday sparkle wore off quickly when Liz arrived at Longbourn on Monday to find Mr. Collins waiting for her.

She had never liked their lawyer. Mr. Bennet had hired him years ago, mostly because he was the cheapest one they could afford that still had a reputation for getting the job done. But he'd always looked at Liz in a way that made her feel kind of slimy. And she always had the feeling that he wasn't quite telling them the whole truth. It was silly, of course. There'd never been anything untoward in their dealings with him, but Liz could never quite squash that feeling.

It wasn't something one wanted to deal with first thing on a Monday morning, either.

"Hello, Mr. Collins," Liz greeted him as she took off her coat and sat down behind her desk.

"Hello, Liz."

She tried to smile at him, but she had a feeling it came out looking more like a grimace. She wished her father was here, but in his now semi-retired status, he'd decided to sleep in a little bit. Liz gathered her courage. Here was a prime opportunity to prove that she could handle things. "What can I do for you today?"

"Oh, I've just come to check that all the paperwork is getting done. You know it's time to renew the lease and your non-profit status, which, of course, determines your tax-exempt status for next fiscal year."

"I know. It's all under control."

"Is it?" Mr. Collins paused. Liz remained silent. "Oh, well, good."

"Can I do anything else for you? Since you've come all this way?" Liz tried to give the impression that she was very busy and needed him to leave.

"Umm...well, I was hoping that I could just have a look at all the paperwork and everything. Just to check that it's all going well."

"Is that really necessary?" Liz didn't remember any other time that Mr. Collins had come to Longbourn just to check their paperwork.

"If you'd rather I just contacted Mr. Bennet, I'd be happy —"

That did it. "No, no," Liz assured him. "Just let me get all of it together here."

Liz shuffled through the papers at her desk and then got up to grab some of the binders from the shelf behind her. She started a pile on the desk in front of the lawyer. He made the motions of flipping through the binders, but Liz got the impression that he was watching her more than he was looking through the files.

"And, uh, have you started to fill in any of the electronic forms yet?"

"Yes, I have. They're right here on this flash drive." She showed him the small drive attached to her keychain.

"Excellent. It looks like you are in good shape. So I shall take my leave. Thank you for your time." And just like that he was out the door.

Liz was relieved and irritated at the same time. It was not how she'd envisioned starting her morning. And now she also had a disorganized stack of papers on her desk.

The holiday shine grew even dimmer after Mr. Collins' Monday visit. Many of the children had come down with colds, so practices for the Christmas party were nearly useless. Then the caterer called to change the menu, which wouldn't have been a big deal except that Kitty happened to answer the phone and made it sound like the end of the world until Liz had straightened everything out.

And somewhere in the mix, Charles Bingley disappeared. No calls, no texts. Nothing. Jane tried not to show it, but Liz knew her sister was hurt and disappointed. Liz was disappointed for her. Charles had seemed like such a nice guy. They tried to reason that he was just busy, but Liz could see that Jane was hurt and worried for the kids.

On top of everything else, Liz kept misplacing things. From her keys and her coffee mug all the way up to some of the paperwork they needed in order to renew their lease. She'd nearly had a panic attack about that. Now was not the time to be getting careless. Not when Longbourn itself was on the line. It would ruin the holiday if she had to tell everyone that the center was closing.

The only bright spot was the continual presence of George Wickham, who seemed to make himself quite at home in Longbourn, to the delight of Lydia. But even Wickham had bad news for Liz.

On Thursday morning he was in the office when she walked in.

"Good morning, Liz. You are looking lovely today," he said. The man knew how to brighten a girl's day, that was for sure.

"Morning, Wickham," Liz answered.

"How are things?" He sat in the chair across from her desk and they chatted as she settled in for the morning. It was a friendly, light sort of banter until Wickham mentioned Mr. Darcy.

"So...Darcy, huh?"

"What?" Liz had only been half paying attention.

"Darcy...was here...Friday night. How do you...uh...know him?"

"Oh, he's Charles Bingley's friend. They came together." Liz remembered now the curt greeting the two men had exchanged. Now she was paying attention, unable to resist the gossip (a trait she had inherited from her mother, unfortunately). "Do you know him?"

"Hmmph," Wickham made a derisive noise. "I know Will Darcy very well."

"Now you have to tell me," Liz insisted.

Wickham hesitated. "I knew him at law school. We were in the same year and we had some of our classes together."

"That doesn't seem so bad."

"No, not until he got me kicked out of the school." Wickham threw out the statement in a haphazard way.

"What?" Liz gasped.

"Yeah, in our second year he told our professor that I had been copying off of him during one of our exams."

"But you weren't, right?" Liz was fully on Wickham's side.

There was a gleam in Wickham's eye. "Well, he'd said he would help me. And we had been studying together, so our answers *were* similar. And of course they believed the rich boy whose daddy had donated money to the school."

"And they kicked you out?"

"Yep."

"Wow, I had no idea. I can't even imagine." Liz was flabbergasted. Mr. Darcy had seemed uptight, but to get his friend kicked out of school? That was despicable.

"So be careful of him, okay?" Wickham asked, getting up to go.

"I will," Liz answered. "I definitely will."

When They Meet with an Obstacle, Mount to the Sky

AFTER THEIR FEW encounters with each other, Liz had no trouble believing that the surly and rude Mr. Darcy had indeed been so dastardly as to get the charming Wickham kicked out of school. She was almost happy that he and Charles hadn't come around this week, although she wished that Charles would come for Jane's sake.

So Liz was not feeling particularly kindly toward Mr. Darcy that Saturday morning when he suddenly appeared before her as she stood in the cereal aisle at Meryton Market.

"Mr. Darcy." Liz spoke first. He was carrying a basket and was also clearly shopping. He did not look surprised to see her.

"Ms. Bennet...Liz...good morning." The words were uttered formally.

"I've not seen you here before."

Her directness caught him off guard. "Oh...I...I...usually do my shopping later in the day. But I'm busy today and wanted an early start."

Since directness disconcerted him, she kept on with that strategy. "You didn't come here to see *me* by any chance, did you?"

"What? I..." He was completely ruffled now. Liz quite enjoyed his discomfort. Until, that is, he turned the tables.

He smiled.

Mr. Darcy smiled.

And Liz found it...dazzling. His entire body seemed to relax into that smile. And suddenly she couldn't remember that he'd ever been any other way. It was entirely disarming just at the moment she thought she had the upper hand.

But her inclination to like him went away as soon as he opened his mouth again.

"I *am* here because of you, in fact. I was wondering...if...if you would want...to go out with me sometime?"

And it all came rushing back to her. His rudeness, his refusal to help hang decorations, his treatment of Wickham. He'd probably even been the one to keep Charles away. Liz threw everything into the pot of her delicious soup of hatred.

"Go out with you?" Liz repeated the question. Mr. Darcy's smile faded a little. Good.

"Yes, I was hoping...at least, I thought..." He stuttered.

"No."

"No?" He acted like he'd never heard the word before. His entire body went rigid again. The smile disappeared completely. The scowling, stiff man she'd first disliked was back. Liz had no trouble now imagining Mr. Darcy as a spoiled child who always thought he would get his way. Liz took great delight in bursting his bubble.

"I won't go out with you. Ever." She spat the words at him.

"May I ask why?" He was completely cool about it. It was infuriating. Liz wanted to make him as upset as he was making her.

"Why? I wouldn't care if I never saw you again. You are rude and ill-mannered. You refused to help me at the party. I suspect that you kept Charles away from Jane this week..."

"I was trying to protect him."

"So you admit it!" Liz was aware that her voice was getting louder, but she couldn't help it.

"Yes, I have no reason to hide it. Charles is my friend. I saw that he was falling in love with your sister and that she didn't return his feelings. I saw nothing wrong with telling him what I thought. It's my duty as a friend to keep him safe."

"Safe? From *Jane*? I suppose it never occurred to you that she's really shy and barely even shows her feelings to her family!"

"I...I didn't know." He looked genuinely confused.

"No, you didn't. And just like always, you bent everyone to your will."

"Excuse me?" His voice was growing softer, even as Liz's grew louder. Somehow it came across as even more angry than her own.

"Wickham told me everything." Liz could almost laugh now. She had caught him out in all of his spoiled, rich-kid ways. Well, he wouldn't get away with it this time. He couldn't just manipulate her family and friends like that.

"Wickham?" Mr. Darcy spit the word from his mouth as if it were poison.

"Yes, he told me all about how you got him kicked out of law school."

Mr. Darcy let that hang in the air. The accusation floated above them like a thunder cloud about to let loose. Suddenly, Liz felt wrong and she didn't know why. For a very long minute he just looked at her.

When he finally spoke, his words were measured. "Thank you for telling me this. I won't bother you again." And he turned and left the aisle.

Liz stood there, unable to say anything. She had expected him to fight back or explain himself. In her family they yelled at each other until things were sorted out. That was the kind of confrontation she expected, maybe even wanted. Anything but what he had done. His calm promise to leave her alone was disconcerting.

As she finished her shopping, Liz wavered between righteous anger and feeling like she should find Mr. Darcy and apologize. But then she got angry about feeling like she should apologize. She had never given Mr. Darcy any indication that she wanted to go out with him. Had she?

For the rest of the weekend, Liz threw herself into making sure everything was ready for the holiday. The Christmas party was in less than two weeks and everything needed to be perfect. But even as she did all of this, always in the back of her mind she was reviewing the few words she'd ever spoken to Mr. Darcy and parsing them for any meaning she might have misread. But always it came back down to him actually admitting that he had split up Charles and Jane and not denying that destroyed Wickham's law career. Hurt her family and friends and Liz could be a vengeful fury.

SOON GAVE ME TO KNOW I HAD NOTHING TO DREAD

UNFORTUNATELY, BEING A vengeful fury was exhausting work. And with virtually no sleep all weekend, Liz was not doing so well come Monday morning. *What a difference a week makes,* she thought as she opened the door to Longbourn. Last Monday morning she had been riding high on plans for Christmas and showing her father that she could take over running the business side of Longbourn.

Now this Monday morning she was fretful and worried about everything. She felt like it was all going wrong. First, they'd made her coffee wrong at Mansfield Perk. And then she'd slipped on some ice. Not enough to fall over, but enough to bruise her ego. Then the calls had started as soon as she'd sat down at her desk. Most of them were easy, just concerned parents calling to say their child wouldn't be coming in due to a cold. Or parents worried about the Christmas party. And by the time the phone calls had stopped, her sisters had arrived. Each one insisted that Liz had to help them with something.

It all resulted in her not getting to sit down to do the paperwork until three o'clock in the afternoon. Liz flipped open her laptop and checked her email. As usual, there were a hundred things that everyone else thought were urgent urgent urgent. She worked her way up from the earliest one, patiently answering questions and reassuring parents that the party was still happening and no, they didn't need to be worried about anything.

After twenty of these and similar emails, Liz wearily clicked on the next one. She was not prepared for what she saw.

Ms. Bennet,

I should begin by telling you that this email is not an attempt to ask you out again.

Liz stopped reading. Her eyes flicked up to the email address. mrwilldarcyesq@pemberley.com. That was legit. She scrolled down to the end, past a huge block of text and saw his name: Will Darcy.

Mr. Darcy had emailed her. Liz contemplated saving the email for later. It wouldn't do to be fuming in the office alone for the rest of the day. But that same streak of curiosity that had made her ask Wickham about his past made her plunge right in now. It was either that or be distracted by it for the rest of the day. And she'd already been distracted enough by Will Darcy.

She began to read.

Ms. Bennet, *(so formal!)*

I should begin by telling you that this email is not an attempt to ask you out again. *(Good.)* I was mistaken in your feelings and I am sorry for how I approached you in the store the other day. You can be assured that it will not happen again, if we do come into contact with each other. *(Geez, it sounded like she was a disease he would try to avoid. "I'm sorry Mr. Darcy, you seem to have come down with a case of the Liz." "Oh no! But I wore my protective mask!")*

It seems that I was mistaken about the feelings of your sister, as well. I hope you will believe me when I tell you that I did nothing out of malice. It's only that Charles has become so popular so fast, he has women hanging around him constantly. Women who are only looking for fame and do not really care about Charles. *(Could he really think that about Jane? Ugh. Who does he think we are?)*

Forgive me, I did not mean to imply that you or Jane are only interested in Charles for the fame. I have seen that you are caring people and I believe you really do like Charles for himself alone. I only wished to protect him as his friend. *(Hmmph.)*

There is another, more serious, charge that you laid at my door. I decided to write this email because I think you deserve the truth. I will leave it up to you as to whether or not you believe it. I know that Wickham can be very charming. *(Much more charming than you.)*

So it seems that Wickham has told you I got him kicked out of law school. I can only imagine what the details were. Perhaps something about me reporting him to the professor for cheating? That is true, I will admit. But it is the last in a very long string of offenses. Offenses that finally came out once Wickham was caught cheating. He may tell you that we studied together and that is accurate. But did he also tell you that he stole term papers from other students and passed them off as his own? *(Really? That is...not good.)*

All of this might have even been acceptable,

had it not been for the biggest offense and the real reason he was kicked out of school: Wickham was selling "study drugs" to the other students. Once he was caught cheating, the school got wise to his other activities and expelled him immediately.

There was a hearing in which all this came out. All of this and more. This next part I will ask you not to share with anyone. I'm telling you because I feel that you need to know, but it would devastate the other party involved.

Wickham enlisted my younger sister to help him obtain the drugs he sold to the other students. Unbeknownst to me, he sought out Georgiana and wooed her. That's an old-fashioned word, I know, but it fits exactly what he did. She was so enthralled with him that she would have agreed to anything, I think. All of this came out in the school hearing. It was embarrassing for Georgiana and for me. And ever since, I believe that Wickham has blamed us for his bad fortunes. I don't know what he's doing right now, but I was not happy to see him at Longbourn the other night. I would like to believe that he has changed, but I'm not sure I can.

I know I have not been wrong to trust you

with this information. I do it so that you can understand and possibly help your sisters as I could not help mine until it was too late.

Sincerely,

Will Darcy

Liz read it through three times before she understood all that Mr. Darcy had written. Could it be true? What he said about Wickham? Could the charming man that had swept her whole family off their feet really be so nefarious? That seemed the appropriate word for it...nefarious. Liz could hardly believe it. It must just be a way for Mr. Darcy to get back at Wickham.

But then, what did he really have to gain by sharing all of this? It wasn't exactly complimentary toward his own family. And he wasn't trying to get her to go out with him. She knew little about Mr. Darcy, but he didn't seem like the gossipy, vindictive type. He hadn't even put up a fight in the store...Liz's feelings went back and forth all afternoon.

As they walked home that evening, Jane held Liz back while their sisters walked ahead.

"Liz, you'll never believe it." Jane bubbled with excitement.

"Believe what?"

"Look." Jane held up her phone for Liz to see. It took her a second to focus on the screen and realize what it said there. *Missed call from Charles Bingley.*

"Really, Jane?" Liz was excited and a little confused at the same time. If Charles was calling her sister again, that meant that Mr. Darcy had probably talked to him. But Darcy hadn't mentioned anything like that in his email.

What was his game? Was he really just a good—if a little too stiff—guy trying to do the right thing? Had she misjudged him so completely?

Liz fell asleep that night with those questions whirling in her head. And woke up the next morning without any answers.

Tuesday started a little better than Monday. She was still thinking about Darcy's email. But her coffee was perfect and she didn't slip on the ice. Sometimes it was the little things...

When she turned on her computer, though, things got a lot worse. There was an email from Mr. Collins. The subject line was written all in caps and labeled only *PAPERWORK?* Liz dreaded opening it.

Ms. Bennet,

I am concerned about your lack of communication re: the lease and non-profit paperwork due soon. I should remind you that not getting the paperwork in on time will result in dire consequences, including a potential loss of the property. You know the developers are circling the neighborhood and would relish getting their hands on your land. I have already had many calls from people wanting me to get you to sell.

Please let me know where you are with the paperwork. Finished with it would be the best reply I could receive.

Mr. Collins, Esq.

Ugh. He had to add that "Esq." just to get her goat. Liz could picture the man twirling his mustachios like an old-timey villain as he wrote the email. It hit her in just the right spot to make her both angry and worried. Of course she knew the consequences for not getting the paperwork in. She'd dealt with the letters from the developers offering the Bennets incentives if they would only let their lease lapse and give up the property. It made her burn with rage to have Collins bring it up again.

And the email was copied to her father, too. Great. Mr. Collins seemed to be deliberately making her look bad in front of her father. In fact, her father came in not long after and casually asked her about it. He didn't mention Collins' email, but she knew that's where his worry came from.

"So..." Mr. Bennet drawled. "Everything going okay?"

"Yes, Dad. I have everything under control."

"I know you do, Liz," he said. "But you would tell me if you needed help?"

"Of course. But I'm telling you that everything is fine. I almost have the paperwork complete and ready to send to Collins. You don't have to worry."

"I'm not worried."

Liz laughed. "I know you are! And you only came in here today to check up on me. So shoo. Go out there and help your other daughters. Or go home and help Mom do something. She'll probably have some project or other for you to do."

"That's what I'm running from," Mr. Bennet mumbled with a smile. They laughed together as he left the office.

But the truth was, as Liz quickly discovered, that all was not as well as she'd made out. The binder with all the paperwork wasn't where she'd left it. She looked everywhere in the office. She really thought she'd put it back on the shelf. She'd made a habit of it, just to make sure she never misplaced it.

Liz went out into the main room and asked her sisters. Luckily, her father had gone home to help with whatever project their mother had made up. The women started a search for it. No one could remember seeing it outside of the office. By mid-morning, Liz was in full panic-mode. She even went home and scoured her rooms for it. But there was no trace of the binder.

"At least I have the flash drive," Liz muttered to reassure herself as she walked back.

But the tiny bit of faith she'd managed to build up deflated after a thorough search of the office and a hasty dumping out of her handbag on the desk revealed that the flash drive was missing too.

Liz decided not to cry. But the tears came anyway. And with the tears came the doomsday thoughts. Everything was ruined. Christmas would be the worst they'd ever had. They'd lose the center and it would all be her fault. What's more, she'd managed to misjudge and possibly offend the people who might have helped them. And worst of all, she couldn't tell her father any of this and get his reassurance that it was all going to be okay. She'd ruined everything.

After half an hour of wallowing in her misery, Liz's optimistic nature took over and she started to make a plan. She would have to work night and day to redo everything. But she *could* do it. All was not lost.

Liz was swiping the last tears from her eyes when Lydia entered the office. Her normally buoyant and boisterous sister sat gingerly on the edge of the folding chair next to Liz's desk.

"Hey, Lizzy?" she asked in a timid voice.

"Yes, Lyds?"

"Can I tell you something?"

Liz didn't think she could handle any more problems today, but she said yes anyway. "What is it?"

"Well, first off, you have to promise not to tell Dad."

This did not bode well. Lydia had Liz's full attention. "Out with it."

"You promise?" Lydia looked actually scared. She wasn't trying to get away with charming Liz out of whatever trouble she was in.

"Sure, I promise not to tell Dad. Now what is it?"

Lydia suddenly burst into tears and the story came pouring out. "I think I...I did something bad, Lizzy. I think you're gonna hate me. But I swear I didn't know. I swear it."

Liz's body was throbbing with adrenaline now. What on earth was going on? "Lyds, calm down. And then tell me what it is you think you've done wrong."

"You're gonna be mad at me," Lydia wailed, her tears intensifying.

"No, I promise I won't, but you have to tell me." Liz was on her last reserves of control now.

"Well, I know you're looking for your papers..."

Liz's heart dropped. "What happened to them?"

"Well, I c...caught W...Wickham in here the other day. He was looking around for something. He told me not to say anything to anyone about him being in here. I just...I just wanted him to like me...But I think maybe he took your papers..." Lydia's sobs had died down into hiccups.

Liz couldn't believe it. Until she could. Wickham. He'd been here. And Lydia had caught him snooping around. Liz remembered back to the times he'd been in the center. He'd always somehow found his way into the office. And after what Darcy had written to her about Wickham's past...

"And then I was looking on his phone the other day when Mr. Collins called him. Isn't that our lawyer's name?"

"Yes, it is." Liz was stunned.

"I asked him about it and he got mad at me. I don't know what's up, Lizzy, but I'm sorry." Lydia started to cry again.

"Oh my god," Liz realized that she believed her sister. And she believed Mr. Darcy. And she'd been completely taken in by Wickham.

"I'm sorry, Lizzy. I'm so sorry. I didn't think he was doing any harm."

"Lyds, have you seen my little flash drive that I kept on my keychain?"

Lydia shook her head. "Did he take that too?"

"I don't know," Liz sighed.

"Was that important?"

"It was. Very important. That binder and the flash drive had all the paperwork for renewing our lease. If we don't get it in on time, the landlord will probably sell the building to the developers that keep coming around."

"Oh no!" Lydia began sobbing again. "It's all my fault."

"No, no," Liz assured her sister. "It just means we have to work harder now to redo everything."

"Is it a lot of work?"

Liz knew that if Lydia panicked then the whole family would hear of what had happened. And the very last thing she wanted was for her father to worry. So she lied to Lydia. "No, it's not too much work." Liz tried to be chipper about it. It had only taken her the better part of the last two weeks to even figure out the beginning of it. Not too much time at all.

"And you'll let me help, if I can?" Lydia asked. Maybe she really was growing up. Lydia from a year ago might not have cared about anybody else.

"I will let you know if I need help. But the best thing you can do now is make sure the kids have a great dance to show us at the party, okay?" Liz tried to smile at her sister.

Lydia nodded. "I can definitely do that."

"Good. Now get back out there. I've got some work to do." Liz smiled half-heartedly and Lydia got up to leave.

"Liz," she stopped in the doorway and turned back toward her sister, "I really am sorry. I'll try to call him and see if he'll tell me anything."

"Thanks, Lyds. I'm not gonna hold my breath about him picking up the phone. Gotta just start over again."

"You're awesome, you know?" Lydia smiled at her big sister.

"I know."

HE SPOKE NOT A WORD,
BUT WENT STRAIGHT TO HIS WORK

BUT LIZ DID not feel at all awesome. It took very little for her to believe the worst of Wickham. If her suspicions were correct, Wickham was working with Mr. Collins to sabotage their paperwork. Liz suspected that the lawyer had probably pulled a deal with the developers. It was too awful to think about. Mr. Darcy's words about Wickham kept ringing in her head. And the fact that he had used Darcy's younger sister made sense. Wickham had picked Lydia out of them all and exploited her. She couldn't even be mad at Lydia. The girl was only looking for some attention and Wickham had taken advantage of that.

Liz sat in the office for a long while just staring at her desk and thinking. She knew she needed to make a plan and get to work, but it was all just too exhausting to contemplate. She had already spent most of her time these last weeks getting the paperwork together. And to start from scratch...

So after about an hour, she decided to walk down to Mansfield Perk. Liz knew she was merely stalling, but maybe a change of scenery would do her good. And at least she would have coffee.

A little bell rang as she opened the door. The smell of coffee and baked goods, just on the verge of going stale, wafted over her. Liz breathed it in deeply and headed for the counter.

"Liz?"

The voice startled her. She spun around. Standing next to the little stand that held the milk and sugar and napkins and coffee stirrers was the very last person she'd expected to see.

"Darcy."

He had stopped stirring something into his coffee and stood looking at her. Liz looked back. She didn't know what to say. There were warring thoughts in her head. She should apologize and thank him for his warning about Wickham. She should walk out of here right now and never come back. She should carry on like nothing had happened. She should, she should, she should...

And then Liz noticed the tall, thin, beautiful woman next to him. His girlfriend? Liz reddened at the jealousy that unexpectedly boiled up. He'd just asked her out a few days ago and already he had moved on? The woman was looking back and forth between Liz and Darcy. Finally, she nudged him. He looked around at her. She raised her eyebrows and nodded her head toward Liz.

"Oh, sorry," Darcy said to the woman. "Liz, may I introduce you to my sister, Georgiana?"

Sister. A little of Liz's tension drained away.

Georgiana thrust her hand out excitedly toward Liz. "My brother can be so formal. I almost think I should curtsey to you, Liz."

Liz enthusiastically shook the proffered hand.

"Are you the Liz who runs the community center down the street?" Georgiana asked.

"I wouldn't exactly say that I run it, but..."

"Oh, no no. My brother insists that you do and are doing a great job of it, too."

"He does?" Liz glanced at Darcy, who was looking down into his coffee with quite a bit more concentration than it warranted.

"Yes, he does. He's talked of almost nothing else since Charles dragged him there a few weeks ago."

"Has he?" Liz asked. She was beginning to enjoy this. Darcy looked like he wanted to dissolve into his coffee cup.

"Oh, but you must have come in here to get something and here I am keeping you from it. I should never keep anyone from their coffee." Georgiana led her toward the counter. With a few quick steps, she had moved behind the counter and was grabbing a cup. "Now, what can I get you? Can I surprise you?"

"Sure. Surprise me." Liz had already been surprised so much this afternoon. What was one more thing? She was definitely surprised that Georgiana seemed to work here. She came here often and knew she had never seen Georgiana before.

"You work here?" Liz asked as Georgiana hurried between machines.

"Yep. I do now. In a way." She laughed as if something was funny. Liz didn't get it.

Darcy came up beside her. His voice wasn't loud, but for Liz it seemed to block out all the other noise in the cafe. "She's being modest. She owns the store. And a few others."

"Stop bragging," Georgiana chastised Darcy.

"I can't help it. I'm a proud big brother." Darcy smiled at his sister. This didn't jell at all with the picture she'd had in her mind of him. But then, nothing much was as it seemed to be lately. The rush of Wickham's betrayal and all that it meant came back over her.

"A big brother who needs to stop checking on his little sister because she is a capable adult woman now." Georgiana had finished making the coffee and was moving toward a few of the empty armchairs in the corner.

As they settled in, Liz asked Georgiana about owning the place.

"Well, I have my business degree. And people always need coffee, so..."

"It's a little more complicated than that," Darcy chimed, the radiant smile still on his face. "She's too modest about herself." The last was directed toward Liz. The smile distracted her from what he was saying. "Georgiana invested in one franchise a few years ago while she was still in school. And since then she's been learning the ropes and acquiring more stores in the area."

"This one is just my most recent purchase. The owner was ready to retire and I just happened to be ready to expand."

"Just happened to nothing," Darcy joked. Liz saw the way he looked at his sister. It was the way she looked at her sisters. A look full of love and pride and exasperation. The way only siblings can look at each other.

"Darcy encouraged me and helped me. He's a brilliant lawyer, you know." Georgiana couldn't resist a bit of bragging herself. Darcy's coffee had suddenly become quite interesting again.

"Is he?" Liz asked. If she didn't suspect that his rates were more than she could afford, she might hire him to go after Wickham.

"Well," Georgiana popped up out of her armchair, "I need to get back to work. Can't slack off all day like my big brother here..." She winked at Liz in a confiding way. Liz liked Georgiana Darcy a lot. It was a wonder she had turned out so different from her brother. "Liz, it was really nice meeting you and I'm sure I'll see you around some more."

With that she moved off and left Darcy and Liz sitting in awkward silence. They both sipped at their drinks. Liz wasn't sure what to say to the man. So much had passed between them in so few days of knowing each other. She decided to stay on neutral ground.

"Your sister is really something." Liz smiled at Darcy. He smiled back.

"Yes, she is. She won't ever tell you herself, but she

was the top of her class in school and did it all while actually managing her businesses, something the other kids can't say."

"You're really proud of her, aren't you?"

Darcy nodded and looked over at his sister, who was cheerfully helping a customer. "I really am. It's strange to watch your younger siblings grow up. But it makes you happy to watch them grow into successful, good people."

"Yeah." Liz thought of Lydia. Her sister had spent so many years being nearly spoiled by their mother and father, and yet she had fessed up today without trying to play the pity card. She'd owned her mistake and tried to make it right.

Liz blurted. "Darcy, I think I need to apologize to you."

He responded quickly and turned his head away, as if embarrassed. "There's no need, really."

"No, there is," Liz insisted. She willed him to look up at her. He did. For the first time since she had known him, she really looked at him. He looked back at her in a way that made her feel safe, made her feel like he cared. It struck Liz hard.

She spoke in a rush. "The truth is that I've been a horrible judge of character and I think it's going to cost me everything." Tears welled up in her eyes.

Darcy's eyebrows knit in concern. He leaned toward her and spoke softly. "Liz, what is it? What's happened?"

And just like that, she was sharing. It suddenly seemed so easy.

"Christmas is all in disorder and Dad put me in charge of everything. I've made a mess of it all after I promised everyone it would be the best Christmas ever."

"What's going on?"

"All the kids are sick and I don't know if they'll be able to do their performances. And then the parents keep calling and I feel such a responsibility to all of them. And then our lawyer keeps checking up on me."

"Lawyer? Why?" Darcy interrupted.

Liz sighed heavily. The tears threatened again. This was the real root of all her problems. "It's time for us to renew our lease and do all of our non-profit paperwork. If we don't get everything in on time, we could lose the center and everything my family has worked for. And those kids..."

"But I'm sure you have the paperwork done, right?" Darcy had more confidence in her than Liz did at the moment.

"That's the problem. I had most of it done, but..." Liz blushed deeply. How could she tell Darcy that his warning about Wickham had been perfectly correct? That she'd been so blinded by his good looks and charm that she'd not even thought he could do anything bad.

"What is it?"

"Wickham."

"Wickham?" There was steel in his voice. She felt him go rigid and hated herself for it.

"You were completely right about him and I should have known it."

"What has he done?" Darcy asked.

"He made up to Lydia so that he could get into my office and steal all the paperwork."

Darcy stared at her. "Did you have backups?"

Liz nodded. "I did. But I think he stole my flash drive, too. And I think he might be in league with our lawyer in some way..."

Darcy didn't say anything. He only glared at the table.

"I feel so stupid. Even after I knew what he had done, after you told me what he had done, I still let him hang around." Something else occurred to Liz. "Oh no! And now we have no Santa either!"

Darcy was startled. "No Santa?"

"Wickham had agreed to be our Santa. But hell if I'm letting him anywhere near my family or the center ever again. What am I gonna do?" It was a rhetorical question thrown out into a universe that seemed to want her Christmas completely ruined.

Darcy reached over, put his hand gently on her hand, and squeezed lightly. It was so simple. And yet...Liz felt a little more at ease, a little bit reassured. Someone was on her side. She looked up into Darcy's face. He was smiling gently at her.

"I'm sorry to dump all of this on you...it just happened and—"

"Not at all. I wish I could do something to help." His hand was still on her hand. Liz found that she liked it there.

Her phone started to ring. It was Jane.

Liz stood up and Darcy rose with her. "I have to

go. They need me back..." She didn't quite know how to say goodbye. It had never been a problem for them before. Should she shake hands? After what she'd just dumped on him, shaking hands seemed a little too formal. Liz leaned forward for a hug and found herself in Darcy's warm embrace. Yes, that was the adjective to use. His hug was like being next to a campfire and feeling that intense flame warming the very center of you. He smelled good and felt good.

Abruptly, Liz took a step backward. A little embarrassed at her sudden feelings, she looked at the ground and muttered "thank you" before rushing out the door into the cold. She was halfway back to Longbourn before she could face the fact that she'd blown it with Darcy. Of all the burdens she'd shouldered today, that one suddenly felt the heaviest.

AND AWAY THEY ALL FLEW LIKE THE DOWN OF A THISTLE

THE REST OF the week didn't get much lighter. The only bright spark was that the badgering emails from Mr. Collins stopped. She hadn't even answered his last ones, too angry at him to trust herself. The worst was that she couldn't come out and accuse him. She had no proof of anything.

Liz still didn't know what to do about the paperwork. She'd tried copying from previous years, but that only went so far. There was all the accounting to be done again. With that and the planning for the Christmas party, it became clear that Liz needed to confess to her father and get his help on things. She didn't want to admit that she'd failed, but she couldn't risk losing the center because of her own pride.

Near the end of the week, she called her father and asked him to come down to the office. He turned up wearing a gaudy sweater and tunelessly humming a Christmas carol. He plopped down in his seat and laughed.

"I'm going to need to dust off my desk, I haven't been here in so long."

Liz felt even more guilty than she had before. She started with the small ask. She knew that was the way to build up to the big thing she had to tell him, the big thing that would destroy all of his confidence in her. She steeled herself for it.

"Well, Dad, it seems that Wickham will no longer be available for the party."

"Good riddance," he said with a note of disdain in his voice. "If I ever see that man again, I'll hit him for hurting my little Lydia. She can be a silly girl, I know, but no one deserves to be dumped like that. And so close to Christmas."

"Yeah," Liz agreed. She didn't know quite what story Lydia had told their father about why Wickham would no longer be around, but apparently it was a good one that covered Liz's ass. "But since he won't be here, we need a Santa. I know I told you I'd find someone else this year, but—"

"Say no more about it, my Lizzy. It is my pleasure to do it. To be honest, I think your mother likes it too." He waggled his eyebrows significantly. Liz groaned and laughed.

"Dad, stop! I don't need to know that about you two. Eww." Liz was grateful for the laughter. Maybe it would soften the blow of what was going to come next.

"There's something else, too..." Liz started. Her father kept grinning. "It's about the paperwork."

"I was wondering when you were going to tell me. You've been so humble about it!" He was still grinning at her.

Liz didn't understand. "Humble?"

"Yes, for getting it all in early! I'm so proud of you, Lizzy. I knew you could do it, but I never expected this."

Liz was completely lost. What on earth was her father talking about? "Dad, I don't understand."

"It's lucky how it all worked out," he explained, not realizing that Liz was hearing this for the first time. "That Mr. Collins called me to say he was going on a long vacation and then Mr. Darcy of all people called to offer his help. It was almost like a Christmas miracle."

"Mr. Darcy?" Liz's heart thumped wildly.

"Yes, he called to tell me that he'd like to take us on as *pro bono* clients. Can you believe that? One of the partners at Pemberley Law Firm! Taking care of us! He's going to take over from Mr. Collins. And he told me he wanted to start with the paperwork that's due."

"He did?" Liz was utterly bewildered, but the pieces were slowly coming together.

"Yep. So I sent him all the financial stuff so he could check our accounting. He said he wanted to verify the work you'd sent him as well as familiarize himself with the business. Couldn't have been nicer about all of it. Can you believe it?"

No, Liz couldn't believe it. She hadn't sent Mr.

Darcy anything at all. Hadn't even talked to him since she'd spilled everything at Mansfield Perk.

"And then I got confirmation from him just this morning that the paperwork was in and everything was set for next year. Well done, my dear. I guess this means I *have* to retire now. And I can't say that I'm sorry about it either. How about we grab the girls and head out for a celebratory dinner on me and your mother?"

"Okay," Liz agreed. In a daze, she followed her father from the office and rounded up her sisters. All the time she was thinking about Darcy. He hadn't verified her work as her father had thought. No, Darcy had actually *done* all the work. But why? Why would he spend his time and energy doing that?

"Lizzy," Jane ran up and slipped her arm through her sister's. "Bingley just texted me and confirmed that he'll be here for the party."

"Awesome." Things were falling back into place. Liz could hardly believe it. "Did he say anything about Darcy?"

"Darcy? No. But I would think after the way he's acted at all the other parties, we wouldn't want him there anyway, right?"

"Right," Liz agreed. How could she tell her sister how wrong they'd all been about Darcy? Or how much Liz owed him?

BUT I HEARD HIM EXCLAIM, 'ERE HE DROVE OUT OF SIGHT...

DAYS FLEW BY in a whirlwind of Christmas activity. Liz haunted Mansfield Perk as much as she dared, hoping to see Darcy. But he never showed. A few times, Georgiana was there and insisted on giving Liz free coffee, saying that anyone who could make her brother smile deserved it.

Liz glowed inwardly each time Georgiana said this. Her feelings about Darcy had changed so much over the past week. No longer did he loom in her imagination as the scary, scowling, unhelpful specter hanging over their parties. Now she craved another one of those hugs.

Longbourn was one big cacophonous jumble by the night of the Christmas party. The kids had mostly recovered from their colds and were in various corners hastily practicing their songs and dances. The adults milled around with plates of food in hand, chatting joyfully to each other and comparing notes on what their Christmas plans were. The main room was decorated to the nines and the tree looked magnificent in its corner, surrounded by all the gifts that would be given out to the children or donated to other children around the city.

Mr. and Mrs. Bennet were holding court, like Santa and Mrs. Claus welcoming everyone to their home. They had kind words and big smiles for anyone who wandered into their path. Jane, Mary, Lydia, and Kitty all buzzed around the room, making sure their props and instruments were in order for the performances.

Liz stood in the shadow of the office doorway and watched the festive activity. She felt oddly alone in the midst of so many beloved people. They all had a purpose, but her job was already over. Darcy's face floated through her imagination. Again she thought over all that had passed between them. From the first impressions to the last, from scowl to smile, he had saved her and her family and no one but she knew it.

A hundred times she'd thought about calling him. Just to say thank you, of course. And a hundred times she'd put the phone away without even dialing. How on earth could she ever say thank you for all that he had done? Liz felt even more alone tonight because of her knowledge. How close they had come to losing this place. How close they had come to no Christmas at all.

When Charles Bingley arrived, he had an entourage of smiling, bubbly people behind him. Liz's heart leaped to her throat. She stood still as she waited to see his face. But after a few agonizing moments it was clear that Darcy had not come.

Liz had no time for disappointment, however. Kitty was coming to fetch her while the other girls ushered people to their seats. It was time to begin. Without Darcy.

Charles had agreed to be their master of ceremonies for the evening. Liz watched as he enthusiastically introduced each act and applauded the most for the kids when they had finished. They had put on successful parties in the past, but this one seemed to have an extra shine on it because Charles was here. The children were doing their very best to impress their famous new friend.

A few times, Liz caught Charles looking at Jane and it made her smile even as her own heart ached. Charles was a special man and Liz was happy for her sister. But it made her want Darcy around even more.

After all the kids had performed, it was finally time for Santa. Liz had noticed her Dad slip out a few minutes ago to put on the Santa suit and grab the bag of candy he would give out. Charles got up, following his cue, and announced that he had brought with him a very special friend.

"Can you guess who it is?" Charles asked.

"Santa!" The kids and adults all yelled together.

"That's right. It's time to bring out my main man!" Charles gestured to the doorway and there Santa appeared.

Right away Liz knew something was wrong. It was

definitely not her Dad in there. The suit hung off of this person in all the wrong places and the belt was hanging loose. The red cap drooped too low and the beard was crooked, like it had just been stuck on in a hurry. When the bedraggled Santa gave his first weak "ho ho ho," Liz knew for sure it wasn't her father. Had something happened? She started to panic. But before she could move to check on things, Santa stepped toward the microphone and began to speak.

"'Twas the night before Christmas, and all through the house..."

Liz recognized that voice. But it couldn't be. She squinted in the dimness of the Christmas lights and tried to confirm her suspicions.

"I hope you all will have a very merry Christmas!" He spoke. "Now come up and get some candy."

There was a rush toward him, but Liz stood still. It *was* him. Darcy was Santa. Liz's smile couldn't have gotten any bigger. She watched him as he spoke earnestly to each of the children and listened patiently to what they wanted to get for Christmas. His Santa laugh got stronger as he settled into the role. He made a lot of people happy. He made *her* happy.

What a change from the first time she'd seen him. Charles had eclipsed Darcy then, throwing his beaming smile over everything and leaving Darcy in shadow. And that had seemed to suit him. But now Liz only had eyes for the man in the Santa suit.

And he hadn't even looked at her. The first truly nice man—no, more than nice: smart, kind, handsome —and she'd blown it. He'd said so in his email, hadn't he? She didn't need to worry about him asking her out again. He'd helped them out because that, after all, was the kind of man he was. But Liz had no reason to hope that things had changed.

She turned to go into the office and sulk.

"Liz?" Darcy's voice was hesitant behind her.

She composed her face, unwilling to show him any emotion, and turned around. "Hi."

"Hi." He'd taken off the hat and beard. The children were opening presents now in little groups throughout the main room. She and Darcy had a little bit of privacy at the back, close to the office.

"Good job on being Santa," Liz said.

"It was nothing." Darcy shrugged. They stared at each other until Liz remembered that it was her turn to speak.

"Darcy, listen, I..." Liz was interrupted by a burst of laughter from behind them. Darcy remained silent. After a pause, she continued. There were things she should say to him. And who knew when she'd have another chance?

"Liz—" He took a step toward her.

She barreled on, determined to say what she needed to say. "Darcy, I have to say thank you. A million times thank you."

"You don't need to thank me." Another step toward her.

"I *do* need to thank you. For everything. You've made a Christmas miracle for these kids...and for my family."

Darcy took another step forward and caught her

eyes in his gaze. He was close enough that she heard his whisper. "I did it all for you."

"For me?" Liz squeaked out the question with what little air was still in her lungs. His proximity was doing strange things to her insides.

"I told you awhile ago that I would not ask you out again. You made your feelings toward me very clear." He paused. Liz stared at him. "If you still feel the same way..."

"I don't," Liz interrupted. "My feelings...are not the same." Liz watched the muscles in Darcy's face relax. She didn't realize how tense he had been. It reassured her. "In fact, my feelings are about as opposite as they can be from what I told you before." She smiled shyly.

"Are they?" His eyes dropped briefly to her lips.

There was that squirmy feeling again. Liz tried to play it off. She spoke lightly. "I can't believe you did all that paperwork..."

"For you." He leaned closer.

Liz stumbled over her words. He was so close. "And I assume...I assume you told Charles to call Jane..."

"For you." Closer.

"And Santa?"

"Ho ho ho." The words made soft bursts of air against her mouth as his lips finally touched her lips.

From the front of the room near the dazzling tree, Mr. Bennet boomed out. "Merry Christmas to all, and to all a good night!"

ABOUT THE AUTHOR

Kimberly Truesdale is a teacher and storyteller who has a line from *The Great Gatsby* tattooed on her arm and has worn out at least five copies of *Anne of Green Gables*. Kimberly's first novel, My Dear Sophy, told the story of how the Admiral and Mrs. Croft from Jane Austen's *Persuasion* first meet. Her second and third novels, *The Wrong Woman* and *A Prince for Aunt Hetty* kicked off the Unexpected Love series of sweet historical romances with atypical heroines.

You can connect with Kim on her website http://kimberlytruesdale.wordpress.com, or on Twitter at @KimTrues. You can also email her at AuthorKimberlyTruesdale@gmail.com.

Made in the USA
San Bernardino, CA
31 March 2019